Stonebridge

by

Linda Griffin

Stonebridge

Cover Art by *Jennifer Greeff*

The Wild Rose Press, Inc.
PO Box 708
Adams Basin, NY 14410-0708
Visit us at www.thewildrosepress.com

Publishing History
First Edition, 2023
Trade Paperback ISBN 978-1-5092-5235-0
Digital ISBN 978-1-5092-5236-7

Published in the United States of America

Did she detect something tangible now? A faint trace of perfume? Something unfamiliar and suggestive of roses. Now I'm imagining things, she told herself sternly. She hoped the light hadn't given her away and she still had time to wait undiscovered for the trickster to appear.

She leaned back against the wall and waited, listening to the silence. The house was almost too quiet, as if nobody lived there. Nothing creaked or shifted or fluttered in the darkness. But for the knowledge that she didn't have long to wait, the silence would have gotten on her nerves. As it was, the hair on the back of her neck prickled. She shivered a little. Like most old houses, Stonebridge was drafty.

The silence was oppressive and in some way alive. An inexplicable chill ran down her spine. She saw nothing, heard nothing. She didn't even have a definite sense of someone else in the room. She was simply unnerved for no reason. For a few seconds more she stayed in the shadows of the music room and then, with an almost physical sensation, her composure shattered.

Rynna fled. She ran for the stairs and clambered up them, slipping and stumbling in the dark, half-choked by terror and gasping for breath. At the top of the stairs, she ran full tilt into someone hurrying down the hall, and before she had time to register who it was, she screamed.

Praise for Linda Griffin and...

BRIDGES:

"If you enjoy vintage romance with a classic vibe, pick up *Bridges*. Brilliantly written, this is one of the best books I've read this year."

~N.N. Light's Book Heaven

"Thank you, Linda Griffin, for this beautiful and poignant romance."

~Anastasia Abboud, author of Tremors through Time

"An engaging and sweet-natured love story featuring an unlikely couple."

~Kirkus Reviews

GUILTY KNOWLEDGE:

"Griffin has a gift for romantic suspense...An involving mystery elevated by vivid characterizations."

~Kirkus Reviews

THE REBOUND EFFECT:

"*The Rebound Effect* by Linda Griffin is a suspenseful psychological thriller that did not disappoint."

~Joanie Chevalier for Readers' Favorite

Dedication

To Carolyn and Anne,
who let me borrow (and misspell) their surname

Acknowledgement

An earlier version of this book was published by
Winston-Derek Publishers, Inc. in 1994.

Chapter One

Stonebridge Manor, Brenford County, Virginia
April 1958

The house itself was magnificent. As the Bentley came around the curve and crossed the gray stone bridge that had given the estate its name, Stonebridge Manor loomed ahead. It was imposingly Georgian and as sternly handsome as the ancestral portraits in Grandfather Dalton's picture gallery. Rynna caught her breath and leaned forward for a better view. She had been told it was built in 1734, and she knew enough about architecture to translate that into the austere lines of a child's drawing— symmetry in bulk, every corner squared. Nothing had prepared her for the tall narrow windows with their segmental arches, the light gray stonework, the elegantly framed doorway, the pattern of small panes in the dormer windows, the encroaching ivy, or the enormous oaks that flanked the drive.

"It's beautiful," she said, and Ellery, the chauffeur, glanced at it indifferently and murmured something meant as agreement. But he saw it every day and always from the viewpoint of a servant. She shouldn't wonder if its charms were lost on him.

He stopped the car in front of the solid paneled door and came around to help her out of the car as if she were elderly or an invalid. He was a little reserved, not unfriendly but keeping a proper distance. He swung her suitcases out of the trunk and, carrying them without visible effort, led the way up the broad stone steps.

The door opened before they reached it, and a young woman in a spotless cap and apron smiled a greeting. Rynna had never seen anyone dressed like that outside of a movie, not even in Grandfather Dalton's formal household. The people in this house were seriously rich. "Hullo, Miss," chirped the frilled cap. "We're so glad you've come at last." She stood with her hands together at her waist, a broad smile on her face, but she might as well have curtsied.

The chauffeur waited in stoic patience with the suitcases until the maid nodded toward the stairs and said, "Miss Pamela's room." Rynna was startled. This woman was not old enough to have known her mother, yet she said "Miss Pamela" as if she were referring to someone who might waltz into the room at any moment. "It's a lovely room," she continued to Rynna. "I'm sure you'll like it."

"I'm sure I will," she said with automatic politeness, but she wasn't sure she wanted to be assigned to the room where her mother spent her girlhood. Did it occur to them that she might not? Her grief still had sharp edges sometimes. She still awoke in the middle of the night to a single naked thought: I want my mother.

"I'm Lucy, by the way. You'll meet the others later. Now, if you'll come this way, Miss—they've been waiting for you in the library. She's been very anxious." Again a smile, sincerely friendly, and Lucy scurried down the hall ahead of her. Rynna followed, taking in winding stairs, handsome railings, cornices of polished wood, and fine paneling. This house would have to be reckoned with or it could easily overwhelm her.

As they approached the library, the steady murmur of a single voice could be heard, the unmistakable rhythm of someone reading aloud. The voice was masculine, the accent undistinguishable, the tone faintly bored. She braced herself for she knew not what and entered the room in Lucy's wake. After the exterior and the spacious hall, the library was smaller and darker than she expected, but it was beautifully paneled and furnished, with an immense fireplace, two walls covered with bookshelves, and rugs of the deepest plush. It had a dry, powdery odor that might be just musty old furniture and drapes.

"Here she is at last," said Lucy and backed gracefully out, leaving Rynna alone to face the strangers she had come to live with. Her great-grandmother, Edwina Demeray, sat in a straight-backed armchair near the fireplace, overdressed for the season in old satin and lace to her chin. Her back was straight, her gray hair perfectly coifed, her dark eyes lively in a face only sketchily lined with age. She didn't look much more than sixty, and she must be over ninety. The hands that rested on the arms of the chair were covered with ornate rings, and necklaces of pearls hung to her ample bosom. Rynna was thoroughly intimidated.

The young man with the open book still in his hands was seated only a few feet from the old lady, but he could have belonged in a different century. If Mrs. Demeray was Georgian, he was at least Edwardian. His straight dark blond hair touched his collar in back, and he had a high forehead and aristocratic nose—a scholar if she had ever seen one. He wore a long-sleeved pinstripe shirt, rather like an early Arrow shirt ad, gray linen slacks, and wire-rim glasses. All he needed was a straw skimmer and a rowboat. He was seated instead in a shiny metal wheelchair.

They stared at her as if they were expecting someone else. An awkward silence lasted until Mrs. Demeray said, "She does look a little like Pamela."

"A little," agreed her companion, and to Rynna, "You should let your hair grow."

"I like it short," she said. Why was she on the defensive already? She had been invited—more than that, commanded—to live here.

"Forgive me," Mrs. Demeray said, as if she could read her mind. "We must welcome you to Stonebridge. I trust your journey was not too fatiguing, my dear?"

"It was fine, thank you—" She faltered—what was she to call this formidable woman? "Your majesty" might be insufficient.

Again she seemed to have read her mind. "You may call me Grandmother," she prompted.

"Yes, Grandmother," she said, and it was very natural, after all. Why had she lopped off a generation? To further the illusion of youth, or the fantasy that this awkward city-bred girl was her beloved Pamela back again?

"And this," she went on, holding out a bejeweled hand in a gesture both imperious and fond, "is your Cousin Theodore."

"Ted," he corrected swiftly.

"I despise nicknames," Mrs. Demeray said, "and he will tease me so. Your own name, my dear—surely Rynna is a nickname?"

"No, it isn't," she said, "but I believe it was intended as a derivation of Edwina."

4

"Ah, I see," the old lady murmured, rather pleased. "Pamela was such an imaginative child. Tell me, my dear: was she happy in that place?" She spoke as if Colorado were on the far side of the moon.

"Yes, Grandmother. At least she was until Daddy died. After that, she sometimes talked of coming back here."

"Dear Pamela," Mrs. Demeray said. "Well, Theodore, we mustn't keep this child standing here as if she were giving a school recitation." She pulled a velvet rope beside the fireplace. Rynna was fascinated. It was something else she had seen only in movies. Almost immediately Lucy appeared, and Rynna understood that she was being dismissed. "Dinner's at seven," her great-grandmother said and gave Lucy a crisp nod. Rynna followed Lucy out of the room as Ted cleared his throat and begin reading again, as if he hadn't been interrupted.

Lucy led the way up the stairs and down another hall and opened the door to a room with a familiar air. It was painted pale blue, like her room at home, but a fireplace stood against one wall, opposite one of those marvelous mullioned windows. The mantelpiece and all the woodwork were cream-colored, and the fourth wall was covered in blue-and-white figured wallpaper. The bare wood floor was softened by an oval rag rug in shades of blue and gray, and the bed was a handsome four-poster with a light blue matelassé bedspread. The view from the window was of expanses of green lawn, tall shade trees, and a distant river.

"Nevertheless," she said with firm resolve, "I'm not staying." It was a lovely room and an entirely seductive house, but she would not live here. She would not live with that dictatorial old woman or rude Cousin Ted or any of their kind. She was a competent human being, and she could live anywhere she liked and get a job to support herself. Of course she could. She had not been so expensively educated for nothing. If she would be hopeless in a typing pool, she certainly knew her way around a schoolroom. Even Great-Grandmother Demeray might find her references adequate for teaching French or piano, or heaven forbid, even algebra. Her own money was tied up in a trust, and she couldn't touch the capital without Edwina's permission, and Edwina wanted her to live here. She wanted her close, wanted to control her life as she had been unable to control Pamela's.

Rynna stood at the window gazing out across the luxuriant grass, and her fists clenched. "I won't," she said half aloud.

A tentative knock at the door interrupted her thoughts.

"Who is it?" She hadn't been in the room long, and neither Ted nor her great-grandmother could have maneuvered the stairs so quickly. She hoped it was Lucy and not another strange face.

The door opened and a curly head under a starched cap appeared. "It's only me, Miss. I don't want to bother you. Oh, just look at you!" The girl who bounced into the room was younger than Lucy, younger than Rynna, possibly not out of her teens, and she bubbled with vitality. "Oh, Miss, you do look nice!" She put her hands to her rosy cheeks. "That jacket is ever so becoming." Rynna had yet to hear the kind of Southern accent she'd expected here, but this girl sounded distinctly British. "But—oh, Lord, I am forgetting my manners. I'm Cecile, Miss, and Lucy said I could—I mean to say I'm to be your lady's maid, and I shall be ever so happy to serve you, Miss."

"That's absurd," Rynna said without thinking. "I've never had a maid. I don't need a maid, and besides—"

"Oh, but, Miss, I shall be ever so good, I promise. I'll take such good care of your clothes and brush your hair and help you with anything at all, anything you say. Oh, please, let me. If you say I won't do, Lucy will think I did something to upset you. She told me I mustn't chatter on and—oh!" She gasped and her hands flew to her mouth.

Rynna laughed. She couldn't help it. "It's all right, Cecile. I'm not going to complain to Lucy or anyone else. It's just that I've never lived in a house like this before, and I've never had servants. I wouldn't know how to act. I certainly wouldn't want to give orders to someone who's lived here longer than I have. This isn't my house, you know. I'm only a poor relation."

Cecile thought that was a good joke. "But you will let me be your maid, won't you, Miss? I won't be troublesome, I promise. I'll be ever so quiet and stay out from underfoot, and the minute you need me I will come like a flash. I would like it ever so much, Miss."

"But why?"

"Why, Miss?" She was mystified.

The obvious dawned on Rynna. "What would you be doing otherwise?" she asked.

"Oh, no, Miss, not only because it's a better job. It's that you're so young and pretty. We all saw you arrive, and I was so excited. They all said how lucky I was. Your clothes are so smart and all."

"That's very nice," she managed to say, half-choked with amusement, "but I don't think I'll be staying long, and I don't need a maid." The girl's chagrined expression prompted her to add, "What I could use while I'm here is a friend."

"Oh, Miss!"

"And you mustn't call me Miss. It's ridiculous. My name is Rynna."

"You're ever so nice," Cecile enthused. "I knew you would be. We all said so. And pretty, too. The only pictures we'd seen were when you were just tiny, so we didn't know, but you look ever so much like her. It's quite eerie."

"Do you think so?" Rynna caught a glimpse of herself in the dressing table mirror. "Grandmother said," and she did her best to approximate the expression and grudging tone of the elderly Mrs. Demeray, " 'She does look a little like Pamela.' "

"Oh!" Cecile was surprised. "I suppose you do, a bit. It's only logical since she was your mother, but it wasn't Miss Pamela I was speaking of, you know."

Rynna stared at the artless young face. "What do you mean?"

"They wouldn't have told you," Cecile said, "but they're sure to have noticed. Why, Miss Rynna, you are the very image of Miss Rosalind."

Rosalind.

After Cecile backed out, leaving her to rest before dinner, Rynna lay in her mother's comfortable four-poster bed and thought about Rosalind. Her mother had told her amusing stories about her childhood in this house and bits of family history, but had shared tantalizingly little of her memories of Rosalind, which seemed to be pervaded with sadness. They were cousins, raised as sisters, closer than most sisters, devoted and inseparable friends. After the early deaths of their respective parents, both girls and Pamela's brother William were raised by their grandmother, Edwina Demeray, at Stonebridge.

Their idyllic friendship was shattered when Rosalind married against her grandmother's wishes and left Stonebridge forever. Pamela continued to write to her, without Mrs. Demeray's knowledge, but after her own marriage Rosalind's letters inexplicably stopped. She suspected interference from her grandmother or Rosalind's husband but was never able to prove it. Her resilient hope of family reconciliation ended with Rosalind's tragic death.

Now they were all gone—Pamela and her husband, William and his wife—at least those two died together, as devoted as the day they were married—Rosalind and her disfavored husband. The girls had moved away when they married, so only William was buried in the family plot with Edwina's husband and sons. Edwina had outlived two generations of her descendants. No wonder she was so imperious.

****

Dinner was difficult, and Rynna's determination to escape hardened. Mrs. Demeray dominated the conversation, explaining the history of the house and the family who had lived in it for generations. Ted, who must have heard it all before, had his mind on other things, and his attitude toward Rynna was too disinterested to be hostile.

The food at least was satisfactory, and when she was not being grilled about her education and her father's business, she was free to enjoy it with only an occasional "Yes, Grandmother" expected. The cook had excelled with the roast beef, tender and succulent, simmered in a rich gravy with potatoes and carrots. Dessert was rice pudding with plump warm raisins and plenty of cinnamon. Ted's table manners were impeccable, but he was as indifferent to the delicious meal as he was to her.

As the dessert dishes were cleared away and she prepared to rise from the table with the aid of a silver-headed cane, Mrs. Demeray announced, "We must have Jason to dinner one day next week."

"Jason?" Rynna asked, surprised. "Rosalind's son?"

"Yes, of course, dear, your cousin Jason. We're all that is left of the family now and we should not lose touch. He lives in town. He has a fine law practice."

"Sharp practice," Ted said. He was not indifferent to Jason.

"Theodore," said Mrs. Demeray, giving him a stern warning. She got to her feet, steadying herself with a hand on the table. Rynna rose too, in case she needed help, but she didn't seem to.

"Yes, Grandmother," Ted said meekly. He was mocking her, matching her tone exactly.

Mrs. Demaray, quite aware of what he was doing, said, "Theodore!" again in exasperation.

"Yes, Grandmother," said Ted in an entirely different tone, and a look passed between them that astonished Rynna. She wouldn't have thought either of them capable of so much affection and humor. She was aware more than ever of being an outsider.

"Now, my dear," the old woman continued, "would you like to see the rest of the house?" Her voice held more command than invitation.

"Yes, I would," she said, wary of Ted's derision.

"By all means, give her the grand tour. I'll be in my

room." He backed and pivoted the wheelchair with practiced skill and disappeared into the hall.

"He's not being unsociable," Mrs. Demeray explained with patient indulgence. "He's working on his book."

"Book?" echoed Rynna.

"Yes, dear, his book. Nearly every evening now. Very time-consuming, that book. It's all about minerals and things, terribly dry. His father would be astonished, but you never know what interests a boy will take up." She made it sound as if Ted were ten years old and playing with a crystal radio. Rynna supposed he was about thirty and was pleased to have recognized him as a scholar.

As they came out into the hall, stepping fairly quickly in spite of the cane, they could hear the creak and clatter of the old-fashioned lift taking Ted upstairs. The fact that they never modernized something so essential was another symptom of their living in another century.

Mrs. Demeray led her from room to room, pointing out family heirlooms and explaining bits of related history. The rooms were dustily elegant but far removed from reality. Even the names belonged to another time: sitting room, drawing room, library.

What did so few people do with all these rooms? The presence of so many shelves filled with books was encouraging, but she was afraid they would prove to be like Ted's, all about minerals and things and terribly dry.

The music room was something quite unexpected. The walls were papered in a shade that was almost coral and the wood was a deep, rich brown, aged to perfection. The piano, though polished to a high sheen and recently dusted, wore the neglected air of an instrument seldom played. Whatever else they might be, the remaining Demerays must not be music lovers. But I am, Rynna thought defiantly, and sat on the wide mahogany bench. She was afraid Mrs. Demeray might object, but she only stood by, waiting. Rynna raised the lid and fingered the keys experimentally.

She played softly, without self-consciousness, from oh-so-familiar memory. The piano had a different quality than the one she was used to at school, more resonant, even more impressive than the one in Grandfather Dalton's house, and yet she was at home here. Playing Chopin on this magnificent instrument in this elegant, tranquil room was perfectly natural. What was it that made this room, out of all of Stonebridge, so special? Nothing in the room, taken by itself, not even the piano, could explain the warmth and charm and keen sense of belonging she experienced here. The room itself was welcoming her, calling her home.

As she played she admired the delicately figured wallpaper. Was the pattern of leaves and tiny flowers somehow familiar? Finally, her gaze came to rest on the vivid painting above the mantelpiece, a portrait of a woman in her early twenties, seated gracefully in a heavy armchair, wearing rose chiffon and pearls, her thick, dark hair piled high, lips curved in a slight smile.

"It's Rosalind."

"Yes," said Rynna, with a little shock of recognition. She couldn't remember having seen pictures of Rosalind, but she must have. She searched for the resemblance to herself Cecile had mentioned, but it evaded her. Her dark hair, of course, and she remembered Ted saying critically, "You should let your hair grow."

"This was her favorite room," Mrs. Demeray said. "She played beautifully." Her voice held a shade of coolness, as if Rosalind had not been forgiven.

I'm not Rosalind, Rynna reminded herself, and I'm not Pamela. I will not stay in this house one minute longer than necessary. She recalled her first impression of the house, the feeling that it would overwhelm her if she wasn't careful, and resolved that she would not be seduced by a fine piano and the portrait of a young woman who had liked pink and married unwisely. Her hands stilled on the piano keys, and the spell was broken. By the time they moved on to the next room, she had forgotten what it was she sensed or imagined in the music room.

When the downstairs tour was completed, they rode the slow, creaking lift to the second floor. Mrs. Demeray opened the door to her own bedroom, permitting Rynna a quick glimpse of velvet draperies, lace bedspread and canopy, and highly polished furniture. The old woman told her, straight-faced, that Edmund Randolph had once slept in the room. As they passed another closed door, the rapid staccato clack of a typewriter identified it as Ted's, and Mrs. Demeray explained that it was once his father's. The next room had been Rosalind's, but now it had a stark, abandoned quality and was being used primarily for storage.

"And this, of course," she said as she opened the door to Rynna's room, "was your mother's. Dear Pamela always liked blue. I suppose you knew that."

"Yes, Grandmother." She should have said more but was choked by a wave of fresh grief for the pretty, generous-hearted girl who had lived here and designed her daughter's room after this one.

Mrs. Demeray hesitated in the doorway. Perhaps it had just occurred to her that Pamela's death was recent. She didn't simply vanish from the face of the earth when she left Stonebridge. The old woman was momentarily confused and embarrassed by the evidence of Rynna's emotion, but she quickly recovered and said, "I expect you're tired. I hope you sleep well."

"Yes," said Rynna faintly. "Thank you, Grandmother."

After the old woman retreated down the hall, Rynna closed the door and lay on the bed. She closed her eyes and tried to detect some familiar scent or vibration. If the music room could retain a trace of Rosalind's personality after so many years, shouldn't Pamela have left some impression here? She concentrated but sensed nothing and after a few minutes she dozed. Instead of her mother she dreamed, if the confused images of half-sleep could be called dreams, of the gray stone bridge, the winding staircase, and Cousin Ted's mocking voice.

A discreet rap on the door invaded the dream, and she stirred. "Who is it?"

"Cecile, Miss."

"Oh, yes, come in," she called, sitting up, rather groggy.

"Are you all right, Miss?" Cecile asked as soon as she was inside. "You look that tired."

"Yes, I am tired. It was a long trip."

"You must go right to bed, then," she said decisively. She picked up a hairbrush from the dresser. "Let me brush your hair. That's always relaxing. Just you sit still." She perched on the bed behind Rynna and brushed with easy, expert strokes. "Such pretty hair," she murmured. "You should let it grow, Miss."

"Now don't you start." Rynna found she couldn't be cross with Cecile, not in that comfortably drowsy moment. She relaxed under her capable hands. "Grandmother showed me the house," she said. "I love the music room."

The steady rhythm faltered for a second, and Cecile said softly, "I like it too, but Lucy won't go inside if she can help it."

"What? Why ever not?" Rynna pulled away and stared into the girl's suddenly guarded face.

"Oh, Miss, it's— Lucy says it gives her the creeps."

"That lovely room?"

"Yes, Miss, but Lucy says there's a ghost in this house."

"A ghost?" Rynna couldn't keep the scorn out of her voice. Starched, efficient Lucy believed in ghosts?

"Yes, Miss," said Cecile, a bit defensively. "But things go on in this house nobody can explain." She lowered her head and continued brushing Rynna's hair.

"But surely you don't believe in ghosts?"

"I...I don't know, Miss. I suppose you think it's silly."

"Very silly. I think you've all been shut up here together too long. You ought to get out more, go into town."

"Oh, I do, on my days off. I go to church and that."

"And do they believe in ghosts in your church?"

"Oh, no, Miss. I do see what you mean."

"Please stop calling me 'Miss.' You can call me Rynna. I'm not much older than you are, and I could use a friend. If I'm to be shut up in this drafty old place with my awful relatives, I'll need you to keep me sane."

Cecile was speechless for a moment and then said,

"I'll do my best to be your friend. I'm so glad you've come."

Soothed by Cecile's kindness and her skill with the hairbrush, Rynna faced no difficulty in falling asleep in the strange bed. As she drifted off she considered whether it was fair to dismiss Lucy's belief in a ghost when she herself had speculated about lingering traces of personality in a room. If anything in the world might be called a ghost, wasn't that it? Faint impressions left behind like the hint of perfume after someone passed through a room? But if that was all Lucy meant, why would she find it creepy? Or refuse to enter the music room?

Rynna slept deeply and did not dream, but once during the night she found herself wide awake in the dark room. She was not conscious of having heard any sound but still thought she had been abruptly awakened. She lay still, listening, but heard nothing. Everyone was apparently asleep, and she could not detect so much as a whisper. She would have expected a house so old to settle and creak, but at least within the walls of Pamela's old room stillness reigned.

Then she did hear a muffled thud, which appeared to come from beneath her room. She considered the layout of the house from Mrs. Demeray's tour, and yes, it might be the music room directly below. Was it possible to hear anything from the room below when not so much as a rustle or creak issued from the bedrooms on the same floor? Through the fireplace or a connection between heat registers? Or did she only imagine a sound she was listening for? Rynna shrugged and rolled over, ready to slip back into sleep.

Clearly, distinctly, a single note rose from the fine

old piano. She had absolutely no doubt that it emanated from the music room and she was meant to hear it, and instead of being frightened or doubtful, she was reassured and welcomed and comforted.

Rosalind was here.

Welcome home.

"Thank you," Rynna whispered in the darkness, and she slept again.

Chapter Two

In the morning of course, Rynna felt foolish and certain she had dreamed it. She didn't mention it even to Cecile, who would have believed her all too eagerly. That was how ghost stories got started. Somebody dreamed something and described it to someone else with a little embellishment, and imagination took over.

She got up early, dressed, and found her way down to the kitchen, a large, warm room that invited her nearly as much as the music room, on a different level. Mrs. Lester, the stout, stern-faced cook, took a dim view of young ladies invading her kitchen, and Rynna set herself the task of winning her over. If she could feel no kinship with the Demeray family, she must find it among the servants. Compared to a solitary tray in her room or breakfast in state in the vast, chilly dining room, the kitchen glowed with warmth and friendliness.

Modern equipment had been installed, but the atmosphere was still that of an earlier century. Rynna liked the high ceiling and tall cupboards, the wide, plain wooden table, the sturdy iron pots, and long-handled cooking spoons. She liked Mrs. Lester, who concealed a dry wit and generous spirit behind her severe expression, and she liked Jenny and Marie, the cheerful, hardworking girls who did Mrs. Lester's bidding. They were almost identical in their blonde prettiness, but Marie was quieter than Jenny and had a charming

Southern drawl. The enticing smells of breakfast fresh from the oven completed the picture.

They were kind enough, feeding her bacon and eggs and fresh, hot biscuits with strawberry jam, allowing her to sit on a high stool and take a turn at stirring the oatmeal, but she remained an outsider. They were only waiting for her to leave so they could relax and be themselves without being interfered with or spied on or condescended to. In addition to the fact that she was a stranger and belonged to the family upstairs, they of course noticed the resemblance to Rosalind's portrait and kept giving her quick, appraising glances to see how she measured up. They would probably discuss it as soon as she left.

Discouraged, Rynna returned to her room. She could have rung for Cecile, but it would be silly and pretentious. She would have preferred to knock on the door of Cecile's tiny room at the end of the hall, but that too might be an intrusion. Could Cecile really be her friend, or did she consider the suggestion condescending? Did she prefer to preserve the distance between them and keep her thoughts and feelings to herself?

Once again Rynna determined to leave, to find a way to support herself and free herself from Stonebridge forever.

She stood at the window and gazed out at the sunlit grounds. Under the trees it would be cool and private, invisible from the house. If she wasn't planning to stay long at Stonebridge, she might at least get a taste of the place that had once been home to her mother. Pamela, a tomboy well into her teens, used to climb those trees and skip stones across the river. She and William and their friends played football on the lawns while Rosalind practiced diligently on the piano. Pamela had played well enough, but with Rosalind music was a passion.

Rynna shook her head impatiently. Why did her thoughts drift to Rosalind? "It's this damned house," she said aloud. She put on stout walking shoes and a warm jacket against the early spring wind and went downstairs. A murmur of voices came from the library—not Ted's this time, perhaps Grandmother giving instructions to one of the servants. Rynna passed the door quietly and slipped out the back.

The weather was cool and sunny, perfect for a stroll, and she headed toward the river. Once among the trees she couldn't be spotted from the house, and her oppression lifted. She was free for the moment.

Free—and lonely. Everyone she cared about was dead. She needed someone to depend on, and there was nobody left. Cecile promised to be a friend, but she was so young and only cared about Rynna's pretty clothes. As for the remaining Demeray clan—Grandmother, Ted, the unknown Jason, Rosalind?—Pamela was all they had in common, and Pamela was dead.

The fresh wave of grief overcame her again. *I want my mother*. She wandered along the bank of the river and stood gazing into the flowing water, reliving the terrible evening of her mother's death.

She had been waiting in the relentless white corridor, sipping scalding, strong coffee, and the doctor came to her—a departure in itself. She was apprehensive immediately, but when he told her, she could only stand frozen in numb disbelief, warming her cold hands around the waxy paper cup.

"It isn't possible," she said. She stared at the closed

door of her mother's room, but she didn't go in. The doctor asked if she wanted to see her, and she shook her head. She wanted to hold onto the image of Pamela alive, hopeful, laughing.

The doctor asked if she wanted something, and it was a moment before she understood. No, she didn't want anything, no sleeping pill, no tranquilizers, no oblivion. She wanted to feel the full weight of it as soon as she could feel anything. No blunting the pain, no blurring of memory. In a way she owed her mother that. The memory was still fresh, and she had never regretted the decision. Later, after she left the hospital, she strode alone down dark, quiet streets, and it rained a little, and her tears were entirely natural and necessary. Afterward she went home to bed and slept without a sleeping pill. In the morning, and every morning thereafter, she awakened to a world where Pamela Demeray Dalton no longer lived.

As Rynna stood at the river behind Stonebridge Manor, a desperate ache filled her throat and chest, but she couldn't cry. She had come beyond that relief now.

An unexpected grating sound jarred her out of her reverie, and she turned to see Ted making his way down the slope. She was instantly enraged, as if he were intruding on her private grief with deliberate intent.

He rolled toward her until the wheelchair struck an obstacle on the rough ground not five feet from where she stood. He looked up with a faintly bored and mocking expression and said, "You're not thinking of jumping in, are you?"

"Would you mind?"

He didn't hesitate. "Yes. It would be so tiresome. Another funeral, for one thing. We've had enough funerals around here, wouldn't you say?"

God, he was hateful. She turned her back on him without answering. Her eyes stung, and she blinked, forbidding tears. She wished he would go away.

"Well, that was pretty tactless, wasn't it?" he said. "Pamela left here a long time ago. It's not as if we've just lost her. More like getting her back."

"I'm not Pamela." She glared at him and would have said more, but he held up a restraining hand.

"Take it easy. That was tactless too, wasn't it? Sorry. I guess I'm a little out of practice."

"A little," she agreed. She wanted to tell him to go away and leave her alone, and she reminded herself this was his home, his river. She was the intruder here.

"It's this shortage of cousins," he continued. "Just you and good old Jason. I wouldn't waste tact on Jason."

"You don't like Jason," she surmised.

"He's not my favorite cousin."

So far, Jason was Rynna's favorite cousin. She certainly didn't care for this one. He was too blunt and too clever, always joking and always with a bitter edge. She would have said as much, but he beat her to it.

"You're prettier than he is anyway. Not much friendlier. Stuck up, I guess."

"Thanks," she said. "I don't like you either."

He raised his eyebrows. "I guess you are a Demeray at heart," he said. He tried to shove the wheelchair forward again, but it wouldn't budge. "Damn rocks," he said and instead set the brake and pushed himself to his feet.

Rynna reached out to help him, but he stopped her. "I *can* walk, you know," he said. Holding onto the wheelchair and then to the nearest oak, he took a few stiff, cautious steps and leaned against the tree. "What's the matter?" he asked in his familiar mocking tone. He had caught her staring. "Oh, yeah, I suppose you think everybody in a wheelchair is paralyzed."

"No, I just…" She didn't know what she had started to say. He was taller than she expected.

"Yeah, I get a lot of that," he went on. "If I go into town, perfect strangers will come up and ask me what it was like in Korea. Damned if I know. I was 4-F. Consolation prize for not being able to play football. My dad really wanted me to play football. Damn near broke his heart."

"Why are you so disagreeable?" Rynna asked. What annoyed her most was that she didn't know how to take him. He was mocking her and everything else, and yet she couldn't be sure he wasn't just brutally honest.

"Am I?" he asked. "I thought I was using my best company manners."

She shook her head. "Sharpening your wits," she said, "at my expense."

"No." He shook his head, unsmiling. "No, I'm not." For the first time it occurred to Rynna that life might have contrived to give him such a bitter edge. "You'll like Jason better He's a sweet-talker, our Jason."

"Why don't you like him?"

"Oh, no, I'm not going to fall for that one. I told you you'll like him, and if I say anything against him you'll be convinced I eat babies. Assuming you don't think so already."

"Do you?"

"Not me," he said. "I'm not so sure about Jason." Before she could say anything, he raised a hand in a forestalling gesture. "No, I'm sorry, I take it back. Mr.

Wyatt is a fair-haired angel of light. A paragon of the legal profession and a real charmer with the ladies. If all the judges were female, he would win every case. Not that he loses much anyway, you understand. One way or another, he is a winner."

Rynna wasn't much interested in Jason, and she wouldn't learn anything objective about him from Ted anyway. "Did you know his mother?" she asked instead.

"Rosalind? No, she flew the coop before I was even born, or so they tell me. I do remember *your* mother."

Rynna stiffened. She did not want to hear Ted Demeray's version of Pamela's life at Stonebridge. She was in no mood for cynicism.

"I remember her laughing," he said. "She laughed a lot, and she smelled wonderful, and she was always kind to me. Excellent qualities in an aunt. When she left, everyone knew she was happy to be leaving, happy to be going to the man she loved. I cried when she said goodbye to me. I missed her for a long time."

The ache rose in Rynna's throat again, but with a difference now, not self-pitying grief at being left alone in the world, but instead a shared sense of the loss of a special person. If she had nothing in common with the mature, derisive Ted, she could at least identify with the little boy who had lost a beloved aunt. They were kin. You didn't always love your relatives, or even like them, but still they were kin. She understood too why Mrs. Demeray liked to have him read aloud. Without the tone of boredom or mockery, his voice was low-keyed and expressive, with a subtle hint of his Virginia breeding. She felt closer to him than she was ever likely to again, and she couldn't say anything of the sort. He would only say something cutting again, and in her present frame of mind she would probably burst into tears.

When she said nothing, standing silently facing the river, Ted shifted against the tree and said, "I'm sorry."

"Oh, no!" She turned quickly, anxious to assure him he hadn't offended her. "I'm glad you told me that. It helps. Thank you."

He shrugged, started to say something, and stopped. With a little shock of pleasure, she realized she had done the impossible. She had embarrassed him.

****

In spite of the conversation at the river, Ted paid no attention to Rynna at dinner, which was a tasty sausage lasagna followed by angel food cake. He abandoned even the pretense of sociability and brought a book to the table. Mrs. Demeray did most of the talking, and he didn't listen to the conversation, concentrating on his book and absentmindedly eating whatever was set in front of him. He must be the despair of the servants, Rynna thought. Imagine trying to please a man who was eternally cynical and didn't even notice what he was eating.

Only once did he appear to be aware the women were even in the room. When Mrs. Demeray mentioned again that they should have Jason to dinner, Rynna could almost feel him tense, although he was halfway down the long table from her. Mrs. Demeray had already begun to plan the meal and mentioned that she would ask Mrs. Lester to make one of her special chocolate pies. "It was always dear Jason's favorite," she explained.

Ted made a sound that could only be called a snort and turned a page.

"Did you say something?" Mrs. Demeray asked him.

"Nothing, Grandmother," he said sweetly and kept his eyes on his book.

Mrs. Demeray smiled faintly and returned to the menu.

Rynna was astonished. These exchanges were a game, and they both enjoyed it. She baited him. The lordly old woman loved to get a rise out of him. Was Jason invited to dinner to meet her or to give Ted a chance to battle with his favorite adversary? What a family!

After dinner, with Mrs. Demeray gone early to bed and Ted diligently typing away in his room, Rynna yanked the silky velvet rope by her bed and waited for Cecile's soft knock. She needed to talk to somebody with whom conversation was neither an ordeal of endurance nor a series of unseen pitfalls.

She convinced Cecile to sit instead of fussing with her hair or clothes and opened the conversation with, "Tell me about Jason."

"Jason Wyatt?"

"Of course Jason Wyatt. Grandmother keeps calling him a dear boy, and Cousin Ted obviously hates him. I'll never learn anything reliable from either of them. Tell me what you think of him."

Cecile blushed. "Why, I hardly know him, Miss."

"Don't you dare get secretive with me," Rynna said. "And don't call me Miss."

"I'm sorry. I forgot. But he doesn't come here very often. I've only seen him a few times."

"But you were impressed, I see. He must be very handsome."

"Oh, yes! He is terribly good-looking, and he isn't married yet either. Some of the girls are truly smitten."

"Not you, though."

"No, of course not," the girl said and blushed again. "He does seem very nice and—and…"

"Desirable?" Rynna suggested.

"Gentlemanly," said Cecile. "But some say he takes after his father."

"And what was his father like? Surely nobody here now could have known him. I understood Rosalind married him without her grandmother's consent and they never lived here."

"That's true," admitted Cecile. "But there was lots of talk, you know. There's always talk."

"Probably much exaggerated," Rynna reminded her. "What did they say about his father?"

"He was extremely jealous and had terrible rages sometimes. Some say he beat Rosalind. Others say he made her life hell in other ways."

"That's nonsense. Why would she have left this beautiful house to marry a man like that? If he didn't treat her well, she could have come back."

"I don't think so, Miss Rynna. When she left, Mrs. Demeray said she wasn't to come back. She said, 'If you go to that man, I don't ever want to see you again.' "

"How terrible. But she must have forgiven her, and she's fond of Jason."

"They say she sees Rosalind in him, and she likes him, but she can't stand to have him around too much. He's like Rosalind, but he's like his father too, they say."

"So, if he's handsome and gentlemanly and takes after his father, then his father must have been a good person too. Grandmother just couldn't forgive Rosalind for defying her. She may have spread lies about him herself. He was probably a perfectly nice man and devoted to Rosalind."

"Oh, no!" Cecile shook her head decisively. "Nobody knows exactly what happened between them, but everybody knows he killed her."

"What?!"

"Jason's father killed Rosalind. He murdered her. It isn't just talk. He was convicted of murder."

"Are you sure? My mother never told me any of this."

"Oh, yes, everybody knows, Miss—sorry, Rynna, everybody in town knows about it. It didn't happen here, but it was in the papers. He strangled her. He broke her neck."

"Poor Jason," Rynna said at once. The weight of so much tragedy made her restless, and she rose and went to the window.

"Yes, it was a very sad thing," Cecile said. "His father died in prison, and Jason was raised by relatives on his father's side. He didn't come back to Brenford until he was grown."

Rynna turned to meet the girl's eyes. "What does Ted have against him, then? If they never met until they were grown up, it's a little late for cousinly rivalry."

"I don't know why," said Cecile. "But I do know they don't get on. They go at it fiercely sometimes. It's another reason he doesn't visit very often, I guess. Mrs. Demeray doesn't like it when they fight."

"I bet she doesn't," said Rynna, trying to digest what she knew about Jason now. Ted said he was a sweet-talker and she would like him, but he didn't himself. Grandmother said he was a dear boy with a fine law practice. Cecile said he was handsome and gentlemanly, but some said he was like his father, a jealous man with terrible rages. And his father killed his mother when he was a child. Rynna could hardly wait to meet Jason Wyatt.

****

The room was less unfamiliar the second night, and she slept soundly. She dreamed intensely about her mother and woke to the dark, silent room with the taste of tears on her lips. The hands on the old-fashioned Baby Ben alarm clock on the bedside table stood at 2:15. The memory of her dream was too painfully fresh in the lonely darkness, and she cast about for something else to think about, some plan for tomorrow, something to convince her morning would come.

A single low, shimmering note echoed from the music room below. She sat up, listening hard, her heart pounding. The sound wasn't repeated. She hadn't dreamed it. It was real music. Once might be her imagination. Two nights in a row could not be.

Cecile said there was a ghost in the house. Lucy was afraid to enter the music room. Last night, jet-lagged and half asleep, she had been convinced it was Rosalind. Tonight she was sure of nothing. Was somebody in the house playing a trick? Someone who was familiar enough with the house to know she would hear and the others wouldn't be disturbed? She would not have put anything past Ted, but doubted he was physically capable of going downstairs unheard. He could have put one of the servants up to it, though. Or could it be Cecile, stung by Rynna's dismissal of her ghost theory? "Things go on in this house nobody can explain," Cecile had said. Rynna doubted it. An explanation existed for this, and she would find out what it was. She would tell nobody what she had heard. If it was Ted or Cecile, they would give themselves away by watching for signs the trick was working. She would give them no satisfaction.

Amused, she thought, Ted is right. I am a Demeray.

Chapter Three

When Rynna came downstairs in the morning, Ted was alone in the dining room, reading a thick volume and eating sausage and buttered toast.

"Good morning," she said and waited for him to lift his head.

"Good morning," he said brusquely. He seemed surprised and a little annoyed but managed to rise to the occasion. He gestured at the covered dishes on the sideboard and said, "There's oatmeal and sausage and I think some eggs. If you'd like anything else…"

"That will do," she said, and busied herself filling a plate.

"I could ring for more toast," he offered. "This is cold."

"No, thanks." She took a seat and started eating, and Ted picked up the bell and rang it, not so imperiously as Mrs. Demeray, but certainly as if he were accustomed to such things. She could detect nothing on his conscience. She assumed he wanted to get back to his boring book but was obliged to be polite to this inconvenient female relation.

Almost immediately one of the girls Rynna recognized from the previous morning in the kitchen appeared at the head of the table.

"Yes, sir?"

"Oh, Jenny, please bring Miss Dalton some fresh

toast."

"That's not necessary," Rynna said, furious with him for ignoring her.

"We have some lovely hot biscuits, Miss," Jenny said. "Maybe you'd like that better."

"Yes, I would. Thank you, Jenny."

"Biscuits, then," said Ted, "and strawberry preserves or whatever you have."

"Yes, sir." Jenny managed to give the air of having curtsied without doing so and left as silently as she had appeared.

As soon as she was out of hearing, Rynna said, "My God, you're a grouch. I told you I didn't want any toast, but you had to get that girl up here for nothing, and you didn't even thank her."

Ted stopped in the middle of spearing a bite of sausage and stared at her. "For God's sake," he said. "Obviously, you weren't brought up with servants."

"No, I wasn't, and I hope I never learn to treat them the way you do."

"Oh," he said, amused. "You've seen my horsewhip, then?"

"It wouldn't hurt you to be polite."

"I'm sure you were polite enough for both of us. I'm not imposing on Jenny by asking her to do her job, you know. They have little enough work with only the two—three of us. We don't entertain much, and if Grandmother didn't keep them all on as if there were still a houseful, they'd be out of work, wouldn't they?"

"So you're a humanitarian," she said sarcastically.

"No," he said. "Grandmother is, in her way."

Jenny reappeared with biscuits and jam and asked prettily if Rynna would like her to pour the tea.

"No," said Ted. "She doesn't want to overwork you. Beat it."

"Yes, sir," said Jenny, unperturbed, and left. Ted held out his hand for Rynna's cup and poured the tea himself.

"Sugar? Yes, I thought so. You want to watch out for her anyway."

"Who? Jenny?" She split a warm, flaky biscuit and spooned in a dollop of jam.

"Yes, our sweet Jenny. She's a sly one. Listens outside doors and such. I suspect she's secretly in Jason's employ."

"Jason?"

"I imagine he slips her the odd dollar now and then. For all I know he may slip her something else as well."

"Don't be crude. You make it sound as if Jason were the enemy." She bit into the biscuit, which proved as buttery and delicious as it looked.

"Oh, yes, he is, and he has a spy in our camp."

"I don't believe it." She murmured her appreciation of the biscuit.

Ted snagged one for himself and shrugged. "Don't then. What are you planning to do today?"

"Are you kidding? What the hell do you think I'm going to do in this place? I'm going to write some letters and figure out how to get out of here."

Ted was nonplussed.

"Don't look at me like that," she said. "If you weren't so wrapped up in your minerals and your stupid family intrigues, you would have noticed it yourself. It's a beautiful house, but there's nothing to do, and the company is pretty deadly."

"Sorry," he said, both amused and taken aback.

"That really burns me up," she said.

"What?"

"The way you hide behind that goddamned mockery all the time. Jesus, you infuriate me."

"So I see," he said, raising an eyebrow, and then he ran out of quips and fell silent. After a moment he smiled, not the familiar, mocking smile this time, but a real, boyish grin. "I think I might get to like you," he said.

"I don't think you'll have a chance," Rynna said. "I have to get out of here before I go nuts."

"I'm sorry," he said, and almost sounded as if he were. "If I'd known you were coming, I wouldn't have sold the horses. What can I do to make it up to you?"

"It's all right," she said. "I was never a very good rider."

"Me neither." He grinned. "My parents liked to ride. I guess they were the last."

"I could play that fantastic piano," she said, "if it wouldn't disturb anybody."

"It wouldn't disturb me," he said, and she found it impossible to believe he knew anything about ghostly notes at 2:15 a.m. "I'd like to hear you play."

"I don't do requests," she warned. "I'm partial to Chopin."

"God—you're partial to Chopin? I thought I did well to get through 'Chopsticks.' I play great typewriter, though."

"Very funny," she said dryly.

"You don't think I'm funny either, huh? Besides being infuriating."

"I'm sorry. I shouldn't have said that."

"A real conversation stopper," he agreed. "Anyway,

if you get too bored you can borrow some of my books. You can borrow any in the library, for that matter, but the best ones are in my room."

"Yeah, I bet. The life history of rocks or something."

"No," he said. "Not the stuff I write. Real books. You want to come up and see my library?"

"I can hardly wait."

After they polished off the sausage and biscuits, they went up together in the lift. They had been at ease for a few minutes across the breakfast table, but barriers were erected again all too quickly. The wheelchair shouldn't have made any difference, but it did. It came between them. She felt awkward standing beside him. She was learning to like this stranger who was her cousin, and morbid curiosity had no place in their relationship. If he was aware of her feelings, he gave no sign. He had surely encountered it all before.

His room was not in any way what she expected. Behind the door, the imposing, historic Stonebridge ceased to exist. The single mullioned window was obscured by plain fabric curtains. The walls were painted a flat off-white—although not much of them was visible. Bookshelves rose to the ceiling on every side. The bed was narrow, with a simple, solid headboard and a heavy brown quilt. A typewriter sat on a strictly functional small desk. It was a schoolboy's room, almost Spartan except for the books. The wall-to-wall shelves surely held more books than the library downstairs.

"There, you see," said Ted. "Real books."

Rynna ran inquiring fingers over a shelf or two and spotted familiar titles here and there. All sorts of books, old favorites among them—fiction, history, biography, every sort of scientific study. She met Ted's eyes where he sat awaiting her judgment. "What did you mean," she asked, "by 'not the stuff' you write?"

"Oh, yes," he said and pointed out the lowest shelf above the desk. She glanced at the titles, recognized them as textbooks, and slid out the volume at the end. *Introduction to Mineralogy* by Christopher Powell and Theodore Demeray. Rynna was impressed to see the familiar name in bold lettering on the cover.

Are you telling me you wrote all of these?" she asked, indicating the entire shelf.

"No, as a matter of fact, I didn't write any of them. Powell insisted on the co-author credit on that one, but all I wrote was the chapter on crystalline structure. His was hopeless."

Rynna put the book down and tried another, halfway down the shelf. On the title page, below two unfamiliar authors' names were the words, "edited by Ted Demeray."

"You edit textbooks?"

"Dreary, isn't it? But it's an honest living. I hope you didn't think I was living off Grandmother."

"I really hadn't thought…"

"No, I suppose not."

"But that isn't what you've been pounding away at since I've been here, is it?"

"Grandmother gave you a clue, did she?"

"She said your father would be astonished."

"Yes, so he would."

"What's it about, your book?"

"Nothing racy, I'm afraid."

"Minerals and things, Grandmother said."

"Grandmother is no scientist." He was evading her questions. The book he was writing was something he didn't want to discuss with her.

Considering their relationship to this point, she didn't blame him, but now she was curious. Who was the real Ted Demeray? She studied the desk, hunting for clues, but the manuscript had been put away. Her gaze fell instead on the container of sharpened pencils and two medicine bottles. One was a recognizable shape with familiar colors, a commonplace over-the-counter pain reliever available in drugstores and supermarkets. The smaller bottle next to it bore a prescription label she couldn't read without prying, but she knew what it meant. It hadn't occurred to her before, and she was so surprised she blurted it out." Are you in pain?"

"None of your business," he said, and when she continued to stare, he added, "Sometimes. It's nothing I can't handle. Don't worry about it."

"I'm not worried," said Rynna and scanned the bookshelves again. "It's just morbid curiosity." The truth was she was chagrined not to have thought of it before. He lived with pain and disability every day of his life. The wonder was not that he was sometimes disagreeable, but that he was not more so. She was sorry she had been so impatient with him, and it was the last thing she could ever tell him.

After a curious silence in which she could feel him studying her, he said, "I'll tell you the truth, Cousin Rynna."

"That could be dangerous."

"Very dangerous," he agreed. "The truth is I've always considered myself lucky."

"Lucky?" After what she had just been thinking?

"Yes. You see, my parents were terrific about everything, and I always knew they loved me. My dad wanted me to be able to play football and enjoy riding the way he did. It was very hard for him. He was a disappointed man, but he was never disappointed in me, only for me. That made all the difference."

"I understand," said Rynna.

"Do you? I hope your children will be so lucky. The other thing is…" He lifted his hands and flexed his long fingers. "It's not my hands. Do you understand?"

She nodded. She understood the inflection more than the words. In his voice, in the slow, unemphatic way he spoke, was the truth he promised. He thanked God every day that the arthritis that confined him to a wheelchair most of his life never affected his hands. He couldn't play football, but he could type. His world was in this room, surrounded by books, sitting at his typewriter. As long as he had this, the rest of the world could go hang. And yet he was not convincing as an ivory tower recluse, either. He had too much humor, too much courage, too many surprises. She suspected more were to come.

She returned to the shelves. "Let me see what I can lay my hands on. Something fat and readable and not too dull."

"*Les Misérables*?" he suggested. "*Gone with the Wind? War and Peace?*"

"No kidding," she said. "I've never read it. It's the title, I think. It sounds so all-encompassing."

"What, *War and Peace*?" He knew the collection by heart, or it was arranged in a system that eluded her, and he immediately rolled to a shelf beyond her and tugged out a large volume. "I can recommend it," he said. "It's not as ponderous as it sounds."

"Thank you." Rynna accepted the book and opened

it to the title page. On the flyleaf in a clear, elegant hand was written, *To my dearest Ted—Happy birthday—from your devoted Sylvia.* "Who is Sylvia?" she asked without thinking.

Ted stared at her as if he had seen a ghost.

"The inscription," she said, gesturing at the page.

"Oh," he said, both relieved and embarrassed. "I'd forgotten it was a gift…"

"From your devoted Sylvia," Rynna prompted.

"Yes," he said brusquely. "You're welcome to it. It ought to be fat enough to suit you. Now beat it. I've got work to do." He swerved the wheelchair quickly away from her, toward the desk.

"Ted, please don't be angry. I didn't mean to sound flippant. I just wondered who she was. I'm sure it's none of my business."

"No, it isn't," he said at once, and then, wearily, "It isn't important. We were…sort of engaged."

"What happened to her?"

"Nothing. She split." He gave her his wry, humorless smile. "She liked to dance," he said.

Rynna left without a word and returned to her own room. How right she had been—more surprises were still to come. Maybe she and Ted could be friends, and she certainly could use an ally in this place, but she would have to be careful not to blunder in like that. What a family we are, she thought, shaking her head. William, Rosalind, Pamela, Jason, Ted, and me—life has dealt us all a few cards from the bottom of the deck.

She settled into the comfortable armchair near the fireplace and opened *War and Peace*. Ted was right—it was not as ponderous as the title suggested, but she bogged down in the battle scenes and gave it up for a while. She went downstairs, past his closed door with the typewriter clattering behind it, and into the music room.

Alone in the room for the first time, she sensed again the subtle charm she had noticed the first night. Although it was not like any room she had ever lived in, she was at home here, and although she would never have chosen those colors, it suited her taste. The comfortable warmth embraced her, in contrast to the drafty hall. The portrait of Rosalind smiled down from above the mantelpiece, beckoning, welcoming.

"Foolishness," she muttered and sat at the piano. She didn't question her feelings about it, at least. Such a fine instrument should be played, and play it she would, whether it disturbed anyone or not. Her fingers explored the keys, sliding easily into familiar patterns on the unfamiliar instrument, and she played softly, humming under her breath. She played her favorite pieces for her own amusement, without worrying about whether anyone would hear, admiring its exceptional tone. She knew she was safe here. No other part of the house could match its promise.

She played for about half an hour before she became aware of another presence. Lucy was standing in the doorway. "Pardon me, Miss," she said. "I didn't want to disturb your playing, but Mrs. Demeray asked if you would come to the library."

Rynna's confidence vanished. She felt like a child being called to the principal's office. Was she to be reprimanded for playing the piano without permission? "Thank you, Lucy," she said, more calmly than she thought possible, and rose from the bench. As she followed Lucy out of the room, she found herself glancing back at the portrait of Rosalind, as if to borrow her courage. And what did she know about Rosalind's courage?

For all her trepidation, Mrs. Demeray smiled kindly enough when Rynna entered the library. She wasn't in disgrace after all. "Sit down, my dear," Edwina said in a tone that was not quite a command, but serenely confident of being obeyed.

"I hope my playing didn't disturb you," she said, easing into an upholstered armchair.

"Of course not. Play whenever you like. Such a valuable instrument should be played by someone who appreciates it. We pay that ridiculous Mr. Pirelli to keep it in tune, and nobody uses it. Theodore will not practice. He's so like his father." She sighed, and Rynna suppressed a smile. She was amused to hear Ted referred to as if he were ten years old. To Mrs. Demeray, they were all about ten years old and always would be.

"I would like to hear you read," Mrs. Demeray said, picking up a weighty volume from the table beside her chair.

"Yes, Grandmother," she said and opened the book. The feeling was exactly like being asked to recite in class. She remembered Ted reading aloud the afternoon she arrived and told herself Mrs. Demeray simply liked to be read to, but it didn't help.

The book proved to be a dry English historical novel, which added to her fancy that Grandmother belonged to another era. She read until Lucy quietly opened the door and peeked in. Lucy put a finger to her lips and gestured toward the old lady, who was dozing in her comfortable chair. Both reprieved and a little guilty, Rynna rose and slipped out, closing the library door gently behind her.

"I thought she'd soon nod off," Lucy said. "She didn't sleep well last night."

"Is she ill?" Rynna asked. Invalids could be the worst tyrants.

"No, Miss. She's in excellent health for her age. But she does have a little spell sometimes and trouble sleeping. It's her heart, the doctor says, but it's nothing serious, thank God."

Yes, thank God, thought Rynna and returned to her room and *War and Peace*.

****

Ted brought a book to the dinner table again, but this time he left it beside his plate and made conversation like a civilized human being. Mrs. Lester had baked a chicken with a special lemon sauce and served it with a delicious green bean casserole and a jelled strawberry salad. As usual, Mrs. Demeray did most of the talking, but Ted ran interference for Rynna, explaining bits of family history and bringing her into the conversation with surprising deftness.

As she rose from the table, she asked lightly, "Why are you being so nice to me? Are you trying to persuade me to stay?"

"No," he said, smiling. "I'll help you escape. I'm sure you'll make it. Nearly everyone does."

Nearly everyone, she thought as she headed upstairs to her room, sooner or later, in one way or another. Everyone, in fact, except Ted.

****

She dreamed she was in a house she had never seen before, sitting on the floor of a bare room with sunlight flooding in through opened windows. She was sitting against the wall, and she couldn't make her muscles work or control her voice, as if she was paralyzed or held by an overmastering force. Other people were in the room, but she couldn't make herself understood. She wanted to explain what was happening to her and who she was, but when she finally managed to make her voice audible, the only word she could say was her name, and it wasn't her name at all. It was Pamela.

She awoke frightened, unable to shake the terrible feeling of being helpless, of being possessed by someone or something. I was having a dream, she told herself, only a dream. Why was it that dreams, so insubstantial in fact, possessed such emotional power? She lay still, taking slow, even breaths, trying to calm herself, waiting for the dream feelings to pass.

A single note emanated from the piano below and then, as she caught her breath sharply, a second. Two notes and again silence.

Rynna glanced at the clock. It was 2:15.

I won't put up with this, she thought. I won't be tricked and manipulated by anyone. I don't care if there is a ghost in this house or a practical joker or Rosalind bloody Demeray. I'm getting out of here anyway.

She glanced at the clock again and considered the other times. She hadn't looked at the Baby Ben the first night, but 2:15 twice in a row was more than coincidence. Very well, she told herself, at 2:15 tomorrow night someone else will get a surprise.

The Demerays might be devious, but the Daltons could be determined.

Chapter Four

Rynna napped in the afternoon and set the alarm for two a.m.

At dinner she gave Ted a challenging look, but he didn't take any notice. He didn't have a book this time, and he and Grandmother carried on a wide-ranging conversation about current events, local politics, and family history while Rynna concentrated on the chicken parmigiana and roasted vegetables. She didn't care about what was happening in Cuba or the World's Fair in Brussels or century-old family stories, not when she had a mystery to solve. She dismissed Ted as a suspect half a dozen times, but he was still the most likely culprit. Or someone he put up to it. He claimed Jenny was in Jason's employ, and that sword could cut both ways.

"When is Jason coming?" she asked into a silence.

"We're boring Rynna," Ted said. "Her mind is wandering." He was right, of course, but it was unkind of him to say so, and she gave him an icy glare.

"Perhaps we are," Grandmother said. "I wish you wouldn't be so blunt, Theodore. It isn't quite nice."

"It's all right, Grandmother," he said. "Rynna isn't company anymore. She already knows I'm not—quite—nice."

"Really, Theodore," she said disapprovingly, but with a hint of a smile, and responded to Rynna with, "Jason has been invited for tomorrow night. I'm sure he's looking forward to meeting you."

"Oh, yes," Ted said. "We all know how he loves the idea of dining with his assorted cousins."

"Theodore," Mrs. Demeray snapped. "Will you stop? I mean it now."

"Sorry, Grandmother."

"I expect you to behave yourself tomorrow night. I've had about enough of your quarreling with Jason. I don't know what your poor mother would say."

"All right!" said Ted sharply. Did he dislike being chided in front of Rynna, or was it the reference to his mother that annoyed him?

Grandmother, satisfied, continued where she had left off about her great-grandmother Hutchinson.

****

The alarm chimed at two o'clock, and Rynna hastily shut it off and lay still, listening, hoping nobody else had heard it. The house was silent. She waited a few minutes to be sure before she got up and dressed in the chilly darkness. She put her coat on over jeans and a sweater and slipped her flashlight into the pocket.

She opened the door and stood listening. Silence. She closed the door carefully behind her and slipped down the hall past Ted's room. She paused for a second in front of his door and listened. No sound, no movement.

She negotiated the stairs one at a time, her bare feet silent on the plush carpet. Halfway down, she leaned over the banister, concentrating intently. No sound from the direction of the music room, no stir from the servants' hall.

She crept in the door of the music room, where she could barely make out the shape of the piano in the darkness. A quick, furtive glance behind her and then she switched on the flashlight and swept the beam around the still room. Nothing lurked in the shadows. She tiptoed to the piano and ran the light across the keys. No visible strings or wires.

She heard a faint murmur and snapped off the flashlight. She ducked back from the door and hid in a shadowed corner where she was sure she couldn't be seen with the overhead light off. She waited and heard nothing more. The sound had been almost inaudible, perhaps just the old house creaking or settling.

She held her arm close to her face so she could read the faintly luminous dial of her wristwatch. It was 2:15. Easy enough to wait where she was for a few more minutes. If the pattern held, the practical joker would fall right into her trap. She leaned against the wall and kept her breathing steady and quiet. Just a few minutes more, a little patience. The house was quiet, peaceful, waiting.

Someone was in the room.

Rynna snapped on the flashlight.

No one was there. She had not heard anything to suggest anyone had come into the room, and nothing had touched her, and yet for a split-second she had been absolutely certain someone was a few feet away. She'd had such a strong kinesthetic sense of a presence that the flashlight was on before she had time for conscious thought.

She switched it off again, feeling foolish, but damn it, she *had* detected something. The sensation was so vivid she had a lingering memory of the other person's scent. Or did she detect something tangible now? A faint trace of perfume? Something unfamiliar and suggestive of roses. Now I'm imagining things, she told herself sternly. She hoped the light hadn't given her away and she still had time to wait undiscovered for the trickster to appear.

She leaned back against the wall and waited, listening to the silence. The house was almost too quiet, as if nobody lived there. Nothing creaked or shifted or fluttered in the darkness. But for the knowledge that she didn't have long to wait, the silence would have gotten on her nerves. As it was, the hair on the back of her neck prickled. She shivered a little. Like most old houses, Stonebridge was drafty.

The silence was oppressive and in some way alive. An inexplicable chill ran down her spine. She saw nothing, heard nothing. She didn't even have a definite sense of someone else in the room. She was simply unnerved for no reason. For a few seconds more she stayed in the shadows of the music room and then, with an almost physical sensation, her composure shattered.

Rynna fled. She ran for the stairs and clambered up them, slipping and stumbling in the dark, half-choked by terror and gasping for breath. At the top of the stairs, she ran full tilt into someone hurrying down the hall, and before she had time to register who it was, she screamed.

"Miss Rynna!" Cecile, completely astonished, snapped on a flashlight of her own.

"Was it you?" Rynna stammered. "Did you…?"

"For heaven's sake, Miss," Cecile exclaimed at the same time. "Whatever is wrong? You look as if you'd seen a ghost."

Trembling from relief as much as the start Cecile had given her, she almost managed to laugh. "What are you doing up?" she asked.

"I thought I heard something downstairs. Did you

hear something too, Miss?"

"No," said Rynna emphatically. "Cecile, tell me the truth. Were you trying to play a trick on me? Last night and…" But the girl's expression of bewildered innocence was unfeigned. Rynna abandoned her suspicions, at least as far as Cecile was concerned. "I'm sorry if I woke you up," she said.

"I should hope so," said a masculine voice, and Rynna jumped. Ted was sitting in his wheelchair in the doorway of his room, dressed in a nondescript brown robe, his hair disheveled, his expression more annoyed than surprised.

"Sorry," she said again. She was sorry to have disturbed him, but she didn't forget he was her chief suspect. Was he awakened by her scream, or by the brief discussion? Or had he already been awake?

"What's going on?" he demanded.

"Nothing," said Rynna. "Cecile, go back to bed. Everything is okay."

"Yes, Miss," said Cecile, but she lingered a minute longer, unsure where her duty lay.

"I want to talk to you," Rynna said to Ted, determined to put an end to the uncertainty.

"What, in the middle of the night?"

"If you can manage to stay awake."

Her sarcasm did surprise him. "Beat it, Cecile," he said and gestured to Rynna to follow him into his room.

She might have preferred a more neutral site, but at least the room was familiar. In the harshness of artificial light, the decor was even more severely austere. This was the room of an ascetic, a disciplined scholar. Did such men play practical jokes? She sat in the only chair in the room, a cane-seated antique that was only marginally comfortable.

"Well?" he said, as soon as the door was closed. "What is all this wandering the halls in the middle of the night?"

"Either you already know the answer," she said, "or it's going to be damned hard to explain."

"What?" He stared at her with a rough approximation of Cecile's bewildered expression, but she was nowhere near convinced.

"All right," she said. "The first night I arrived here and every night since, at about this time"—she didn't miss Ted's automatic glance toward the clock above the desk—"I have heard…"

"What?" *Did* he know?

"Music. Or not really—just a note or two. From the piano downstairs."

"Wait a minute. You were asleep, and you dreamed—"

"No, I was awake. I always woke up shortly before."

"But you were in your room? And you heard the piano? That's impossible, Rynna."

"No, it isn't. I don't know how it works, maybe through the fireplaces, but I can hear it in my room."

"At two o'clock in the morning?"

"I thought someone was playing a trick on me. Cecile said the house was haunted."

"Oh, that," he said. The scorn in his voice was genuine.

"And I laughed. I thought maybe she was getting even, and then I thought maybe it was you."

"Me?" He was amused. "You think I was playing the piano in the middle of the night?"

"No, I don't," she admitted, hesitating to mention

her reasons. "But I thought you might have put someone up to it."

"Oh, I see," he said. "You figured my talents didn't include slipping downstairs in the middle of the night? Ghosts don't use elevators, something like that?"

"Yes, and despite your charming personality, it did occur to me that you might be trying to…"

"What? I can hardly wait to hear this."

"Make me think I'm crazy, like Charles Boyer in *Gaslight*."

"Jesus, Rynna. You thought…" He studied her. "Do you still think so?"

"I don't know. I'm not sure. I guess not."

"So now you're fresh out of suspects?"

"Not exactly. Tonight I waited downstairs to try to catch whoever it was, but I…I got scared." She waited to see if he would laugh. He didn't. "I didn't hear the piano and I didn't see anything, but once I thought someone was in the room. And then I got scared for no reason. I know what you think. You think I got hysterical and talked myself into it, but I didn't. It was all so damned indefinite, and it doesn't prove anything, but it wasn't my imagination, Ted."

"So what do you think it was?" he asked. "You think the house is haunted? Or do you have another suspect for this mysterious sleight of hand?"

"I think it was Rosalind," she said.

Ted was momentarily speechless. "Rosalind is dead," he said finally.

"Yes, I know."

"And you think…? Jesus." He was silent for a long moment, staring at her with something like astonished respect. "I think you're nuts," he said.

"Of course you do. No rational mind believes in ghosts. I don't either. I never did, and I still don't. But I knew the first night it was Rosalind. I never should have doubted it."

"I'm not sure whether this is better or worse than your other theory," he said. "Either I'm trying to make you doubt your sanity, or there's a ghost in the music room."

"I don't think I know what 'ghost' means," she said. "I don't want to use that word because it has too many flaky connotations. I don't know what to call it. 'Spirit' doesn't thrill me either. Presence? I just know it was Rosalind, and I know you think I'm out of my mind."

"I think it is the middle of the night, and you are obviously shaken up. Try this on me again in broad daylight."

"I will. Don't think I won't."

"Okay," he said and, searching for a change of subject to distract her, added, "How are you doing with *War and Peace*?"

"Pretty well," she said, willing to demonstrate how calm and rational she could be and still believe in Rosalind's presence. "I like Pierre, but Natasha is terribly fickle."

"Yes, well, young girls *are* fickle," he said.

"Oh, yes?" she flared. "What do you know about it?"

He grinned. "Feeling better, I see."

There was a discreet tap on the door, and at Ted's gruff invitation, Lucy put her head in. "Mrs. Demeray heard voices," she said. "She wondered if everything was all right." She looked first at Rynna, sitting in the chair in her jeans and bare feet and then at Ted in his pajamas

51

and robe.

"Miss Dalton had a nightmare," he said. "She was walking in her sleep."

"I was not," Rynna protested and then, flushing under his ironic gaze, "Yes, I guess I was."

"Are you all right now?" he asked formally.

"Yes."

"Then beat it, both of you. I'd like to get some sleep."

Rynna slunk meekly back to bed, reflecting that, whatever Ted might make of her conviction, he didn't want the whole house talking about it. No more notes echoed from the piano, but before she drifted back to sleep she detected the slight scent of roses again. She was safe and warm and comforted, as she was the first night under this roof. Rosalind was near.

Chapter Five

Rynna found no opportunity the next day to try the theory on Ted in broad daylight as she had promised. While she couldn't have definitely claimed he was avoiding her, he did manage to stay out of her way. He was working in his room most of the day, and as long as the typewriter was clattering away she hesitated to disturb him.

She played the piano for a while in the afternoon, half hoping to lure Ted downstairs, half fearing he would only come to scoff. She basked again in the simple charm of the room itself, but nothing so definite as a scent suggested another presence. She gazed at Rosalind's portrait. What was behind those mysterious dark eyes and the hint of promise in her smile?

If the survival of the spirit after death was possible, wasn't it logical for her to linger here? Whether or not she was happy with Jason's father, she had met a violent death at his hands. Wouldn't her spirit have fled back to this place where she grew up happy and sheltered, to this room where she learned to make beautiful music on this fine instrument?

Did nothing draw her back to her other home? No music, no love, no comfort? She had a son. Would Rynna be able to ask Jason about his childhood? He was very young when his mother died, but would he remember her happy, laughing, playing the piano, or would he remember shouting, violent arguments, and the terrible night when they struggled, swaying together on the stairs, and hands encircled her slender throat?

They struggled, swaying together on the stairs… How did I know that?

Cecile said everybody knew about it, but Pamela had never told her how Rosalind died, and yet for just a moment she knew exactly what happened, as if she had witnessed it. They were near the top of the staircase, two shadowy figures in the semi-darkness, both voices raised. Rosalind repeated "No!" insistently several times, and he slapped her twice, and when she backed away, he grabbed her arm and then choked her, his thumbs digging into her flesh, and her head was forced back until…

Blackness. Rynna was giddy for a moment before the room steadied and her head cleared. She shuddered, and although she remained seated at the piano, she was every bit as terrified as she had been the night before when she broke and ran for the stairs. Where did that memory come from? Could she have overheard someone talking about it when she was too young to consciously remember it?

Or did she know what happened through Rosalind? The idea of her presence as music-loving spirit returned to her beloved home was romantic. But a Rosalind tormented by the memory of her own death was another matter entirely. She had never taken much interest in the lore of ghosts, but she knew they were traditionally often the victims of violence, dead before their appointed time and lingering in outrage and the hope of revenge.

Horrible. Horrible. Rynna refused to believe it, and she played the piano with gusto as if to shut out the grisly images. She did not believe in ghosts. If the details of Rosalind's murder had been in the papers, as Cecile said, she could research them in the library or newspaper morgue and prove to herself this brief vision was only her morbid imagination. Damn Stonebridge anyway. The house was gloomy enough to give anybody nightmares.

Presently Lucy appeared in the doorway and interrupted her playing to ask her to join Mrs. Demeray in the library. Again she dutifully read to the old lady from a dull novel for nearly an hour. This time Mrs. Demeray didn't fall asleep, but after a while she dismissed Rynna and rang for Lucy. She wanted to make sure all the preparations for dinner were proceeding smoothly.

Finding herself reluctant to return to the music room, Rynna headed upstairs and struggled with *War and Peace* for a while. Her mind wandered, and she had to keep sternly returning her thoughts to the evacuation of Moscow. "I'm getting out of here," she muttered, half aloud. "This place is giving me the creeps."

She was delighted when Cecile arrived to help her dress for dinner. This evening at least would be a diversion. She longed to pump Cecile about Rosalind's murder, but a little discretion was called for. She had made enough of an impression last night, running into the young maid in the dark and screaming as if she had seen the proverbial ghost.

Cecile, regretting how little she could do with short hair, pinned a rose over Rynna's left ear and coaxed her into her most becoming blue chiffon dress. The style—a high waist, half sleeves, and sweetheart neckline—flattered her slim figure. She was ready—more than ready—to meet Jason Alexander Wyatt.

****

Jason was tall, slender, dark-haired, and terribly good-looking, with bold brown eyes, an engaging smile, and well-groomed, wavy hair. He was impeccably dressed for the occasion in an elegantly tailored suit only a highly successful lawyer could have afforded. Even his hands, with their careful manicure, suggested success.

"This can't be Rynna," he said. He clasped her hand in a firm, warm handshake and then stepped back for a better view. "God, you look stunning," he said and in a smiling aside to Mrs. Demeray, "She certainly raises the family standard."

Rynna didn't take this seriously—Ted had warned her he was a sweet-talker—but on the whole the impression he made was a favorable one. He was undeniably handsome, and his manners were impeccable, and in the prevailing atmosphere of Stonebridge, he was a breath of fresh air.

"Our mothers were cousins," he was saying now, "which puts us within the degree of kinship to be considered kissing cousins." He put his hands on her shoulders as he bent his head to claim the privilege. He kissed her full on the lips in an almost impersonal, brotherly way, but with a lingering promise. Nicely done, Rynna found herself thinking. For now at least she could see him clearly, with the cynical view Ted would have taken, but at the same time she was already being drawn in by his apparently genuine charm.

He kissed Mrs. Demeray more dutifully and took her arm as they entered the dining room. "You have more color in your cheeks than the last time I was here," he said. "Either Rynna has brought some life into this mausoleum or some lucky fella's been courting you."

"Don't be impertinent," she said in a tone of mock severity. "I'm in good health, thank you, as I always am."

"And Cousin Ted? You've been well, I hope."

"Terrific," Ted said dryly. His idea of dressing for dinner extended only to wearing a V-neck pullover sweater over a white shirt. He might not even own a jacket or tie.

Jason pulled out Mrs. Demeray's chair and made sure she was comfortable before he moved on to do the same for Rynna. She couldn't see the look he gave Ted as he held her chair, but the one Ted gave him in return was almost contemptuous. Jason had everything he didn't, and simple jealousy would explain his enmity.

Jenny served the first course, keeping her eyes demurely lowered as she carried the soup tureen from place to place, and filled the wine glasses. The perfect servant, discreet and efficient, but Rynna noticed the way she looked at Jason. "Our sweet Jenny," as Ted called her. She might not be a spy, but she was clearly smitten. Cecile had said some of the girls were, and why not? He was dreadfully handsome and charming. The servant girl's dream. Most likely a dozen girls in town dreamed of him as well.

Ted, the only son of an only son, was the presumed heir to Stonebridge and the Demeray fortune, but charming, dark-haired Jason put Ted, with his bland looks and disabled legs, in the shade. Jason was the real catch. She was thinking, of course, of the girls in town, not of herself. They were both her cousins, and she was accustomed, even before meeting them, to consider them as romantically off-limits. But now, exchanging laughing comments with Jason while Ted visibly kept himself in check, the thought surfaced in the back of her mind that she and Jason were only second cousins.

Mrs. Lester had pulled out all the stops for the honored guest, including the finest prime rib topped with sautéed mushrooms, and Jason lavished praise on every dish.

Ted did fairly well at keeping his promise to "behave." Mrs. Demeray ranged far and wide on her favorite subject—the family history—and if Jason was not fascinated nobody would have guessed. Every remark Ted and Jason exchanged bore an edge, but they stayed within the bounds of civility by keeping them to a minimum.

At one point Ted supplied a date Mrs. Demeray was groping for, and Jason said to Rynna, "He's the brilliant one in the family, you know. He has a photographic memory." He managed to make it sound like some sort of idiot savant trick.

He told amusing stories about his court cases with a self-deprecating humor that put him in a better light than blatant bragging. He was a little obvious, a little arrogant, but damn it, he was charming. Little by little, Rynna succumbed to his wit and to the wine and the party atmosphere of having a new face in the house. She liked Jason except for the way he spoke to Ted, but she didn't like the way Ted spoke to Jason, either.

After they finished the delectable chocolate pecan pie, Ted excused himself and rode the lift up to his room. "That book of his," Mrs. Demeray explained. They lingered over coffee and then adjourned to the music room, so Jason could hear Rynna play.

Something was odd about the music room, but in the glow of the wine and his electric presence, she couldn't put her finger on it. Something was different. Something was missing. She didn't puzzle over it for long, though. She had too many other things on her mind. Jason was clearly familiar with the room and didn't even glance at Rosalind's portrait. Rynna longed to ask him what he remembered about her, but it would be indiscreet to do so. He hadn't remarked on the resemblance Cecile had noticed. Maybe the girl had imagined it. How strange that Rosalind's favorite room held something special for her but not for Rosalind's son. Still, it was all so long ago, and he was definitely a man of the present.

She played Chopin without self-consciousness but with a vague unease. Was she forgetting something important? Surely it had nothing to do with Jason, leaning above her, relaxed and smiling in his easy, flattering way. The feeling nagged at her mind for a few minutes, and then she let it go. The evening was too pleasant and the company too congenial for her to be bothered by elusive phantoms.

Jason played too, not well but with a dashing self-assurance and enthusiasm she found hard to resist. He bent his head above the keys and pounded away with furious concentration like a schoolboy, and Rynna laughed in delight.

"Is it that bad?" he asked, grinning.

"You were great," she said. "You should go on the stage."

"I noticed you didn't say concert stage. Vaudeville more likely." He slid into raucous carnival music.

"That's terrific."

He finished with a flourish and stood up to take an exaggerated, hammy bow. "Your turn again," he said. "I think Grandmother would prefer something a little more sedate."

"Indeed," said Mrs. Demeray, who was nevertheless relaxed and smiling. "He is a rascal," she told Rynna later, "but a pleasant one."

The evening was quite successful, and when Jason had gone home and Mrs. Demeray to bed, Rynna sat at her dressing table, smiling at the image in the mirror. She looked pretty tonight—young, happy, flushed with excitement. She hadn't had so much fun in a long time, certainly not since her mother died. She was sensible enough to know it wasn't entirely Jason who had done the trick. She was so bored and restless, so ready for a change, for a good time.

With languid reluctance, she unpinned the rose and laid it on the dressing table. She undressed in the semi-darkness, not wanting Cecile to disturb her mood. She let the party dress fall over the back of a chair instead of hanging it in the closet. She was already getting spoiled, used to servants. She was even beginning to like being called "Miss."

She lay awake for a while, thinking about Jason. Why did he and Ted dislike each other so much? She knew Ted well enough now to know he could make a better effort to get along with someone so likeable. But it wasn't all on his side either. Jason responded in kind. Did anyone remember now how it started? Was any specific incident the basis of the feud? Or had they taken an instant dislike to each other like a couple of mongrel dogs snarling and bristling at each other? Was it something akin to sibling rivalry? Rivals for what? The attention of an old woman living in the past? Did Ted want the kind of public career his cousin enjoyed? Did Jason want Stonebridge? As long as Ted preferred to retire to his typewriter, she would never know.

She slept and dreamed vividly of a darkened staircase, a violent struggle, shouts, and the choking terror of strong hands at her throat.

"No!" She woke herself crying out and lay still, listening, hoping no one else had heard. After last night, she would be getting a reputation for nightmares. But the house remained silent, apparently still asleep. She turned her head to see the clock. It was 2:15.

Now we'll see, she thought, and sat up. She waited through a silent, breathless pause and then…

Not the shimmering note of previous nights, but a harsh, clashing chord, deep and frightening.

Rosalind was disturbed.

Chapter Six

In the morning Rynna again found Ted breakfasting alone in the dining room, but this time he was less annoyed to see her. "Good morning," he said in an agreeable tone. He was eating corn flakes with strawberries. He righted a cup, poured her tea, and passed the sugar. "Did you sleep all right?" he asked politely, but his expression asked something else.

"Yes," she said, "and I had a pleasant evening. You should have stayed."

He shook his head. "No, thanks. Now you can tell me how I did at dinner. Do I get an A for deportment?"

"You'll have to ask Grandmother. Personally, I think I liked you better when you were 'not quite nice.'" She lifted the lids of the warming dishes on the sideboard, finding nothing that tempted her this morning.

"Did you? I'll see what I can do. I have an idea. What would you say to a picnic?"

"A picnic?" She turned, eyebrows raised. It was an unlikely thing to suggest, and she found herself trying to detect an ulterior motive.

"Yes, a picnic. You know, lunch packed in a basket and taken outdoors. A little excursion down by the river?" He smiled at her surprise and added, "Rich people have picnics too."

"All right. Yes, it sounds like fun. I just thought— you're always so busy."

"I believe we have something to discuss," he said. "And…" He raised his voice a shade. "Certain people have been known to listen at doors." Rynna's gaze automatically went to the door, and she couldn't be sure whether she heard a slight rustle from outside. Ted grinned. "You do see what I mean?"

"Yes," she said dryly. "Is there any more cereal? I'm going to get fat if I keep eating bacon and eggs."

****

The day was perfect for a picnic, clear and sunny with a light breeze. Mrs. Lester had packed enough food for six—cold fried chicken, roast-beef sandwiches, oatmeal cookies, a thermos of ice-cold lemonade. Rynna carried the basket, as Ted had his hands full maneuvering the wheelchair down the slope.

They chose a spot near the river with equal amounts of sun and shade, and Rynna laid out the tablecloth. Ted sat under a tree, and she settled on the grass, heedless of stains, and surveyed the lunch arrayed before her. "Heavenly," she said. "Is this what they mean by a spread?"

"No doubt," said Ted, absently rubbing his knees. Rynna bit her lip to keep from asking impertinent questions. He had other things on his mind anyway. "I have a confession to make," he said.

"Something dreadful, I hope."

"Not dreadful, perhaps, but certainly 'not quite nice.' "

"Oh, good."

"I was in your room last night."

She sat up. "What? When?"

"While you and Grandmother and our beloved cousin Jason were in the music room, making an unholy

63

racket. You were right—you can hear the piano clearly in your room. I could hardly hear it at all in mine. Interesting. It's a wonder nobody ever noticed it. Or maybe they did. Pamela might have. I was too young to remember if she ever said anything about it."

"So now you believe me? I'm not crazy?"

"Not so fast. You were right about the acoustics, but it only means it is possible for somebody to play a practical joke on you. Someone who noticed what I never did. Or somebody is playing *Gaslight* with you."

"How do I know it isn't you?"

"I appreciate your crediting me with the imagination to come up with such a stunt, but as you so kindly pointed out, I couldn't have done it without an accomplice. Anyway, if I wanted to drive you mad, I would encourage your belief in the ghost of Rosalind past."

"It isn't funny, Ted."

"I didn't say it was. Anyway, did you hear anything last night, or were you and our guest up carousing past the witching hour?"

"I bet you know exactly what time Jason left."

"I couldn't care less what time he left. I'm trying to play detective here. *Did* you hear the piano last night?"

"Yes."

"Just like the other times?"

"Yes—not quite the same, though. It was different, scarier."

"Escalation? Turning the screws? Or maybe Rosalind doesn't want her progeny in the house. Did you think of that?"

"Damn it, I shouldn't have told you. You think everything is a joke." His flippancy was annoying, but he had also hit the nail on the head. She had known it was true last night, just as she'd known the first night it was Rosalind. Something had disturbed Rosalind last night, and if it was not Jason, what was it? What else was different?

"No, I don't," Ted said mildly. "But you take life too seriously, Rynna."

"I don't take life too seriously, but when something strange is happening, I sure as hell won't dismiss it with flippant remarks like you do. I want to know what's going on."

"So do I."

"Anyway, it doesn't make sense. Why wouldn't she want him here?"

"If I had a son like Jason, I wouldn't."

"Oh, will you stop? It is so damned childish. Grandmother was right. The two of you could get along if you half tried. Jason is very nice, very easy to like. *I* liked him. I thought he was charming and lots of fun to be with."

"Oh, Jesus," he said, and his tone wasn't what she expected. "Not you too."

"What?"

"Nothing." He shook his head. "*Cousinage— dangereux voisinage.*"

"What? I didn't know you spoke French."

"There are a lot of things you don't know. Cousinhood is dangerous neighborhood. It's in *War and Peace*, remember?"

"Sorry. I don't have your photographic memory," she said in a tone reminiscent of Jason's, and thought at once, If Jason can be cruel, so can I.

If Ted noticed the unkindness, he didn't react. "At least *I* didn't have to buy my degree," he said and bit into a roast beef sandwich.

"I've never seen two grown men behave so childishly," Rynna complained. "Jason—"

Ted cut her off. "I don't want to hear about Jason. Shut up and eat."

She had attended more enjoyable picnics.

****

Later in the afternoon, Rynna confided in Cecile. If nothing else, she would be a more receptive listener than Ted. As soon as Cecile settled herself in a chair with a skirt that needed hemming, Rynna sat across from her on the bed and said, "I owe you an apology."

"An apology? Whatever for?"

"Remember when you told me about Lucy and the music room? I was patronizing about it, and I was wrong."

"Oh, no, Miss, you only…"

"I was wrong, Cecile. Very smug and very wrong. What you said is true. Things do go on in this house that nobody can explain. I never believed in such things before, but now I think Lucy is right—not to be afraid, but there is a ghost or something, a presence of some kind, in the music room."

Cecile was staring at her with mixed emotions, as if she suspected she was being conned but was nevertheless anxious to believe, like children enjoying the scary thrills of ghost stories. "Wh-what do you mean?" she asked, wide-eyed.

"I sensed something in the room. I don't know what. Nothing to be frightened of, surely. And late at night when everybody is asleep, I hear someone playing the piano."

"Oh, Miss!" The girl was thrilled and then afraid of

appearing too gullible. "Are you sure?"

"Yes, I'm sure, and I know who it is. It's Rosalind."

Cecile was speechless.

"Don't you think that makes sense?" Rynna asked her. "I believe it because I feel it's true, but it's logical, too. Rosalind was happy here. The music room was her favorite room. In her place, I would want to haunt it too."

Cecile stared at her, needle poised.

"Or do you think I'm crazy too, like Cousin Ted?"

If possible, Cecile was even more amazed. "You told *him*?"

"Yes, and he thinks I'm nuts. Which should not surprise me."

"He's a scientist," Cecile said, as if that explained everything.

"He certainly is. You mustn't tell anybody else about this. Not yet. Most people won't believe it anyway, and we don't want a lot of gossip."

"My lips are sealed," said Cecile so eagerly that Rynna regretted telling her. Cecile probably couldn't wait to run downstairs and tell what she learned.

Nobody needed to gaslight her. She could do the job quite thoroughly herself.

****

That night, Rynna awoke to a feeling of calm contentment. Whatever had disturbed Rosalind the night before had passed. She had a sense of belonging, of comforting connection with Stonebridge and its inhabitants, past and present. She lay still, waiting, and was rewarded, not with a few notes but with a complete musical phrase. She recognized it immediately as the beginning of *Für Elise*. *I can name that tune in six notes.*

Could Ted or Cecile play *Für Elise*?

****

Two days later, Jason called and asked Rynna to have dinner with him in town. The invitation was a reasonable one. With the almost reclusive life led by Ted and Mrs. Demeray, she had yet to see anything of Brenford. Good manners required Jason to return their hospitality, and if the invitation didn't include the Demerays, it was no doubt because he knew they wouldn't accept. She would be the envy of all the eligible young ladies in town, but she still hadn't stopped thinking of him primarily as a charming and likeable close relative.

He picked her up in a sleek silver-gray Ferrari. "Is this what lawyers drive?" she asked.

"This is what this lawyer drives," he said. His tailoring was impeccable, his shirt real silk. She didn't know how much money he earned, but he certainly knew how to spend it. If he was not as rich as the Demerays, he was flashier. Rynna felt more than ever like the poor little church mouse. She didn't know which was worse, Ted's offhand lord-of-the-manor cynicism or Jason's stylish arrogance.

He was pleasant company anyway. He made conversation easy, taking an interest in everything she said and filling in the silences with local color. She didn't have to be on her toes all the time as she did with Ted. If he set traps, they were invisible, and it was very relaxing.

He drove past his office and the handsome turn-of-the-century building that housed the courtrooms of Brenford County. "I'll show you my office sometime," he said. "It's quite impressive. It will impress you with how much of the legal profession is pure paperwork. My files have files. Fortunately, I have a secretary who knows what's what. Sometimes I think she could argue my cases too." He appreciated his secretary—nice touch.

He drove right through Brenford, pointing out the historic sites, such as they were, and escorted her to a small, discreet French restaurant with an elegant menu and inflated prices. Jason ordered for both of them— lobster bisque, goat cheese salad, filet mignon with bearnaise sauce, accompanied by pinot noir, with chocolate ganache crepes for dessert.

"Are you sure you can afford this?" she asked.

"If I can't, I'm in the wrong business."

"Why did you become a lawyer?"

He considered the question. "I don't know. I don't think I ever thought about doing anything else. It was sort of inevitable. In my blood, I guess."

"Was your father a lawyer?"

"No," he said. His tone made it clear the subject was off-limits. "My grandfather was. He was a judge too, and he ran for Congress. Unsuccessfully."

"Are you interested in politics?"

"No. Maybe someday, but right now I'm enjoying what I'm doing too much to think about doing anything else. Would you vote for me?"

"Depends on who you run against."

"Good answer. I'd vote for you regardless."

"For what?"

"Anything you like. I expect you'd stick up for whatever you believed in. Yeah, I'd vote for you." He grinned. "If you're smart, you'll get that in writing."

A great deal of what he said during the evening was in the same vein—good-humored, flattering, and quite meaningless. The unchallenging nature of the conversation allowed her to give the exquisite meal the attention it deserved. The meat was tender, juicy, and perfectly grilled, the wine light and fruity, and the dessert delectably rich.

After dinner they went on to a small club with atmospheric lighting and an excellent band. Jason was a good dancer, better than she would have guessed, and she had a marvelous time. Being away from Stonebridge, breathing different air, would have been enough. She hadn't expected to be so thoroughly entertained. The evening was not only fun but also pleasantly romantic, and it didn't matter at all that he was her cousin.

One reminder of Stonebridge did mar the perfect evening. Circling the dance floor in his arms, flushed with happiness, she remembered Ted's cool dismissal of Sylvia, "She liked to dance." She was overcome with the sadness of that, as she hadn't been when he said it. Ted could never take a girl dancing, and the one woman who had declared herself "your devoted Sylvia" had proved untrue. Maybe she left him for someone like Jason. She would not dare even to think, "Poor Ted," but only, "How terribly sad life is sometimes."

Jason delivered her to Stonebridge at a respectable hour to find the house dark and silent. Nobody had bothered to wait up, and even the servants had retired early. He came in with her and, rather than disturb anyone, said goodbye in the dimly lit front hall.

"I had a wonderful evening," she told him and didn't have to rely on inbred politeness. "Thank you."

"Entirely my pleasure," he said, smiling. "We'll have to do this again." He kissed her, much as he had the first time, when he claimed the privileges of a kissing cousin. No more than that, or not much more. Second cousins.

"Good night, Jason."

"Good night." He kissed her again briefly and left.

Rynna sighed and headed up the stairs to bed.

A light was on in the music room.

She stopped where she was on the stairs and caught her breath. The hair on the back of her neck prickled, but common sense told her she had nothing to fear. Someone must have waited up for her after all. She went back down and into the hall and stood for a few seconds, listening, detecting nothing. Someone—Lucy, who didn't like to go into the room—had simply left a light on. When every other light, save the dim bulb near the entrance, was out?

Was she about to solve the mystery? Did she want to?

The light blinked off.

Rynna waited for somebody to come out of the music room. She expected to see Ted, who was, in spite of all logic to the contrary, still her chief suspect.

Nobody appeared. Steeling herself, Rynna approached the open door. No murmur or rustle betrayed a presence. Was she imagining the faint scent of roses?

She stood uncertainly in the doorway and then decisively strode in and snapped on the light.

Nobody lurked in the corners, and no visible sign of an earlier presence was left behind. No back door or secret panel for a plotter to slip out through? Nothing. Nobody had waited up for her.

Unless it was Rosalind.

Chapter Seven

Except for Cecile, who wanted to hear all about it, Rynna found a singular lack of interest in her evening out. Mrs. Demeray said politely that she was glad she'd had a good time and quickly changed the subject. Ted didn't even pretend a polite interest.

"He *is* handsome," Cecile agreed wistfully as she made up the bed. "But they do say he has a temper like his father."

"I haven't seen any sign of it," Rynna said, dismissing the idea, once and for all, as idle servants' gossip. "He was perfectly charming to me."

She did not tell Cecile about the light in the music room. She didn't tell anyone she had dreamed again of struggling with someone at the top of the stairs, of being choked. She didn't admit, even to herself, that when she managed to glimpse his face in the half dark it was familiar.

For three nights in a row she slept straight through and heard no vibrations from the music room.

****

The third morning after their first night out, Jason called and invited Rynna to a party, to meet some of his friends. That too was a reasonable thing for a cousin to do. She would go crazy if she didn't make contact with people outside Stonebridge. The prospect of real conversation with other human beings, interesting people with interesting lives, was definitely enticing.

The telephone was in the hall downstairs. The Demerays could have afforded a dozen extensions, but that idea did not belong to the century Mrs. Demeray was living in. At least she had been willing to update to a dial phone, bypassing the operator, but it was the only one, and receiving a call involved a servant climbing the stairs to knock on her door. Consequently she had no chance of privacy. Whoever answered the phone would report in the servants' hall that Miss Rynna had received a call from Jason Wyatt.

The location of the telephone meant it was possible for Ted to overhear her end of the conversation. She went into the dining room when she got off the phone, and he was reading one of his boring books as if nothing else existed, his breakfast dishes already cleared away. He probably hadn't heard. Surely he was above eavesdropping.

"Good morning," he said neutrally. He must at least have heard the phone ring, but he didn't ask who'd called. He didn't care. All he cared about was rocks.

"Good morning," she said. Her annoyance must have shown in her tone of voice, and his eyebrows went up.

"Something wrong?" he asked.

"Nothing."

He studied her, and she couldn't read his expression. "Well," he said finally. "I'm going to town today. Would you like to come?"

"You're going to town? Why?" She sat in her accustomed seat and poured herself a cup of tea.

A familiar ironic tone crept into his voice. "I've been known to go all the way to the state line," he said.

"I'm quite a traveler."

"I bet."

"I'm going to the university to use the library. Pretty boring, yes?"

"No," she said. "I'd like to come. I'd like to see the university. I've heard it's a lovely campus."

"If you say so. They have a good library."

While she was dressing for the excursion to town, she considered the timing of Ted's offer to take her along. Did he know she'd accepted another invitation from Jason? Was this another move in the continuing chess game of cousinly rivalry? How classy—an offhand suggestion that she might like to visit a library. She had no reason not to go, nothing to keep her at Stonebridge. Any chance to get out for a while was welcome. Ted certainly wasn't courting her.

Was Jason?

****

In the Bentley, sitting back in plush comfort beside Ted, Rynna asked, "Is this what you meant when you said you would help me escape?"

He glanced at the back of the chauffeur's head as if he were reminding her to be discreet. "No," he said. "But it will do for a start."

She tried again. "What are you going to the library for?"

He told her, and she understood about every third word.

"Sorry I asked," she said. The weather was lovely, and the first part of the trip was smooth and pleasant, on little-traveled roads lined with imposing trees leafed out in new green. Ted pointed out where the river could be glimpsed through the trees.

"There's a waterfall," he said. "You'll have to see that sometime. It's one of your basic tourist attractions."

"Of which there are not many in these parts."

"Not unless you pine to see where Edmund Randolph slept," he agreed.

After a brief, companionable silence, Rynna said, "Ted?"

Something in her voice caught his attention, and he really looked at her for a change.

"I'd like it if we could be friends," she said.

He met her eyes, and his held no mockery. "So would I," he said.

Ted asked the chauffeur to drop them at the front gate so they could cross the "lovely" campus at a leisurely sightseeing pace while Ellery drove around back to the library to pick them up afterward. "I'll be in the library for a couple of hours, but Miss Rynna might like to do some shopping in the village. Yes?"

"Don't call me Miss Rynna," she said. "Yes."

Ellery nodded and withdrew.

"He doesn't talk much," she said as they headed down the long, curving path through the tree-shaded campus.

"No, he doesn't," Ted agreed. "An excellent quality, in servants and in—"

"Don't say it."

He grinned and directed his attention to the buildings they were passing. The dominant style was Greek Revival, with imposing columns and low-pitched roofs. He identified them for her with the same attention Grandmother Demeray had given to the rooms at the manor. This was his world, as much as Stonebridge.

After a few minutes Rynna realized they were

attracting discreet stares. She hoped she had never gaped at a handicapped person, but these people might not be aware they were doing it. Ted showed no sign of being aware of it, until he noticed Rynna noticing. Instead of referring to it directly, he said, in his familiar ironic tone, "I never wanted to play football anyway."

She had been thinking only about the university and Ted, and now that it had been so rudely called to her attention, all she could think about was the damned wheelchair. Many of the buildings, which, after all were more than a century old, had forbidding flights of stairs. Were ramps available somewhere out of sight?

"Did you go to school here?" she asked.

"Here," he said, "and in France."

"France? Really?" She was impressed.

"*Vraiment*. Being filthy rich has certain advantages."

"Are you? Filthy rich?"

He shrugged. "Grandmother is. I work for a living."

"Technically anyway."

He was not offended. "Yes," he said, "but much of life hinges on technicalities."

"What does that mean?"

"Think about it," he advised.

The library was one of the newer buildings, with a lot of glass and artificially aged stone and no stairs. Ted showed her around and then suggested she have Ellery drive her into the neighboring village. "Soak in a little local color," he said, "or spend money. Shopping always improves your outlook."

"Speak for yourself," Rynna said cheekily.

She did stroll through the village, window shopping, but she had a better idea. The university library was sterile and imposing, but in the village she found a smaller, older, more welcoming institution—a branch of the Brenford Public Library. Ted might find all he wanted in the science department of the academic library, but the public library boasted a local history collection and better still, newspapers on microfilm, all nicely organized and thoroughly indexed.

Within fifteen minutes she was reading the *Brenford Gazette* coverage of Alex Wyatt's murder trial. Studying the slightly fuzzy newspaper photographs, she detected little resemblance between Jason and his father. Alex was fair-haired and broader through the shoulders. Jason didn't take after Rosalind either except for his coloring. She would have to look through the musty photograph albums Grandmother was so proud of to find the ancestor Jason resembled.

Nowhere in the generously detailed story did she find any mention of the crime having taken place on or near a staircase. Previous violent arguments were witnessed by servants, and Wyatt admitted having slapped and choked Rosalind. He hinted darkly that she was unfaithful, but no evidence was presented to substantiate the claim. The state's case was strong, and the jury was out for less than four hours before returning a verdict of guilty of first-degree murder. Alexander Wyatt was given a sentence of twenty-five years to life. Cecile had said he died in prison.

Considerably sobered, Rynna walked back to the car. How had Jason, with such a dark background, grown up so bright and charming? He had been raised by his grandparents from an early age, but he must have been scarred by his mother's death. Living with his father's parents, it was likely he had been exposed to Wyatt's version of the story. Could he believe his father was innocent, even blame Rosalind for Wyatt's death? But no, she had not sensed anything like that in Rosalind's favorite room, sitting at the piano alongside her portrait. Jason was apparently indifferent to his mother now, considering her only part of the dim past.

Only Rynna, who had never known her, detected her presence.

Ted had gathered the information he needed and came back with two fat books whose titles she didn't understand. He also brought a book for her. "You should read this," he said, handing her a slim volume. "If you've read it, read it again." The title was *The Hound of the Baskervilles.*

"Why?" she asked, flipping through the pages with their intricately sketched illustrations. "I've never read much Sherlock Holmes."

"Your education has been sadly neglected. You'll love it. It's about a family who live in a gloomy old mansion, and everybody believes in the family curse, but maybe, just maybe, somebody is being manipulated, à la *Gaslight*."

"Oh, terrific," said Rynna, letting the book fall closed. "I can hardly wait."

"Such enthusiasm," he said wryly. "Did you find anything interesting in the village?"

"You might say that. I went to the public library to use the newspaper microfilm." She decided to be honest with him. "I read about Rosalind's murder."

"Jesus," he said. "Why in the world?"

"I'm learning to appreciate family history," she said. "Maybe we have a curse. Maybe we're like the Baskervilles."

"Maybe you shouldn't read it after all," he said. "You have too much imagination altogether."

"Or the rest of you have too little." She sighed and fell silent, gazing out the window toward the narrow thread of the river. She was uncomfortably aware of Ted's eyes on her, as if he could read her thoughts.

"Rynna, do me a favor," he said seriously.

"What?"

"Don't get serious about Jason."

She couldn't read his expression. He was determined to warn her off, but she couldn't understand why. Her personal life was none of his business anyway. "Grow up, Ted," she said, dismissing the entire subject.

****

Again that night in the two o'clock darkness, the opening phrase of *Für Elise* rose from the music room below.

****

The party Jason took her to was a lot more fun than she expected. The informal get-together at the home of a colleague included six couples, all in some way involved in the legal profession, all apparently glad to meet and welcome Jason's attractive cousin. She could easily picture herself as part of this circle of friends, all bright, all articulate and good-humored. One slightly cynical attorney appeared to think less of Jason than the others, but his wife made up for it by being terribly sweet and funny. Rynna struggled to keep all their names straight but felt included at once. What a breath of fresh air this was after Stonebridge.

In the company of so many compatible couples, most of them married, how had Jason escaped their matchmaking? If ever a man had an obvious need for a suitable wife, he did. She considered the possibility that something was wrong with him, something that made him an unsuitable match. Cecile said he was considered a catch but some said he took after his father. But that was nonsense. Nobody in the circle he belonged to would be influenced by such irresponsible gossip. He was a catch, all right. He just hadn't found the right girl yet.

Among all the people she had so far encountered at Stonebridge and in the surrounding area, only two were less than enchanted with Jason Wyatt: Cy Harris, the lanky young attorney with the biting wit, whose antagonism might be professional jealousy or the result of a courtroom rivalry, and Ted Demeray, who could make no coherent case against his cousin and came off as a disagreeable recluse who did not want to share his family domain with a brighter relation.

Rynna could have added a third name to the list, but she couldn't yet accept the connection. When she lay awake at 2:15 the night of the party and a clashing, disturbing chord rose again from the piano below, she still didn't understand why Rosalind was disturbed.

****

On the second evening after the party, Ted delayed his work at the typewriter long enough to join Rynna and Mrs. Demeray in the music room for a while after dinner. This evening was different in every way from the first one, when Jason had kept things lively, and Rynna had been puzzled by something different about the room. The mood was pleasant, a low-key, mellow, after-dinner ambience that made her feel, almost for the first time, that here she was among family. The warmth and charm of the room were just as they had been the first night— the magnificent timbre of the piano, Rosalind's portrait smiling down at her from the mantelpiece, Grandmother placidly settled in the armchair, Ted listening thoughtfully.

When she stopped playing, he stirred as if his mind had been somewhere else and said, "I liked that one. What was it?"

"*Vilia*. Franz Lehar."

"I like it. Play it again."

"Yes, sir," she said and smiled to show she didn't mind his carelessly commanding tone. She played it through again and was aware of his intent eyes on her the whole time.

"Yeah," he said when she finished. "That's nice."

"Any other requests, sir?" she asked and when he shook his head, "Grandmother?"

"Anything, dear. You play beautifully."

Somehow she preferred Ted's compliment. She played Chopin and then, a bit daring, *Fur Elise*. Grandmother sighed as soon as she recognized it. "It was Rosalind's favorite," she said. She spoke calmly, unemotionally, but the hair on the back of Rynna's neck stood up.

Still playing, striving for the right casual tone of voice, she asked, "Can Jason play it?"

Ted left the room without a word.

Grandmother, not surprised by either the question or the abrupt departure, said, "I wouldn't think so, dear."

Ted? No, he said he did well to get through "Chopsticks." He might have deliberately misled her, but Mrs. Demeray had dismissed him as a musician with, "Theodore will not practice. He's so like his father." He was like his father, but she knew nothing about William except a few stories her mother had told her about their childhood. Nothing that would illuminate Ted's character. And Jason? Was he like his father? What was his father like? What did anybody know aside from gossip and the facts of the final tragedy?

She played the opening again and considered that it would not be difficult for someone to learn those few notes. Who knew it was Rosalind's favorite? Who else had Grandmother told? If the piano hadn't been played in years, when would she have had occasion to mention it? Did any of the servants play? Servants always knew everything there was to know about the people they worked for. Or did they? What did Cecile know? Lucy? Jenny? Why was she sometimes so certain Rosalind was here while she still tried to unravel this monstrous practical joke? Why would anybody want to lose sleep to implement such a scheme? What would anybody gain?

She sighed and her fingers rested on the keys. She no longer wanted to play anything. She was trying to solve the mystery of Stonebridge, and it was not one but three mysteries: Ted, Jason, and Rosalind.

****

She went out with Jason again. She wasn't sure why except that she didn't have any better offers. They went to the French restaurant again, where they enjoyed chicken Marengo and a fine Bordeaux, and to a club for dancing, and ended the evening with a stroll by the river, just talking, for a long time. He was excellent company and so easy to talk to.

He did tell her a little about his childhood, about the period after his mother's death when he was living with relatives. He didn't mention his parents, and she knew better than to ask.

The outing was lighthearted and pleasant, except for one isolated moment when he made a slighting remark about Ted and she felt a chill. How could such a charming, civilized man be so hateful toward someone as basically decent as Ted Demeray?

"Jason!" she said sharply. "You can't imagine how tired I am of that sort of remark. Can't you stop this silly feud?"

"I didn't start it," he said.

"I don't care who started it. I don't care what it's all about. As far as I can see, it isn't about anything. It's stupid and childish, and I'm sick of it. I like you both, and I don't want to listen to you sniping at each other all the time."

"Ted—" he began.

"Ted is our cousin, and I'm beginning to feel that he's my friend, and I don't see why you can't get along. I know he can be disagreeable sometimes, but I don't think he means it. When you think what he's suffered…"

"Not as much as he'd like you to believe," said Jason. "He trades on that, you know. He always has."

"Oh, Jason, he does not. You know that isn't true. Why can't you be fair? I like Ted, except when he gets started on you, and I like you. Isn't there some way to put an end to this?"

She couldn't tell if he was convinced of anything or if he was just smart enough to lay off, but he smiled and clasped her hand. "All right," he said. "In the interest of family harmony," and again the evening was easy, pleasant, and thoroughly enjoyable.

Why did she remember Ted quoting *War and Peace*?

Cousinhood is dangerous neighborhood.

Chapter Eight

Ted buried himself in his work during the day, but more and more often he spent part of the evening with Grandmother and Rynna. Sometimes she played the piano, avoiding *Für Elise*, playing Lehar for Ted and Chopin for herself. Sometimes they sat at the table talking for a while after dinner. Just like a family, Rynna thought.

One evening they adjourned to the drawing room so Mrs. Demeray could show Rynna the fabled family photo albums. Ted must have seen them all hundreds of times, but he was perfectly content to sit with some of the older albums open on the table before him and listen to Grandmother's commentary. He was more interested in the early photography than the ancestry represented, but he was ever ready to supply a name or date that slipped Grandmother's memory—Ted as the dutiful grandson.

Rynna didn't care much about the photographs of early Demerays standing with prominent businessmen or politicians. They were all alike behind their large mustaches and veiled hats. As they progressed toward the twentieth century, she took more interest, searching the dim faces for resemblances to Grandmother, Ted, Jason, Rosalind, Pamela.

Finally, she came to photos of her mother as a young girl, some she had seen copies of, some new to her. She found William, a solidly respectable man with a nice smile and large, capable hands, and Clara, thin and lovely, leaning on his arm. Pamela and William as children, climbing trees and playing football. Rosalind, eerily playing the piano in the room where her portrait now hung.

Rynna searched for the face in the newspaper stories, but in vain. No pictures of Alexander Wyatt could be found anywhere. Not even a family gathering with him standing near Rosalind. The many pictures of Rosalind all dated from before her marriage. Rynna's father was in a few pictures, with his arm around Pamela most of the time, or playing tennis with William. Pamela was so young, so happy. Rosalind was simply beautiful.

Rynna flipped another page, and Mrs. Demeray leaned forward to point out the few unfamiliar faces, but Rynna recognized most of them by now, even the ones she had never met. She was unable to pick Ted out of the group of children in a birthday party picture until Mrs. Demeray pointed him out, but then she recognized him in several more. Here he was aged about three, holding Pamela's hand. On a pony with William standing beside him, beaming with pride. And standing alone, squinting into the sun, a sturdy blond six-year-old with swollen knees. This old photograph was the last of him without a wheelchair.

Rynna's eyes stung and the pictures blurred. She thought about William, who wanted his son to play football, and Clara, who loved him so visibly. Of his childhood in Stonebridge's happier days, how he cried when Pamela left, and all the years since, the hopes they had all relinquished. Rosalind and Pamela left and never returned. William and Clara died. And Sylvia, who liked to dance…

"A penny for your thoughts," Ted teased.

Rynna stumbled to her feet and ran from the room. She did not want him to see her tears. He wouldn't understand. He would mistake it for pity. It wasn't. She didn't know what it was. She ran upstairs to her bedroom and sat on the edge of the bed, tearful and confused.

Ted came after her. She heard the lift clanking up from the first floor but couldn't move to shut the door to keep him out. "What is it?" he asked, deeply concerned. "Rynna, what upset you? Listen, if I said something…"

"No, Ted, really."

"Was it your mother?" he asked with unexpected gentleness.

"No, no," she said and immediately wished she hadn't. He would have accepted and understood that explanation. "I can't tell you."

"You'll have to tell me something," he said. "You can't scare me like this and then get mysterious. We're friends now, remember?"

"I can't," she said. How could she explain when she couldn't understand it herself? The overwhelming feeling when she looked at that picture?

"Something in the album triggered this," he said, trying to puzzle it out.

"I wish you could walk," she said fervently. She didn't mean to say it. It just popped out.

"What?" He smiled like someone who hadn't quite gotten the joke. "Are you kidding?"

He didn't see the relevance. Then he thought about it and said, "Jesus, Rynna."

"You don't understand," she snapped. "I knew you wouldn't."

"Yes, I do. I've been here before."

"No, you don't. There's no way you can know how I feel. It's not what you think. It hurts so much…I can't explain it to you."

He put his hand on hers, comforting her, but in an unemotional way. "It's all right," he said. "You're not going to believe it, but I do know what you're talking about. I've heard this before."

"I don't believe you."

"Then don't. I don't care. But don't cry over spilt milk, either."

"That's not it."

"Sure it is. Remember what I told you?"

"I know. You feel lucky. It doesn't work."

"Don't be a baby, Rynna. You have to learn to take what life deals you and make the best of it. You don't think about what you can't have. You think about what you're lucky to have."

"But you still can't walk."

"Yes, I can."

"That's a technicality."

"As I told you, much of life hinges on technicalities."

"Yes, and you can be very glib about things, but you're still…" She hesitated over terminology.

"Wheelchair dependent," Ted supplied helpfully, with a hint of derision. "In other words, I'm a goddamned cripple. So what? So I couldn't play football, and they didn't send me to Korea, and I can't dance. So what? I have two good hands, and I have a good brain, if I do say so myself. And believe me, I have it all over amputees and paraplegics. Look at the way I live—fat city, kid."

Rynna shook her head. "Paraplegics don't have pain."

"How do you know?" Ted asked. "Amputees have phantom pain. How do you know what paraplegics feel? How do you know what I feel? Anyway, sometimes pain is the only way to know you're alive."

She heard no self-pity in the words, but they hurt more than anything else. "What a terrible thing to say," she said. No, what a terrible way to feel.

He could see how upset she was. "Hey, come on," he said. "It's all right. I'm flattered that you care enough to feel this way, but…"

"It's so sad."

"Come on, Rynna, give me a break here. Lighten up." He brushed away her tears. "I don't want you to cry. I don't want you to ever cry for me. I'm fine, and so are you. You're feeling a little blue tonight, that's all. Okay?"

Rynna wasn't sure how she had come to this point, to Ted comforting her because he was in a wheelchair, but she felt very close to him, touched by his concern. "Okay."

"I'll tell Grandmother it was the pictures of Pamela," he said. "Good night, Cousin."

****

Rynna spent more time with Jason as the weeks passed, and she began to take it for granted that he would always be part of her life. A pleasant part, an important part, and increasingly a part that had nothing to do with their being second cousins. He never mentioned Ted anymore, and if she did, he listened with apparent sympathy. On his side, and as far as she was concerned, the feud was over.

She was not so lucky with Ted. He kept his mouth shut most of the time, but he didn't like her going out with Jason. Once, at dinner, when she spoke too warmly of an evening with Jason, he put down his fork and rolled back from the table. "I just lost my appetite," he said.

"Excuse me," Rynna said to Mrs. Demeray and ran out into the hall after him. "Ted, you're behaving like a child. You know that, don't you?"

He turned on her, his eyes blazing. "I know he's a good-looking bastard," he said, "but damn it, Rynna, you're an intelligent woman. Surely you can see through his phony charm."

"Thanks for the compliment," she said and returned to the dining room. He could be childish if he wanted. She was not going to play his game.

****

Rynna loved to stroll with Jason by the river on those warm, humid summer nights, gazing from the bridge into the dark depths, talking desultorily, his arm around her shoulders, protecting her and keeping her close.

"You know," he said, into a companionable silence. "I never felt like this before about anyone. Never." He lifted her chin with his free hand and kissed her, gently at first and then with more urgency. He had never kissed her like that before. Nobody had ever kissed her like that before. It was possessive and a little frightening, but she was safe in his arms, safe and happy standing on the old bridge with Jason. She didn't want to go back to Stonebridge ever again.

"Jason," she said, her voice muffled against his shoulder as she nestled like a child in his embrace, "would you help me do something?"

"Sure, what would you like to do?"

"Leave Stonebridge," she said, and echoing Ted, "Escape. Would you help me find a job and move away from Stonebridge?"

"I'll do better than that," he said. She didn't know what he meant and looked up. He was gazing out over the river with a thoughtful expression. What was he thinking? She didn't ask. The moment was too peaceful, too dreamlike for questions.

****

At dinner the following night, savoring a perfectly seasoned stuffed bell pepper, Rynna wondered aloud why Jason wasn't living at Stonebridge. With so big a house and so small a family, they certainly had room for another cousin. She had been to his apartment, and it was just a place where he slept and kept his clothes. He ate out most of the time, and he worked long hours in his office and at the courthouse. Even more than he needed a suitable wife, he needed a home. Did it make sense to have sent for her to live at Stonebridge when Jason had been living in Brenford for years?

Ted put down his fork and stared at her as if she had finally lost her mind.

"Jason will never live here while I'm alive," Mrs. Demeray said.

"But why not? I thought you liked him."

"Of course I like him. He is Rosalind's son, and I'm fond of him in any case. He's a dear boy."

In spite of herself, Rynna checked for Ted's reaction. He didn't rise to the bait. "But if you have nothing against him… Is it because of his father? The sins of the fathers?"

Mrs. Demeray shook her head. "Stonebridge is

mine," she said. "I will have whomever I like living here. I don't choose to have him live here, and that's all there is to it. You will have the same freedom of choice when the house is yours."

An odd silence followed, and Rynna, slowly realizing what had been said, looked at Ted.

"You're leaving the house to Rynna?" It was not jealousy that registered on his face, not even betrayal, only a deep and terrible hurt.

She had to ask the question for him. "But why?"

"I think it's perfectly reasonable. The house is not entailed, but we have managed to keep it in the family for a great many years. Theodore is the last of the Demeray name, but he has made it clear that he does not intend to marry and have children. I expect you will. I would prefer that the house not pass out of the family."

Rynna wanted to protest that they could keep it in the family in other ways. If Ted produced no heirs, it would be logical for him to will it to her and her children. Why exclude him from the natural succession?

"That's not the reason," he said.

"Don't be impertinent, Theodore. Have I ever lied to you?"

"No." He said nothing more, his eyes on his plate.

Rynna was paralyzed by the tension she'd unwittingly created and only dimly aware of Mrs. Demeray's voice going on about something else.

Ted rode the lift up to his room immediately after dinner, and as soon as she could, Rynna excused herself and followed. She needed to talk to him. His door was ajar, and no clatter of typewriter keys issued from within. She hesitated and then knocked lightly on the half-open door. "Ted?"

"What the hell do you want?" He sounded as he always did—slightly annoyed. Encouraged, she nudged open the door. He hadn't switched on the desk lamp, but he was sitting in front of the typewriter. He barely moved his head as she approached. "Well?"

"I just wanted to talk to you. I don't blame you for being angry. It's as if I'm taking your place, but I never intended to. I didn't know she was going to do this."

"I'm not angry," he said.

Rynna pulled the chair over beside his wheelchair. She wanted to get close to him, to take his hand and comfort him, the way he had comforted her when she cried, but something held her back. She was too unsure of him, too confused about what he must be feeling. He had said so little. "Ted, I'm so sorry."

"Don't," was all he said.

"She was wrong. Stonebridge is yours. You can have it. I don't want to live here. If she leaves it to me, I won't even come back to sell it. I'll give it back to you. I couldn't afford to keep it up, you know. She'll leave you the money."

"I don't want her money," he said. "I don't want the house. It doesn't matter, Rynna." But it did. Of course it did.

"It's your home, Ted."

"I don't give a damn about this house," he said. "It's not as if I don't have anywhere else to go. I've been offered a teaching position at the university, and I can have it any time I want, as long as Fred Sullivan is the department chairman. I could get along fine if she cut me off without a penny. I told you before: Don't waste your time feeling sorry for me. I don't want anything from her."

Very brave, Rynna thought, very independent. But then, why was he so hurt?

"You love that old woman," she said.

Ted flushed defensively and looked away. "Get out of here," he said, not unkindly. "Beat it. I have work to do."

She couldn't say anything else. She left, still confused.

****

"I didn't think Grandmother could be so cruel," Rynna told Jason later as they sat in his car outside the French restaurant, replete with beef merlot and baguettes. "She may not have intended to blurt it out like that over dinner, but she was so cool about it. It was as if she didn't care."

He murmured something sympathetic and skillfully changed the subject.

She was a little sad, and Jason was a master at consoling her and lifting her spirits. She leaned her head on his strong shoulder, and he stroked her hair and spoke soothing, meaningless words. She was so comfortable with him and at the same time slightly giddy with a kind of romantic thrill.

He kissed her and murmured, "I love you, Rynna." It was all she wanted to know.

Later, emboldened by their increased intimacy, she asked if he remembered his mother. "Not very well," he said. He didn't mind the question, as reluctant as she had been to ask it. The past held no emotional reality for him. He remembered Rosalind's smile and her beautiful hair, and he remembered that she played the piano sometimes, not often.

"Was she happy?"

He didn't know. "I was very young when she died."

"Do you remember your father?"

"Even less. It's just as well. He was dangerously unstable, from what I've heard."

"It must be awful," she said, "to know something like that about your parents."

"I remember…" Jason hesitated, as if he was not sure of the memory or was reluctant to tell her what he had never told anyone else.

"What?" she asked.

"He tried to kill me once."

"Oh, Jason! Are you sure?"

"No." He shrugged. "I think he did, though. He wanted her all to himself, and finally even that wasn't enough. He didn't want her to have a thought in her head that didn't belong to him."

"So he killed her."

"So he killed her. Listen, this is pretty depressing stuff. Let's talk about something more cheerful." He tilted her chin with a caressing hand and gazed into her eyes. "Let's talk about you," he said.

****

"You've been seeing an awful lot of Jason," Ted said over tea and fruit and hot biscuits one morning. His tone was almost accusing.

Carefully, aware she was treading dangerous ground, Rynna said, "I think I'm in love with him." She speared a chunk of fresh pineapple as an excuse not to make eye contact.

Ted put down his teacup a little too fast and sloshed the hot liquid onto the tablecloth and his fingers. "Shit," he said. He busied himself with a napkin, and when he finally raised his eyes he looked and sounded calm. "Bit incestuous, isn't it?" he asked.

"We're only second cousins," she said. She had said it to herself a thousand times already.

"Only," he said. "Well, it figures. Cheer up—maybe you'll get over it."

"I wish *you* would. I'm so tired of your snitty remarks about Jason."

"Yeah, well, I'm tired of hearing how tired you are. If you're dumb enough to fall for that guy, it's your lookout."

"Come on, Ted. What do you have against him?"

"Oh, nothing," he said. "Just that he's a complete bastard and he's making a fool of my favorite cousin." He was near tears, and he rolled away from the table, leaving his breakfast half eaten.

He barely spoke to her for a week afterward.

****

On the first chilly fall evening of the year, Jason and Rynna went dancing, and as they slowly circled the dance floor, he asked her to marry him.

"What?" Surely she hadn't heard him correctly, or maybe he was joking,

He gazed at her soberly, his dark eyes devouring her face. "I love you, Rynna. Will you marry me?"

No one had every proposed to her before, at least no one she had taken seriously. Jason was serious.

"Jason, I…" She had no idea what to say.

"I love you," he said again and leaned closer to kiss her sweetly, hungrily. She could drown in his kisses. She could be swept away and lose all sense of herself. She was frightened of the passion he could arouse and of the commitment he was asking for. If she said yes, there would be no backtracking. Her life would be changed and her future settled. How could she give herself wholeheartedly to him when she was still so unsure of herself? She was so far from home, so much under the influence of people she knew too little about. She was in love with him, but she barely knew him.

"Jason, don't," she said, backing away a little. "I need to think."

"I don't want you to think," he said with a teasing smile. "I want you to say yes." He kissed her again, and she could not breathe, could not think. She was aware of the scent of his skin and the beating of his heart. She was lost in Jason.

"Yes." She surrendered. She would marry him. She would give up every other possibility her life might offer and cling to him. He would be her salvation. She would think of nothing and nobody else.

And God help her.

Chapter Nine

Grandmother accepted the news calmly enough. She wanted to see Rynna married, and Jason was a respectable suitor. Events were unfolding a little faster than she expected, but at her age speed was all to the good. She wanted to see the Demeray bloodline extended to another generation. She didn't even pause to question the wisdom of the decision. Her mind leapt ahead to the details of its accomplishment. Naturally, they would have the wedding at Stonebridge.

Rynna was caught between two strong personalities. If she was to have any say in her own wedding plans, she would have to learn to stand up to Jason and Grandmother both. She would. Jason's love would make her strong.

Nevertheless, she didn't relish the next obstacle.

Ted exploded. "God damn it!"

"I won't talk to you if you're going to swear at me," she said. She had confronted him in his room so Grandmother wouldn't hear them quarrel. She hovered near the doorway, ready to make a quick escape.

He controlled himself with visible effort. "I didn't think you'd do it," he said, almost to himself. "I really didn't think you would. Damn it!" He glared, bristling with accusation. "Tell me, Cousin, did you tell him you're going to inherit Stonebridge?"

"That's beneath even you."

"Did you?"

"I don't know. I don't remember." Had she? Yes, but it didn't matter. He was clutching at straws. "Give it up, Ted. Nobody is amused."

"I'm not trying to be funny. Jason is a carpetbagger if I ever met one. I wouldn't put it past him."

"Stop it, Ted. I'm marrying Jason, and there's nothing you can do about it."

She wasn't sure he heard her. He was talking to himself again. "Damn it. I can't believe it."

"Believe it," Rynna said.

"What do you want?" Ted challenged her. "You want to get out of here? You'd marry him to get out?"

"I'm marrying him because I want to marry him, because I love him. But I will be damned glad to get out of this house."

"Christ, *I'll* take you away from here, if that's what you want. If you think marriage is such a bed of roses, *I'll* marry you."

"Don't be ridiculous," Rynna snapped and stormed out. After she calmed down a little, she realized she'd let him get to her again. As unlikely as he was to reconcile himself to the marriage, she would have to learn not to take his sniping to heart. Otherwise it would not be easy to live in this house until Jason spirited her away as his bride.

****

Rynna took a walk along the river. The sky was overcast, but the air wasn't cold, and she wore only a light sweater. She needed to get away from the house, alone, and clear her head. She had so much to think about. She longed for her mother. She could have used her advice and support, and Pamela would have wanted to see her daughter married at Stonebridge. Would she have been pleased that she was marrying Jason? Why did she have the nagging feeling Rosalind was not? It was nonsense, silly pre-wedding jitters. Everybody endured those.

Ted had said nothing more. Either Grandmother had spoken to him, or he was intelligent enough to know opposition would only make Rynna more determined. Everyone else—the servants, Jason's friends—appeared delighted.

She didn't know how long she had been wandering along the river, but it hadn't occurred to her she would be missed as long as she showed up for meals. When she went back to the house, Ted was waiting for her in a controlled fury. "Where have you been?" he demanded.

"Taking a walk. Why?"

"You might have told somebody where you were going."

"Don't tell me you were worried." She was prepared to be as sarcastic as he could be. "I'd think you'd be glad to be rid of me."

"There's something to be said for that," he agreed with grim seriousness. "But I have more important things on my mind. Grandmother's had a fall."

"Oh, no!" Rynna was stabbed with remorse as well as concern. Her mind filled with terrible images.

"Don't panic," Ted said roughly. "It's probably not that serious. The doctor's on his way."

"What happened?"

"She lost her balance. You know it's a little shaky these days. She may have broken her hip."

"Oh, Ted! That can be dangerous at her age."

"It's no picnic at any age," he said. "I'm glad to see

you didn't go off somewhere and do likewise. Life was a lot more peaceful around here before you arrived."

"Really, Ted, you know I wasn't responsible for Grandmother's fall."

"Lucky for you," he said. She couldn't understand him. He was never serious about anything, but it was a dark sort of humor and out of place in such a crisis.

Dr. Moran, a tall, white-haired man who had been the Demeray family physician for many years, arrived shortly with his black bag and an air of calm reassurance. Lucy led him straight up to Mrs. Demeray's room and returned to report to Ted and Rynna in the library. "He says it isn't broken," she assured them and scurried off to spread the good news.

Half an hour later, Dr. Moran himself came in to give them a full report. "She's injured her hip," he said, "but it isn't broken, and it will be fine in a few days, I should think. She's in no pain and resting comfortably. I'd like her to stay in bed for a bit, not more than a week. She's in remarkable health for a woman her age. Nothing to worry about."

"Thank you, Doctor," Rynna said, grateful for such a positive report. "Can we see her?"

She was anxious to reassure herself that Grandmother was no different. Too many other things in her life had changed in the last six months.

"Certainly. I imagine she would like to be read to. As I remember, she is not a good invalid."

Rynna picked up from the table the book Grandmother had last asked her to read. She would be dutiful and make penance for having thoughtlessly gone to the river. And how did Ted manage to make her feel so guilty?

Dr. Moran gave Ted a straight look over the top of his glasses, for all the world like a caricature country doctor. "And how are you?" he asked.

"Nothing wrong with me," Ted said. "If you want another patient, Rynna should have her head examined."

"Very funny," she said and left the library with as much dignity as she could muster.

****

Lying in bed all day was dull for Grandmother, so Ted moved a few of the family albums to her room so she could work on them, and Rynna brought Jason to visit her before their evening out. Listening to the bantering conversation between the two of them was a great deal more pleasant than reading aloud from dusty books. The relationship between Jason and Mrs. Demeray had altered subtly now that he was Rynna's fiancé. Sitting in the room with them, Rynna imagined herself part of a warm and loving family circle.

As they were leaving, they encountered Ted in the hall, and her contentment evaporated. He didn't say anything, but his expression was plain enough. If he'd had the authority, he would have ordered Jason out of the house.

To his credit, Jason tried to make peace with him. "Can't we be friends?" he asked. "For Rynna's sake?"

"For Rynna's sake?" Ted repeated, glancing coolly from Jason to Rynna and back to Jason. "You can both go to hell."

She was furious. Why couldn't he meet Jason halfway? She went out to dinner with Jason, to an Italian restaurant this time, and did her best to relax and have a good time, but she was seething. It was time for Ted to put up or shut up. She was in love with Jason, and this should have been the best time of her life. She would not let one disagreeable cousin spoil everything.

She got home late, but a light was on in Ted's room, so she steeled herself for a showdown and knocked on his door.

He was at his desk, proofreading typewritten pages, and wasn't at all pleased to see her.

"I have to talk to you," she said.

"If it's about Jason—"

"Of course it is."

"I don't want to hear it."

"I don't care whether you want to hear it or not." She took a deep breath and perched on the edge of the cane chair. "I'm going to marry him whether you like it or not, so you'd better get used to it. I know Grandmother must have talked to you about this."

"What's between Grandmother and me," he said icily, "is between Grandmother and me." He put down his pen and gave her his full attention. "Although how she could want your children to inherit Stonebridge is beyond me."

"You can have Stonebridge," Rynna snapped. "This is not about Stonebridge. This is about Jason."

"The proposed father of said children," he reminded her. "She doesn't seem concerned that the heirs to Stonebridge will be washed-out weaklings. All that inbreeding."

"That's nonsense, and you know it. He and I are only second cousins, and there is no other 'inbreeding.' "

"More like incest," he said. "You may be second cousins, but you take more after the Demerays than the Daltons. I suppose you know you look like Rosalind?"

"Cecile said so, but I don't see it."

"I do. The real question is, does Jason? Did you think of that, Rynna? Are you sure it's you he's in love with? Are you sure it isn't Rosalind?"

Rynna slapped him hard, and he was both taken aback and somewhat pleased to have gotten a rise out of her. She was immediately sorry, but refused to say so. She had cut his lip a little, and he put his fingers to it gingerly. Her own hand stung from the force of the blow.

"I guess I deserved that," he said.

"I guess you did, but I shouldn't have done it."

"It could be dangerous," he agreed. He was enjoying her discomfort.

"Shut up," Rynna said. "I am not interested in fencing with you. I am so goddamned sick of you I could scream. Why can't we have an adult conversation?"

"You're the one who resorted to violence," he reminded her.

"I'm sorry I hit you. Now I think you owe me an apology. More to the point, you owe Jason an apology."

"When hell freezes over," he said, and his tone held absolutely no humor.

"Look, Ted, nobody says you have to love Jason. You obviously never did get along, and it's nobody's fault. It's just chemistry or something. I can accept that. But to object to our marriage, to make yourself so disagreeable to him, you have to justify that."

"I don't—"

"You have to have something more concrete than you've given me. If you do have something against him, I want to hear it now. Otherwise I have no reason to listen to anything you have to say. He's going to be my husband. I don't owe you anything."

"I never said you did."

"I want you to tell me what he ever did to make you hate him so much. Give me one example to justify all this. Just one thing, that's all I'm asking."

He was thinking seriously about what she'd said, his gaze steady. For a change he wasn't searching for a way to hide behind a quip. He pivoted away, shoving hard on the wheels, and then back, hesitated, and turned again. Rynna had never seen a man in a wheelchair pace.

"Sylvia," he said at last.

For a moment, Rynna was terrified. Something was behind this, something real. He would not joke about this, and he would not use it to get his way like a sulky child. He would tell her something he didn't want to tell her, something she didn't want to hear. He would ruin her life.

The stab of terror passed, and instead she was filled with guilty compassion for Ted. She had provoked this, and she would be happy with Jason. No matter what he said, it would not be enough to stop her. And he wasn't going to tell her after all.

"Tell me," she said, but she already knew he wouldn't.

He only shook his head and said nothing.

Rynna didn't like his uncharacteristic silence. "I'll ask Jason, then," she said, just to provoke him.

He gave her a faint smile, but still said nothing.

"You'd better put some ice on your lip," she said. "It's going to swell."

No answer even to that.

"I'm sorry, Ted," she said, and left him to his silence.

****

Rynna hadn't intended to mention it to Jason, but if

she planned to marry him she should be able to discuss anything with him. Over braised duck and cherries at their favorite French restaurant, she asked him, in as casual a way as she could manage, if he had known Sylvia.

"Sylvia? Oh, Sylvia Thompson? Yes. She was a…" What had he started to say? "She was smart and pretty, real class. She and Ted had something going."

"What happened?"

He shrugged. "I guess she knew she'd have no life at Stonebridge."

"You didn't have anything to do with it, did you?"

"With what? Her leaving? No, of course not." He sipped his wine, his gaze steady and guileless.

"But could Ted have somehow gotten the idea you did? Is there any reason for Ted to think you had something to do with it? That you somehow came between them? Or in some way encouraged her to leave?"

"Did he say that?"

"No, he wouldn't talk about it. But do you think he might have some reason to blame you?"

"No, I don't think so. I don't think you should take any of this too seriously."

"But—"

"He's not living in the real world, Rynna. You have to make allowances for that."

Was that true? With his undeniable intelligence, was Ted nevertheless harboring delusions? Was Jason his Professor Moriarty? She wasn't convinced, but she had no better answers.

"Are you ready for dessert?" he asked and signaled the waiter.

After dinner, they strolled through the mall near Jason's office, window shopping. They didn't stop at the bridal shop—it would have bored him—but Rynna glanced at the radiant mannequins and her heart skipped a beat. A wedding was meant to be any woman's big day, like an opening night on Broadway. Her jitters were perfectly understandable, and when all the rush and confusion were over, she would be Mrs. Jason Wyatt.

"What are you thinking about?" he asked, noting her silence.

"The wedding," she confessed.

Just then they passed a flower stall and he stopped to select a single pink rosebud. "You should always wear flowers," he said, trying to entwine the stem in her hair. She had not cut it since coming to Stonebridge, and it was nearly as long as Rosalind's had been when her portrait was painted.

"Let me," she said, laughing at his clumsiness, and fastened the flower with a hairpin. "Thank you, Jason. It was a lovely idea."

"You had a rose in your hair the night we met," he said. "That's the way I always think of you. Will you wear flowers in your hair when we get married?"

"I'll wear it up, with a band of flowers. How does that suit you?"

"That would be great," he said. "Come over here. I want to show you something." He led her to a concrete bench under a tree, a little out of the way of strolling shoppers.

Jason pulled a small white box out of his vest pocket. "If you don't like it, we can find something else," he said. He laid the box in her hand and closed her fingers around it. "It may not be what you had in mind. Don't be afraid to say so."

Her curiosity piqued, Rynna opened the box. In a nest of white satin lay an exquisitely old-fashioned gold wedding band. "It's beautiful," she whispered, her eyes stinging with tears.

"Really, Rynna, if you don't want it…"

"I do want it," she assured him. He lifted the ring out of the box and tilted it to show her the inside of the band. The initials RDW were engraved with intricate flourishes.

"We can have the date added," he said. "When you and Grandmother make up your minds. I have nothing to say about it. I know when I'm outnumbered."

"Oh, thank you, Jason. It's lovely," she said and gave him a kiss. "And you do have something to say. Even Grandmother couldn't argue with you. When would you like to be married?"

"As soon as possible," he said. He bent his head to kiss her, and his lips lingered on hers.

"There are people here," she said.

"They can't see us," he said and kissed her again, more boldly, insistently—almost, if she was able to admit it to herself, roughly.

"Jason!" Breathless, a little shaken, Rynna pulled away. "Gently."

"I'm sorry," he said, so sincerely that her disquiet faded at once. "I got a little carried away, didn't I? I'm sorry, darling, I will be patient. It's just that you're so beautiful and I want you so much."

Nothing else mattered, did it, if he loved her?

They drove back to Stonebridge almost in silence. She thought dreamily of wedding plans, and Jason, lost in his own reverie, drove with one hand while the other stroked her hair and settled for a moment on her knee.

"Will I see you tomorrow?" she asked after he kissed her good night.

"I'm afraid not," he said. "I have to work. I have to be ready for court Monday."

"Monday night?"

"I think so. I'll call you. Sweet dreams, darling."

"Good night, Jason."

As she crossed to the stairs, Rynna thought for a moment a light was shining in the music room, but when she turned to look it had vanished. Imagining things.

In her room, she sat at the dressing table, brushing her hair and studying herself in the mirror, until a soft rap came at the door and Cecile let herself in. "Let me do that," she said and slipped the hairbrush out of Rynna's hand. "You will be the loveliest bride ever in this house," she said with perfect confidence, "and this house has seen quite a few."

Why did that nag at her memory, as if she had forgotten an important detail? Rynna shook her head impatiently and tried to think of something besides the wedding. She considered asking Cecile about Sylvia but decided against it. However much she might wish to think of Cecile as a friend, she was still a servant. Questioning the servants would be indiscreet, and she had been reckless enough already. In any case, it was none of her business, and she had no justification for invading Ted's privacy.

"Thank you, Cecile," she said, taking the brush. "Go on to bed now."

Her mind roamed back over the evening—the rosebud in her hair, Jason's kisses, the magnificent ring, RDW. Rynna Dalton Wyatt.

A small chill ran down her spine. She hadn't asked Jason where he got the ring, and he hadn't volunteered the information. Did he buy it somewhere in the city and have it engraved? Or was it an heirloom?

She could no longer remember what Ted had said right before she slapped him.

RDW. Rynna Dalton Wyatt.

Rosalind Demeray Wyatt.

She had forgotten to ask Jason if he thought she resembled Rosalind.

Chapter Ten

The next day was filled with so many details of the wedding plans that Rynna never found time to think about the larger issues. Grandmother's bed was strewn with patterns and fabric samples, and the dressmaker arrived to take Rynna's measurements and consult with them about the dress. They settled on semi-transparent sleeves with lace at the wrists, and a short veil held with a band of white silk rosettes, and spent hours debating the most flattering neckline and skirt length. Rynna was exhausted.

Dr. Moran came to call on Grandmother again and said she could get out of bed in a day or two. With all the arrangements she wanted to make for the wedding, it would be none too soon.

Rynna heard nothing from Jason and visualized him laboring over a legal brief in his stark, lonely office.

With Grandmother in bed, she and Ted dined alone, mostly in silence. The wedding plans weighed on her mind, and it was the last thing he wanted to hear about. He was barely civil anyway, and she suspected something was on his mind, something besides her wedding. Probably rocks, although his work didn't usually make him so surly.

Completely tired out, she headed to bed early and slipped into profound, dreamless sleep. At exactly 2:15, she was awakened by what she thought was a sudden noise, although she couldn't identify it. She glanced at the clock and knew at once what it meant, although it hadn't happened in weeks.

The clashing sound was harsh and discordant, incongruous from so fine an instrument, and carried a chilling note of warning. Rynna shivered and rolled over and tried to shut it out of her mind, tried to go back to sleep. She had nearly succeeded when another, subtler sound caught her attention.

Cautious footsteps on the stairs. She should not have been able to hear them. Was she dreaming, or had she left her door ajar? It didn't matter anyway. It was probably one of the servants. Half-asleep, she couldn't be bothered even to think it through. She only wanted to forget everything and disappear into blackness.

****

The next awakening was more chilling than the last.

Someone was screaming, and Rynna sat straight up in bed, her heart pounding. The clock showed barely seven a.m., and all hell had broken loose at Stonebridge. Panicked, fumbling, Rynna stumbled out of bed, grabbed her robe, and ran into the hall. The screaming was still going on, a terrible sound, cutting right through her. It was coming from Grandmother's room.

Ted was just ahead of her as she ran into the room. Lucy was at Grandmother's bedside, bending over her still form, her face a mask of anxiety. And Jenny, standing at the foot of the bed, her hands to her eyes, was shrieking, "She's been murdered! She's been murdered!"

"Shut up," Ted said harshly, and Jenny gulped and then sobbed quietly, her face in her hands.

"Oh, sir," Lucy said tearfully. "I can't wake her up."

"Somebody call Dr. Moran," Ted said, and Jenny ran out of the room and clattered down the stairs, still sobbing. Lucy yielded her place to Ted and his take-charge attitude and came to where Rynna stood clutching her robe around her. The room wasn't cold, but her teeth were chattering. On impulse, she put her arms around Lucy, and they clung together fearfully.

Ted sought Mrs. Demeray's pulse, holding the thin, frail wrist in gentle, expert fingers. After a moment, he laid her arm back on the bed and pressed his fingers against the side of her neck. "Grandmother," he said softly and then, "She's dead."

"Oh, no. Oh, Ted, are you sure?"

He didn't answer but sat without moving, gazing at the familiar face, now so strangely pale and slack. Rynna thought about her mother's death and how she had avoided seeing her so she could remember her alive. This was what she had feared to see, this absence of life where it been so recently.

"Dr. Moran was here yesterday," she said. "He said she was fine. He said—"

"It must have been her heart," said Lucy.

Jenny clattered back up the stairs and into the room to stutter out her news. "Dr. Moran wasn't there. Dr. Gould is coming. They said Dr. Moran wasn't available, but they'll try to reach him. Only Dr. Gould could come."

"Get her out of here," said Ted. Lucy led Jenny away, and Rynna was alone in the heavily curtained room with her cousin and the lifeless body of their great-grandmother.

"Ted?" Rynna approached the bed with great reluctance. She didn't want to come any closer to death.

It was not Grandmother on the bed. It was death. But Ted was there, and he would be feeling something close to what she had suffered when her mother died. She wanted to comfort him or at least share some of his emotion, something besides this empty disbelief. "Ted?" She put her hand on his shoulder. He didn't react. She knelt beside the wheelchair so she could see his face. "If there's anything I can do to help…"

His eyes were bright with unshed tears, but he spoke calmly. "Stay here. I don't want her left alone. I'm going to get dressed."

She nodded, although the idea filled her with dread. If it was the only thing she could do for him, that's what she would do. It could make no difference now to Edwina Demeray, but she would not be left alone.

She pulled an armchair closer to the bed and sat down, as if she could keep Grandmother company, as if they had a conversation to finish. After a few minutes, she was less chilled, less horrified. Death wasn't such a terrible thing after all.

She was alone in the room for a very short time. Sooner than should have been possible, Lucy arrived with Dr. Gould, a heavyset, middle-aged man, a little out of breath, and in response to Jenny's hysterical ramblings on the telephone, a police detective, a thin, nervous young man who introduced himself as Sgt. Chandler. Rynna could have left then, but she wanted to hear what the doctor said. Ted was still in his room, and he would want to know all the details later.

The doctor examined Mrs. Demeray and covered her face with the sheet. Rynna could not have done it herself and was glad Ted hadn't seen it. "Was it her heart?" Lucy was brave enough to ask. "You know, she did have these little spells sometimes."

Dr. Gould shook his head, and Sgt. Chandler abruptly became more alert and retrieved a small notebook from his pocket. The doctor glanced around and picked up a bottle from the bedside table. "For arthritis pain," he read from the label. "Looks like an overdose. I would assume it was accidental, Sgt. Chandler. A woman her age, with a weak heart—it wouldn't have taken much. I'd guess she mistook the dosage and overdosed on her arthritis medication."

Rynna spoke before she thought. "But Grandmother didn't…" Mrs. Demeray's silver-headed cane had been only for balance.

Sgt. Chandler looked sharply at her and took the bottle from Dr. Gould. He studied the label and then said, into a charged silence, "Who is Theodore Demeray?"

"My cousin," Rynna said.

"I wouldn't jump to conclusions, Sergeant," Dr. Gould said. "If she had a headache, she might have made a mistake."

Sgt. Chandler's expression was pained. "If she had a headache, Doctor, she would have rung for a servant to bring her an aspirin. People who live like this don't rummage in the medicine cabinet."

Rynna didn't understand what they were getting at, but she was upset by the entire tone of the conversation. "I don't understand," she said.

Sgt. Chandler glanced at her and wrote something in his notebook. "We'll want to question the servants," he said. "Where is Demeray?"

"In his room, down the hall." She gestured in the general direction and, realizing Chandler meant to go right out to talk to him, she caught at his sleeve. "Oh, please, don't." She didn't even understand that Ted was a suspect. She only didn't want him to be bothered. "Please don't tell him," she said. "He was devoted to her."

"Was he?" Sgt. Chandler said. He didn't even pause, and she could only follow him down the hall, protesting.

Chandler rapped on the door, and Rynna, wanting to give warning, called out, "Ted, there's a policeman here."

"Come in." His voice was muffled, and she could tell nothing from his flat tone. Chandler opened the door. Ted had just pulled a sweater on over his head, and his hair was ruffled. His glasses were on the desk, and he looked defenseless without them. He glanced at Chandler, ran a hand through his hair, and reached for his glasses. He studied her expression before he spoke to Chandler. "What is it?" he asked. "You don't think…"

"Sorry to disturb you at a time like this," Chandler began, as if it was something he said every day, "but I need to ask you a few questions."

"Jenny kept saying she'd been murdered," Ted said. "I thought she was just hysterical. It looked like natural causes to me. Do you have any reason to think it wasn't?"

Chandler was annoyed, as if he was used to asking questions, not answering them. "Had your grandmother been ill?" he asked.

"No. She fell a few days ago and was bedridden because of her bruised hip. Dr. Moran said—"

"We'll talk to Moran." Chandler was offensively businesslike. "Did she complain of pain or sleeplessness?"

Ted gave Rynna an inquiring look—*What is he*

getting at?—and she answered for him. "No, I think she was sleeping all right."

"Can you think of any reason why she would take medication, then?"

"Medication?" Ted frowned. "What kind of…?"

Chandler held up the small bottle. Ted glanced immediately at his desk where it usually sat beside the larger one. Chandler looked too, and his eyebrows went up. Nobody would have mistaken one for the other. "You keep it in here, not in the bathroom?" Chandler asked Ted. "Was it there last night?"

"I don't know. I don't remember."

"You didn't take any of this last night?"

"No, I didn't."

"Did any of the servants come to your room last night, while you were here?"

"No."

"Anyone?"

"No. I was working here alone all evening."

"Did you hear anything during the night?"

"Nothing."

"Did you—?"

"I slept very soundly," Ted said. "It's a little too convenient, isn't it?"

"Yes, it is, sir."

"What happens now?"

"I would like you to come downtown."

"No," Rynna protested. "Why?"

"Am I under arrest?" Ted asked. Rynna could not understand why he was so calm. Was it all a game to him?

"I hope that won't be necessary, sir. If you could come with me and answer a few questions…"

"He already answered a few questions," she pointed out. "He told you everything he knows. Why does he have to go downtown?"

"Shut up, Rynna," Ted said mildly. "All right, let's get this over with."

"Can I come with you?" She was asking Ted, not the detective.

"Don't be an idiot," he said. "Call Baxter, in the city. Lucy knows the number."

"Baxter?"

"Grandmother's lawyer. He'll know what to do about the arrangements. I don't want you to bother with any of that. And you'd better notify Jason."

Jason. She needed Jason now. Only yesterday her mind had been filled with plans for their wedding. Today everything was upside down. Everything was wrong. The worst thing was that Grandmother was not here. Grandmother would have known what to do. She would not have let the police take Ted downtown to be questioned.

"Ted, I don't want you to go." She appealed to Sgt. Chandler. "Please, this isn't right."

Cecile appeared in the doorway, pale and breathless. "Oh, Miss Rynna. I'm ever so sorry."

Ted, relieved, said, "Cecile, ask Dr. Gould to give Rynna something, a sedative, and make her lie down for a while. And make sure somebody is with Mrs. Demeray. I don't want her left alone."

"Yes, sir." The girl started to leave, and Rynna grabbed her hand.

"I don't need a sedative. I don't need anything."

Ted gave Cecile the kind of look parents exchange over the heads of children, and she clutched Rynna's arm and led her out of the room.

"There's a policeman," Rynna told her. "He's taking Ted downtown. It's all crazy."

"I know. Another one is downstairs talking to Jenny and Mrs. Lester. Come and lie down for a few minutes. You'll feel better." She all but shoved Rynna into her bedroom.

"I don't need to lie down." She was furious. "Ted wants me out of the way, so I won't make a scene. Damn him." The ancient lift clattered to life at the end of the hall, taking Chandler and Ted downstairs. "I don't understand any of this. Why would they think anybody would murder Grandmother?"

"She had a lot of money. The police always think that's a motive. Maybe it was."

"But Ted will inherit all the money. Cecile! You don't think he…?"

"Don't even think about it," Cecile soothed. "Just lie down for a few minutes."

"No. I have to call Mr. Baxter."

"I'll do it. I'll take care of everything."

"I have to call Jason," Rynna insisted, and the girl yielded. They hurried downstairs together. The front door stood open, and a uniformed police officer was right outside. Beyond him two patrol cars were parked in the driveway. Ted was sitting in the back of one, waiting patiently while Sgt. Chandler conferred with another officer.

Cecile spoke briefly on the phone, told Rynna Mr. Baxter was on his way, and discreetly backed out, leaving her in the dubious privacy of the front hall. She dialed Jason's number and his ever-efficient secretary put her through at once.

"What's wrong?" he asked before she could say anything.

"Oh, Jason, Grandmother's dead."

He whistled. "Jesus. That's really rough, Rynna. Her heart?"

"No, they think an overdose. They think—she might have been murdered."

"What?!"

"The police think Ted did it. It's insane."

"Christ, what a mess. Sweetheart, I absolute have to be in court this morning. I'll get away as soon as I can."

"Wait. Can you do something about Ted? He should have a lawyer. They're taking him downtown."

"Did he say he wanted me to?"

"No, but..."

"He might not want me to represent him. You know how he is. If he asks, I'll do whatever I can. Don't worry." His tone surprised her. He wasn't concerned about Ted. Did he care about Grandmother?

"Jason, I need you here."

"I'll come as soon as I can," he promised. "I have to run, Rynna. I'll be there soon."

After she hung up, she went upstairs and dressed and then went back down and into the music room. She didn't touch the piano but gazed at Rosalind's portrait. "We've had enough funerals around here," Ted had said. Now only three of them were left: Ted, Jason, and Rynna. The curse of the Demerays. She sat on the piano bench for about fifteen minutes and gradually grew calmer, comforted. Rosalind understood. Whatever happened, Rosalind would be here.

Baxter came, an old-fashioned, conservative gentleman, a bit stuffy. He was saddened by Mrs.

Demeray's death, but he was extremely efficient about everything. He knew where her will and insurance papers were kept and what financial ends to tie up and who to contact about funeral arrangements. As Ted had promised, he knew what to do about everything, and she didn't have to worry about anything. He even called the police station and spoke to someone in a dryly chummy tone and reported back that Ted was not under arrest and would likely be home in a few hours.

The detective who questioned the servants talked briefly to Baxter and then asked to interview Rynna. He was so average in appearance and manner that he must have deliberately cultivated that image. She was glad it wasn't Chandler. She sat with him in the library, avoiding Grandmother's favorite chair. He nudged his chair a little closer to hers and retrieved a small notebook from his pocket.

He asked a lot of questions, as if he hoped to find something out by simply exhausting her. She was sure he had asked all the same questions of the servants and was comparing her answers to determine who was lying. A methodical man, Sgt. Yates.

The best way to shorten the ordeal was to be as cooperative as possible, but some of the questions set her nerves on edge. He asked about Grandmother and Jason and each of the servants. How long had she lived at Stonebridge? How well did she know Mrs. Lester? Ellery? He asked about her wedding plans and about Grandmother's will.

"I haven't seen it," she said.

She was embarrassed to find how little she did know about Stonebridge and its occupants. She was the newest arrival, and it was usual for the servants to know more about the family than anyone else did. Sgt. Yates would find her answers disappointing.

He asked a lot of questions about Ted, more than anybody else, more than was reasonable. What did they know that she didn't? Yates was more interested in what she knew that the police didn't and was clearly not satisfied with the little information she provided.

"What's wrong with his legs?" he asked finally. They suspected Ted of giving Grandmother an overdose of his arthritis medication, and Sgt. Yates had to ask what was wrong with his legs?

Rynna's patience snapped. "What the hell do you think is wrong with his legs?"

****

Jason arrived about an hour later, and Rynna simply walked into his arms and took shelter there. She was so glad he had come, so glad he even existed. Jason would take care of her. Death would not touch her.

He apologized for taking so long and explained that he too had been questioned by the police. Rynna hoped he hadn't told them his theory about Ted not living in the real world.

"Mr. Baxter called somebody at the police station," she told Jason. "He said Ted wasn't under arrest. Why did they have to take him down there?" She leaned back in his embrace and studied his face.

"It's the best way to question a suspect. Take him out of his own environment, isolate him from the situation. He doesn't know what else is happening, and he's surrounded by police, by the physical reality of the legal system. It's intimidating even if you're innocent." He had no doubt dealt with a lot of Sgt. Chandlers over the years.

"I think you should be there," she said.

Jason shook his head. "If he wants a lawyer, all he has to do is ask. It's not likely to be me, is it?"

"Mr. Baxter, then."

"I'm afraid Baxter's line is wills and trusts."

She had no other options to suggest and took Jason's hand. They went into the music room. "You don't think Ted could have…"

"If the police had a case, they would have arrested him. Now, would it be too much to ask that we not talk about Cousin Ted for five minutes?"

"I'm concerned about him."

"I know you are, and I'm concerned about you." He kissed her and then studied her face for a moment. "Are you all right?"

"I think so. It's hard to tell. I think this is one of the worst days of my life. I'm so glad you're here, Jason."

"I'll always be here for you," he promised. "Whenever you need me, I'll be here. I'm going to take such good care of you, Rynna."

Lucy came in, hesitating in the doorway, and asked Rynna what she wanted to do about lunch. Except for coffee shared with the police officers, nobody had had any breakfast. Rynna was surprised to discover she was hungry. That empty feeling was not just nerves. She appealed helplessly to Jason, and he told Lucy they would have lunch in the dining room in half an hour. Rynna was about to thank Jason for thinking for her when it hit her.

Lucy had consulted her. Grandmother had died and left her this incredible Georgian house.

She was mistress of Stonebridge.

Chapter Eleven

Although she was hungry, Rynna couldn't eat much. She nibbled on celery sticks and crackers while Jason put away a plate of sandwiches. He told her about his morning in court, and she relayed Baxter's advice on funeral arrangements, and then they lapsed into silence. She had too much on her mind for conversation, even with Jason.

They were still at the table when a car stopped in front of the house. Rynna ran into the hall, where Lucy was already opening the door. A police car was parked in the driveway.

A uniformed policeman took the wheelchair out of the back seat. On the day they visited the university, Ted had managed the broad stone steps on his own, but today Ellery strode over to the car and lifted him effortlessly in his arms.

The policeman rolled the wheelchair into the hall, held it steady for Ellery, touched his cap to Rynna, and left without a word. Ted looked pale and tired, but Rynna, overwrought all morning, was so glad to see him she hugged him. He was embarrassed and a little annoyed, and then he gazed beyond her to Jason, who had just come into the hall.

"Jason," he said with a curt nod. His tone was at least civil, acknowledging his right to be there as part of the family.

"What happened?" she asked. "What did the police say?"

"They don't have any answers," he said in a familiar dry tone. "Only questions."

"You look beat," Jason said. "It must have been rough." Ted stared at him, and in a different tone, as if he hadn't intended to say it, Jason asked, "What did you tell them?"

Ted's expression was unreadable. "I told them if it came right down to it, I would have been much more likely to kill Rynna."

"Oh, Ted." She couldn't tell if he was joking or not. This was no time for jokes. It was true, at least as the police would view it. She had usurped his position here. She had inherited Stonebridge. As long as Grandmother was alive, his world was secure, and he could hope she would change the will again in his favor.

"You're safe, then, Rynna," Jason said. "Since he told the police he has a motive, he can't possibly do you in now." He *was* joking, and Ted was not amused.

"I don't want to deal with you right now, Jason," he said. "I really don't." It was, as Grandmother would have said, not quite nice, but even Jason was not offended. Anybody could see Ted was tired and grieving. He was also, for the first time since she had known him, visibly in pain.

"What can I do?" she asked.

"Nothing," he said. "I'm going upstairs." He didn't even glance at Jason as he passed him.

They stood in the hall while the ancient lift creaked and groaned its way to the second floor. Lucy, hovering in the doorway, spoke first. "Shall I call Dr. Moran?"

Rynna made her first decision as mistress of

Stonebridge. "Yes," she said, and as Lucy went out she said to Jason, "I bet the goddamned cops still have that bottle."

****

Rynna waited for Dr. Moran in the library. Was it only a few days ago that she and Ted had sat here together, waiting to hear about Grandmother's fall? Now a coffin lay in the little-used parlor, and everything was forever changed.

My dear Miss Dalton," Moran said, taking her hands in his. "I am so sorry." It was odd that he was comforting her. He had known Grandmother longer than she had.

"Thank you," she said. "It's still so unreal to me. I keep thinking she should be here. She would know what to do."

"She was a great lady. She will be missed." Was that true? Hadn't most of the people who belonged to her past died before her? She had lived such a reclusive life of late, but Dr. Moran's memory of her extended to an earlier time. Rynna had arrived at the end of the story.

"Is Ted all right?"

"Oh, yes, nothing to worry about. I gave him a shot and he'll sleep through the night."

"It scared me," she confessed. "It was so much worse."

"Emotional stress doesn't help. But it's nothing serious. Now can I give you something to help you sleep?"

"No, I don't need anything," she said. She was a little annoyed by his casual manner about Ted, although it was what he would prefer himself. "Please don't tell him I asked," she began hesitantly, "but isn't there anything that can be done? I mean I've read about hip replacements." She knew how foolish she sounded, trying to tell him his business, but he smiled kindly.

"Knees are more complicated," he said, "Some experimental surgeries have been done, but it's not the miracle you're hoping for, Miss Dalton."

She didn't ask why. She didn't want to know. Her eyes filled with tears, and she remembered Ted saying, "I don't want you to ever cry for me." All right, damn it, she wouldn't. She would be as strong, as grown up, as any of them. She would be a goddamned Demeray.

Dr. Moran saw her tears. "You know what he would say. I expect he had enough 'Poor Ted' treatment as a child to last a few lifetimes."

"Not from his parents," she protested. If she ever believed anything Ted said, she believed that.

"No," Dr. Moran agreed. "Not from William and Clara. Not from Mrs. Demeray either." They sat in silence, drawn together in the realization that everything Edwina Demeray had represented was gone. An era had ended.

She found Jason in the music room after the doctor left. He was standing near the doorway, waiting for her, not looking at Rosalind's portrait. But he must have seen it a hundred times. She took his hand, and they sat together on the piano bench. Rynna leaned against him, seeking reassurance. Whatever comfort she could usually find in this room was not present now. There was only Jason.

"Everything okay?" he asked.

She nodded, understanding that he was referring only to Dr. Moran's visit. She wanted to play the piano, to comfort herself, to reach out for Rosalind, but she had too great a sense of restraint. Grandmother was dead, and not even sad music was appropriate. In any case, she wouldn't want to disturb Ted.

She stirred. "Jason, what do you think really happened?"

"Does it matter?" he asked. "What happened happened. We'll probably never know."

"Do you think Ted could have killed her? Really?"

"You want my opinion?"

"This time I do."

He considered for a minute and then said bluntly, "No, I don't think he would have the nerve. Not that it would take much to sweet-talk an old lady into taking a few pills."

"Jason!" She was shocked that he could speak so casually of someone he had bantered with a few days ago.

"Sorry," he murmured.

****

Much later, lying awake, too tired to sleep, Rynna remembered for the first time the footsteps on the stairs the previous night. Even now she could only recall them dimly, as if it were a dream, but it wasn't, was it? She had dismissed the incident last night, but if Grandmother was murdered, it might be important, and she knew exactly what time she had heard them.

Rosalind knew something. Rosalind had warned her. But if the footsteps had anything to do with murder, Ted was not a suspect.

Jason had said Ted wouldn't have the nerve. That was Jason's opinion. But he was right that it would not have taken much. Not sweet talk, not any sort of persuasion. Grandmother would have trusted Ted completely. And he was not the sweet talker in the family.

****

In the morning, Rynna and Ted met over breakfast as they had so many times before. Nothing had changed, and everything was different. A subtle difference showed in the way the servants spoke to her, a difference that puzzled her at first. Of course, their jobs were on the line. They viewed her as having power over their lives, and she didn't even control her own.

While she ate her perfectly poached egg, she told Ted about the footsteps, and he was barely interested. "Should I tell the police?"

"By all means," he said. "You wouldn't want Chandler to think you withheld evidence."

"I won't talk to *him*. I think he's a bastard." She wanted Ted to tell her what happened downtown, but he would not be drawn out. He wasn't concealing anything. He was indifferent.

"He's only doing his job, Rynna."

"What do you think really happened?"

"I don't know," he said. "I don't care. It's over."

Was it? No official pronouncement was made, but it was generally accepted that the case was closed. The police could produce no tangible evidence, no promising suspect. They could not rule out either suicide or accident.

Other things appeared to be generally accepted during that confused, depressing period too. Without knowing how it had come about, Rynna found her future settled. She didn't remember even discussing it with Jason, but it was now assumed they would live at Stonebridge after they were married. She had a guilty memory of telling Ted he could have the house, that she didn't care about it. His suggestion that she was marrying Jason to get away had an element of truth. She had looked forward to what even Ted had called escape.

But, no, she loved Jason. She wanted to spend the rest of her life with him. "Where" did not matter. *Whither thou goest.* Stonebridge was a beautiful house, a place of long, rich history. She belonged here, and Grandmother had known that. The house would be different now, not a place she needed to escape. It would be her home, hers and Jason's, and they would return it to its former glory. They would fix it up, modernize it, entertain in the style it deserved. Rynna had a small trust fund—small by Demeray standards—and with Jason's income they would have enough to live quite comfortably.

Ted's options had changed too. If she knew him at all, she knew he would end up at the university eventually. But he had a great deal of money now, and he could do other things if he wanted to. He could live in Europe. He could go anywhere. What was there in Stonebridge to hold him now? Memories? Grandmother had lived in the past. Was the past a place he wanted to stay in without her?

Rynna couldn't say anything to him about his plans. Nothing in their relationship to this point would allow her to verbalize the change in their positions. The house was hers now, but when she talked to him she couldn't say "my house." In vague plans and dreams of what she might do with the house in the future, she could think of it as hers, in the same way she could imagine Jason as her husband. But Ted had called the place home for thirty years, and she was still little more than a visitor. She couldn't even tell if he had thought about it yet.

The day of the funeral, Jason called and said he

would meet them at the church, so Ted and Rynna were to ride together in the Bentley. Rynna found nothing suitable in her wardrobe, so Cecile had taken in an old black dress of Grandmother's for her to wear. Ted wore a dark suit—she was a little surprised that he owned one—and he was so different, so soberly handsome and dignified, that she was a little shy of him.

In the car, Ted spoke to her in a tone that was both impersonal and intensely bitter. He *had* thought about their new relationship, and it was hard to tell whether he was angry with Grandmother or simply so resigned to the situation that it didn't matter what he said. Even Ellery's discreet presence didn't hold him back. "There have always been Demerays at Stonebridge," he said. "Now it ends. The name won't continue here. It's damned unlikely it will continue anywhere."

"That's your choice to make," she said. She wasn't sure it was a choice, but she needed to say something. Letting him carry on like that was worse than fighting with him.

He didn't rise to the bait. "You would think Grandmother wouldn't want Wyatts to have Stonebridge," he went on relentlessly, "after what happened to Rosalind."

"That's unfair," she ventured. She didn't know what to do or say. He was so hateful like this, so frightening.

"Life is unfair," he agreed. "So the Demeray name leaves Stonebridge forever. As for the Demeray bloodline…"

"Ted…"

"It's reached a sorry conclusion, hasn't it? Jason is a cheap shyster, and look what a pushover you turned out to be."

He could not insult her if she didn't let him. "I'm not a pushover," she said, "and Jason is an expensive shyster, if you please."

But she couldn't joke him out of this mood. "Yes," he said grimly. "You haven't learned how expensive."

"Stop it, Ted."

"What you ought to do," he continued, in a curiously impersonal way, as if her life were a scientific puzzle, "is marry me, just so your children would be called Demeray."

"Very funny."

"At least my name is Demeray. That may be a technicality, but it used to be important to Grandmother."

"No," she said, trying to match his tone. "You're the one who is so fond of technicalities."

Fortunately, the church was not far, and the conversation was cut short by their arrival. The weather was appropriately overcast with occasional drizzle, and the small, quaint stone church nearly blended into the dull gray sky. The building was as old as Stonebridge and a veritable monument to architectural barriers. It didn't have a wheelchair ramp, and the steep stone steps were a challenge even to Rynna's young legs. Ellery had to drag the wheelchair up.

The funeral was brief and low-key. A few people Rynna didn't know were in the church, but it wasn't an impressive turnout.

At the graveside in the large family plot, she and Jason stood together under the protection of his umbrella—it was drizzling again. Ted was on the other side, with Ellery standing impassively behind him. Ted was bareheaded and oblivious to the weather, if not to the entire proceedings. Lucy, Mrs. Lester, and Cecile huddled together, and one of them sniffled audibly as the minister spoke. The service was altogether quite grim and sad, and Rynna suspected Grandmother would not have approved.

When it was over, Ted spoke briefly to Ellery, and they left without even glancing at the others. Rynna shook hands with the minister and thanked him warmly to make up for Ted's bad manners.

"I haven't been up here before," she told Jason. "Shall we look around?"

He wasn't particularly pleased, but he assented. No Wyatts were buried here—Rosalind was elsewhere—but plenty of Demerays. Some of them were names she recognized from the family albums, but others were unfamiliar. With a feeling of discovery she found Edwina's husband—they were side by side again—and their two sons, Edmund, who was her grandfather and Ted's, and Robert, who was Jason's. A little farther on, William and Clara were buried with a single headstone, a single death date. Together in death as in life. "I always knew they loved me," Ted had said, and all that love was lost in one terrible moment.

"Depressing," Jason said. She didn't think so, but he was edgy, so they left without exploring any further.

He drove fast, as he always did, and by the time they crossed the bridge they were right behind the Bentley. As they swung into the drive, Rynna's heart skipped a beat. A police car was parked in front of the house.

The Ferrari jerked to a stop, and she glanced at Jason. He had turned rather pale. Her first thought was that they were here to arrest Ted after all, but no, an ambulance was parked beyond the police car.

"Now what?" Jason said sharply, opening the door.

An ambulance? Her mind stumbled numbly against possibilities. Who was left in the house? Who stayed behind when they left for the funeral? Only the two girls, Jenny and Marie, in the kitchen. An accident in the kitchen?

No accident. Standing in the doorway were Sgt. Chandler and Marie, with Lucy's arms around her. Marie was sobbing. "Jenny," Rynna said. *Oh, God, Jenny, young and pretty and eager to please.*

Between Marie's sobs and Sgt. Chandler's matter-of-fact remarks, the all-too-simple story came out. While everyone else was at the funeral and Marie was washing the breakfast dishes, Jenny had hung herself.

For a few terrible minutes, Rynna wondered if it was her fault. Ted had implied something between Jason and Jenny, and if it were true, even if it was primarily in Jenny's mind, the news of their upcoming marriage could have driven her to this act of desperation. But his reaction to the news did not suggest any involvement. His concern was all for Rynna. He appeared almost relieved that the latest tragedy involved only a servant girl. Jason had said Ted didn't live in the real world, and Ted was the only one who had hinted at a connection between Jason and Jenny.

Sgt. Chandler was more interested in the fact that Jenny had said, "She's been murdered," even before they were sure Grandmother was dead. No conclusive evidence existed, no ends were neatly tied. Jenny's case was closed, as Grandmother's had been. The police were not satisfied, but they had nowhere to go with it.

When everything settled down a bit, Rynna discussed it with Ted over a late lunch in the dining room. He had handled everything with such straightforward efficiency, contacting Jenny's family and talking to the police, that she found it hard to remember the bitter exchange in the car. Grandmother's death had knocked him off his feet emotionally. Jenny's death interested him as a psychological puzzle. Was there a connection?

"Jenny had no reason to kill Grandmother," he said, "and if she did she wouldn't be fool enough to yell 'murder' before anyone else did. Jenny might have been emotionally unstable, but she wasn't stupid."

"But why did she kill herself? And why now?"

"Guilty knowledge," he said, trying out the phrase. "If she didn't do it, maybe she knew who did, or thought she knew."

"Who?"

"You tell me," he said. "You're the one who heard footsteps on the stairs. What did they sound like?"

"I was half asleep. I wasn't even sure I heard anything." She wasn't hungry, but she made herself take a few bites of cucumber salad. It was oversalted. Mrs. Lester was in mourning.

"Is it possible it was Jenny?" Ted asked.

"I don't know. It could've been. It could've been anybody."

"Are you sure it wasn't me?"

"If it was, you've been putting on a hell of a good act."

He smiled faintly and asked, ever so casually, "Could it have been Jason?"

"Of course not," she said automatically. It could have been Jason. As she'd said, it could have been anyone. If it came right down to it, it could have been Ted. But it wasn't Jason, and she wouldn't feed Ted's paranoia.

"That wasn't very convincing," he said.

"Not to you anyway. You have a one-track mind." She put down her fork, giving up on the salad.

"And we still don't know what Jenny knew."

"You tried to imply something between Jenny and Jason. Are you suggesting he killed Grandmother and Jenny knew it?"

"What do you think?" he asked.

"I think you're crazy, and it really is boring, and Jason doesn't live in this house. He doesn't even have a key." She pushed her plate away.

"That's right," he said. "Somebody would have had to let him in. Through the kitchen, maybe."

"Stop it."

"It scares you, doesn't it?"

The idea did scare her, and it made her furious. She knew better. She took a deep breath and struck back. "You told the police if you were going to kill somebody it would be me."

"That's what I said."

"If Jason were going to kill somebody, don't you think it's more likely it would be you?"

Ted didn't even blink. "I'll keep my door locked," he said.

She honestly could not tell if he was serious. She never could.

Chapter Twelve

Rynna didn't see much of Jason for the next couple of weeks. He was working hard, tying up loose ends, arranging trade-offs with other lawyers, clearing his calendar so he and Rynna could have a long honeymoon trip. As their plans took shape, the wedding date was advanced a little so Jason could be back for an important case in February. "Besides," Jason said, smiling, "it's hell to wait. I was never much good at waiting for anything."

She didn't object. She had a great deal to do, and without Grandmother's help now, but after those first maddening months at Stonebridge, it was a pleasure to be too busy. Cecile, with her youthful enthusiasm, contributed her own definite ideas about the dress and was more help than Rynna would have expected. Lucy was constantly busy too, talking to florists and caterers and calling the dressmaker about fittings.

When she told Ted the wedding date had been moved up, he reminded her that Grandmother had not been dead a month. "Why the indecent haste?" he asked. "Is he afraid you'll come to your senses?" The conversation was taking place in the library, where he was doing an inventory of the books.

"Don't you ever get tired of being hateful? Grandmother would want us to go ahead, and you know it. I'm as sorry as you are that she didn't live to see it, but she wouldn't want us to delay on her account. Anyway, it isn't the timing you object to. It's Jason."

He wasn't about to argue with that. He was silent for a moment, and then he said quietly, "Don't do it, Rynna. Don't."

"It's my life, Ted."

Again he was silent, and finally, resigned, he said, "All right, it's your life. I wash my hands of it. But don't say I didn't warn you."

"I have to talk to you about something else," she said reluctantly, already guessing his reaction. "I want you to give me away."

"That's not funny."

"Give me a chance, Ted. There isn't anybody else. You're my only living male relative, and I wouldn't want anyone else. Jason's friends I barely even know." She had briefly considered Mr. Baxter, who had behaved kindly enough *in loco parentis*, but he wouldn't do. He was too stuffy and still a stranger. "I want you to do it."

"No."

"Please, Ted, it's such a little thing, and it would mean so much to me. You wouldn't have to walk me down the aisle or anything. All you have to do is sit in front and say 'I do' when the minister asks—"

"I don't," he said. "I don't give you to Jason. It's too much to ask."

"It's only a formality."

"Not a chance, Rynna. I'm not even going to be at your damned wedding, so forget it." He punctuated the remark by shoving a book back on the shelf harder than necessary.

"Don't say that. You have to be there."

"Jesus, Rynna, you really are merciless. I said *no*."

He pulled out another book.

"You are the only family I have. Attending the wedding does not have to mean you approve of it. I want you to come, Ted."

"If you say you won't get married unless I'm there…"

"I'm not that dumb. I will get married without you, but I will never forgive you."

"I'll survive that too. You've been a damned nuisance from the day you arrived." He returned his attention to the list he was making.

"Theodore Demeray, you will come to my wedding, whether your heart is in it or not. You will represent the family because you still believe in it in spite of your smart remarks. Grandmother would want you to."

He had no answer to that. Grandmother would have wanted him to. He would have enjoyed arguing with her about it, but in the end he would have been there.

Rynna reviewed the text of the service with Jason and Reverend Holloway to make sure they all agreed on it. They made a few modifications to the traditional service she had heard so many times at the weddings of her school friends. They replaced the old-fashioned "obey" and eliminated "Who giveth this woman to be married to this man?" She worried a little about "If anyone can show just cause why they may not be lawfully joined together." The phrase was an invitation. But what could Ted object to? Marriage between second cousins was legal, and his opinion of Jason was irrelevant. Nevertheless, she was relieved that the line was not in the ceremony.

She never did have the conversation she dreaded about Ted's plans. She accepted that he would stay on at

Stonebridge while she and Jason were away. He had decided to take a teaching position at the university, but first he would finish his book. He implied that with Rynna out of his hair, finishing it would be an easy task.

When Jason wasn't with her, Rynna missed him, and sometimes she doubted her decision to marry him. Did she know him? Who was he? When he was so busy in town and she was alone at Stonebridge with wedding plans and Ted's stubborn opposition, she had a lot of time for doubts.

But when he arrived, doubts vanished. He was so vital, so charming, and so much in love with her. How could she doubt that her life with him would be wonderful? Wasn't it beginning with a dream trip, a fairy-tale honeymoon?

He escorted her to another party, nominally in their honor, and she got to know his friends a little better. Their attitude toward her was subtly different than it had been. She was less of an outsider now that she was marrying him, but she was still a mystery to them. The women especially were appraising her, in a friendly way, to be sure. They were passing judgment on her qualifications for joining their circle. She thought she passed. Bonnie Harris was the friendliest, and they could have been friends except for the slight tension between Cy and Jason. She liked Cy well enough, though, and surely professional disagreements could be set aside.

Jason was busy in town the day before the wedding, but he called and talked to Rynna, who as usual was feeling jittery and tearful in his absence. "Not losing your nerve, are you?" he asked.

"No, just going a little crazy. I'll be so glad when this is all over and I don't have to think of sixteen things at once."

He calmed and comforted her, as he always could. The conversation was thoroughly satisfactory, except that she was standing in the front hall the whole time. She planned to have telephone extensions installed as soon as they returned from the Bahamas.

That night, for the first time since Grandmother's death, she was awakened at 2:15 and heard the sound of the piano from the music room. A warning or a plea, or was it all her imagination? She slept again almost at once, but somehow sensed—or did she dream it?—that Rosalind's presence filled the room.

In the morning, she had no room for any other thoughts or memories. Even before her eyes were opened, she thought, This is my wedding day. She would not see Jason again until she stood with him in front of the altar in the small stone church to become his wife.

Jason's wife. Mistress of Stonebridge. A tall order for someone who didn't always feel grown up. Again and again that morning she stopped and took a deep breath to calm herself.

The dress was absolutely perfect. Cecile buttoned it up the back with tiny pearl buttons in satin loops and arranged the veil over Rynna's dark hair. Facing herself in the mirror, Rynna's nerves steadied. It was so lovely, so right. There was no room now for the smallest doubt. Cecile removed the veil and adjusted the band, striving for absolute perfection, and Rynna, a little breathless, said, "You've been wonderful to me. So much extra work."

"Everybody loves a wedding," Cecile said. "It's worth all the work, and you'll see I was right. You will be the most beautiful bride Stonebridge has ever seen."

Ted was waiting in the hall when she came downstairs, Cecile following her with an anxious eye to details. "My God," he said, stunned. "You look…"

"Beautiful," Cecile prompted.

Ted was momentarily speechless. "Beautiful," he agreed finally.

Rynna didn't much like the way *he* looked. He wore the same shirt he had worn to the funeral, and his hair was neatly brushed, but he looked ill, as if he hadn't slept. "Is it really all right?" she asked. Why was his opinion so important to her when he caused so much trouble?

"It's great," he said. "It's perfect."

"Thank you." On impulse, she bent and kissed his cheek. "I'm so happy, Ted."

He didn't answer. He had promised to be on his best behavior today—Grandmother would have insisted—so he couldn't say anything. It was too late for objections now. It was too late for anything except getting through it with the minimum of fuss.

She remembered—did Ted?—the last time they rode together to the church. This time he was silent. She recalled the intermittent drizzle of that day and said, "At least the weather's nice."

At the church she waited with Cecile in a small anteroom, listening to the murmur of many voices and the muted notes of the organ. Cecile fussed over her, straightening her skirt, checking her bouquet of white roses and baby's breath. They spoke in hushed voices, and Rynna was on the edge of a nervous giggle. The atmosphere was so solemn, so scary, but at the same time she could have floated down the aisle.

Finally, the organ swelled into the "Bridal Chorus"

from *Lohengrin,* and Cecile opened the door and stood back, smiling. "You're on," she whispered.

Rynna clutched her bouquet and stepped out at a slow, careful pace. The church was full, mostly with Jason's friends, and she sensed the presence of every one of them, not as an audience she was nervous about performing in front of, but as people who had shown up to share and celebrate and support. Winter roses, amaryllis, camellias, and yards of white ribbons bedecked the pews.

Jason was even more than usually handsome in his dark suit. He stood in front of the altar, watching her as she came down the aisle, and the expression on his face was worth every bit of planning and fuss and confusion. She felt precisely like a bride, like every storybook image she had ever seen. So proud, so happy, so beautiful.

Reverend Holloway cleared his throat. "Dearly beloved…"

Rynna looked at Jason, and he smiled, his beautiful, dark eyes shining. My husband, she thought, trying it out, my husband Jason.

"Forasmuch as marriage is a holy estate ordained of God, and to be held in honor by all, it becometh those who enter therein to weigh with reverent minds…"

She listened to all the words, gave them her full attention, but it was hard to concentrate under the force of so much emotion.

"Into this holy estate this man and woman come now to be united."

Pamela should have been here, she thought. Pamela would have been so proud. And Rosalind?

"Jason, wilt thou have this woman to thy wedded

wife, to live together after God's ordinance in the holy estate of matrimony? Wilt thou love her, comfort her, honor and keep her, in sickness and in health, and forsaking all others, keep thee only unto her, so long as ye both shall live?"

Jason, very serious, his voice steady: "I will."

"Rynna, wilt thou have this man…"

She gazed into Jason's eyes. Yes, she would love him, comfort him. "I will." Her own voice, firm but nearly breathless, surprised her.

Now he was taking her hand, speaking to her as if they were alone. "I, Jason, take thee, Rynna…"

Holding onto his hand, gaining strength from him, she repeated those so-familiar words. "I, Rynna, take thee, Jason, to my wedded husband, to have and to hold from this day forward…"

He slipped Rosalind's ring onto her finger, and it was accomplished. She was a married woman.

"Forasmuch as Jason and Rynna have consented together in holy wedlock and have declared the same before God and in the presence of this company, I pronounce them husband and wife. What God hath joined together, let not man put asunder."

What God hath joined together…

"God almighty send you his light and truth to keep you all the days of your life. The hand of God protect you, his holy angels accompany you, God the Father, God the Son, and God the Holy Ghost, cause his grace to be mighty upon you. Amen."

Jason bent his head to kiss her, and she felt so beautiful, so cherished, so *married.* The organ again, Mendelssohn this time. The music was always the same, always so familiar, and at the same time it was completely special for her and Jason.

Everything was simply perfect.

They stood on the steps of the church while people gathered around, smiling, congratulating, snapping camera shutters. She was a little like a celebrity, the center of attention, but it was not real. Reality was his hand in hers and the old-fashioned gold wedding band on her finger. Rosalind's son. Rosalind's ring.

She shook her head to clear it. The past was past. She and Jason were the future. Rynna Dalton Wyatt. Mr. and Mrs. Jason Wyatt.

Most of the guests came back to the house, to the front parlor festooned with white streamers, the elegant wedding cake in the dining room, punch and champagne and a giddy whirl of conversation and laughter.

Rynna was in a wonderful frame of mind, more relaxed than at the church, but still buoyed up by happiness. Now she could take off her shoes and sit down and loosen her hair, but she was still the bride, still wearing the dazzling white gown. She held Jason's arm possessively, and whenever she glanced at him he was looking back, smiling.

They cut the cake and then pretended to cut it again for the camera that didn't flash the first time. They sipped champagne and danced the first waltz, Rynna in her stocking feet, feeling as if she could do anything she wanted today. Today was all hers.

A couple of times she spotted Ted, not looking particularly happy, but behaving himself as promised, eating wedding cake and chatting with Jason's friends. She was a little worried about him, although she wasn't sure why, and she set the thought aside. Not now, not today.

Jason glanced at his watch and Rynna, the dutiful wife, followed his cue and slipped upstairs to change into her blue traveling suit. She removed the wedding dress carefully, tangling it a little in her hair, and laid it neatly on the bed for Cecile to take care of.

She glanced around the blue-and-white room that had been Pamela's and then hers. When they came back, she and Jason would move into the redecorated master bedroom, and this room would be empty again.

She hurried back downstairs and stood with Jason to say goodbye to an endless crowd of well-wishers—the servants, his friends, Reverend Holloway, and his wife. And Ted. He was slightly flushed, but behaving with icy self-control, so she couldn't tell whether he'd been drinking too much champagne. "Goodbye, Ted," she said. "Thank you for being here."

"Can I kiss the bride?" he asked. A reasonable enough request.

"Of course." She had taken her hair down, and she let go of Jason's hand to hold it back as she bent to receive Ted's kiss. By then she had been kissed by half of Brenford.

But Ted was not just another well-wisher, claiming a traditional privilege. He was in love with her, and if she hadn't known it or admitted it before, there was no denying it then.

She left on her honeymoon with Jason, still shaken and haunted by Ted's uncousinly kiss.

Chapter Thirteen

Jason and Rynna flew to Vermont, rented a car, and drove straight to the lodge where they would spend the first week of their honeymoon. Jason was a wonderful traveling companion. He was funny and charming and put her entirely at ease.

The lodge was expensive, comfortable, and a cliché of pseudo-rustic style. Rynna thought it was awful, and she loved it. They had found the perfect setting, a place they could laugh at together.

In their room, after Jason over-tipped the bellboy and closed the door behind him, they both laughed in delight. He heaved a sigh of relief and put his arms around her. "Now it's just us," he said. "Now the rest of the world doesn't matter." He kissed her mouth and her throat, and his hands caressed her hair and the length of her back. "Till death us do part," he said.

"I love you," she whispered, leaning against him, feeling heavy, almost sleepy, with so much love. He unbuttoned her blouse, and she pulled away a little, kissed him, and said, "Wait, let me…"

"Now," he said urgently, but his hands were gentle. "Now," and he was kissing her so sweetly, so lovingly.

"Yes," she said, and he lifted her in his arms as if she weighed nothing at all and carried her to the enormous bed with its faux log frame.

"Mrs. Wyatt," he said and undressed her with

capable hands. The urgency of his passion communicated itself to her, and she was ready for him, trembling with anticipation and confused desire.

"Jason," she murmured, drawing him closer. "Jason."

He was a skillful lover, but for him it was not so much an act of love as a supreme act of possession. Rynna wanted nothing more, only be to be possessed, to belong to him. She had a feeling not of helplessness but of power. Such power she could wield to give him pleasure, to bind him to her. *What God hath joined together.*

The weather held, the skiing was fine, and the food was excellent. Before it could have palled, it was time to give up the powdery slopes and the corny lodge and progress to the next stage of this adventure that was life with Jason.

They drove straight through to the home of his cousin Ian Wyatt and arrived too tired to feel awkward. Rynna was hazy with fatigue and found it easy to smile and greet Ian, his wife Janet, two tall teenage boys, and a shy little girl. The house was charming, small but comfortable, and decked out festively for Christmas. The children were polite and curious, and Janet gave them coffee and showed them to their room.

Happy and tired, Rynna nestled in Jason's arms. She liked lying with him, belonging in his arms, without even thinking of making love, and then thinking of it, and asking, her voice muffled against his shoulder, "Would they hear us?"

The next day, her head clearer, she was introduced to more cousins and a few uncles and aunts. Some of them had traveled a long way to spend Christmas together. She liked the continuity. Why had Jason abandoned this community of extended family? Why did he move to his mother's hometown, to memories he didn't share? There was no suggestion from any of the Wyatt cousins that they remembered or cared about the tragedy that had befallen his parents. To them he was simply Jason, and they loved him in an offhand, teasing way that she liked. They welcomed her too, told her how pretty she was, how lucky Jason was, explained who they were, how they were related, showed her snapshots, and told her family stories. She had never felt so accepted.

They stayed with the Wyatts for three days, and then it was time to leave. After so much intense sociability, they were ready to be alone again. Janet kissed Rynna and said, "Come back real soon," and Ian said to Jason with a man-to-man wink, "You take care of her now."

They flew to the Bahamas, and it was like Vermont all over again. Instead of the ski slopes, they had the hot white sand and the warm blue water. They swam, lay in the sun, and smoothed suntan oil over each other's warm skin. They locked the door of their clean, cozy private bungalow and pretended the rest of the world did not exist. They made love, not with the haste of the first night, but slowly, luxuriously, tasting the delicious freedom of time. They were drunk, crazed, stoned with love.

Rynna was so happy she didn't even know what month it was, what year, or what planet they were on. She was deaf and blind even to her immediate surroundings. She saw only Jason.

The second Monday in the islands dawned with a slight overcast, but it burned off soon after they arrived at the beach. Rynna had forgotten her sunglasses, and

Jason, the ever-thoughtful husband, volunteered to go back for them.

She was lying on her stomach on a large towel on the nearly deserted beach, her head resting on her folded arms, her eyes closed against the glare, when heavy footsteps approached. "Thank you, darling," she murmured, turning over to take the sunglasses.

"You're welcome, I'm sure," said a strange voice, an amused masculine voice.

She sat up, flustered, to find a man in his late twenties, tan and muscular, with sun-bleached hair, smiling down at her. "I'm sorry," she said. "I thought you were my husband."

He took a lingering look at her swimsuit-clad figure and said, "I wish I were." He grinned so good-naturedly she couldn't take offense and glancing beyond her, said, "I suppose that's him now."

Jason was coming down the slope with her sunglasses in his hand, and he had seen the stranger. "Yes," she said, "That's Jason."

"Too bad," he said, still smiling. "I'd better move on, then. Have a good day." He headed down the beach without a backward glance.

Jason, a little out of breath, held out the glasses and asked, "Who was that?"

"Nobody. He just stopped to say hello, I guess. Thank you." She took the sunglasses, put them on, and lay back on the beach towel.

"You guess? He didn't want to say hello to me, though."

"I guess not. Come here. Give me a kiss, please."

He kissed her, but his mind was elsewhere.

"Don't let me stay out too long," she said. "I don't

want to burn."

He didn't answer. He sat beside her and stared down the beach, frowning.

"Jason?" She caught his hand and pulled him down to lie close to her. Everything was exactly as it had been before. Wasn't it?

Later, locked in their room, they were again isolated, divorced from the rest of the world, from reality. No other world existed, only Jason and Rynna. While he was making passionate love to her, Jason said in an unfamiliar tone, "You belong to me," and her entire self, her body, her mind, and her heart agreed.

"Yes," she murmured, "Yes." Nothing had changed.

They lingered at lunch in the tiny café they had discovered on the first day, sitting at a small table with a clean white tablecloth, feeding each other the best bits of crab meat and tropical fruit and talking in low voices, as if keeping secrets from the rest of the world. They didn't even register the presence of other customers in the place, but as they got up to leave, Jason counting out bills to pay the check, someone rose from a nearby table and approached them.

"Well, hello," he said, smiling, and after a second of confusion, Rynna recognized the young man on the beach.

"This is my husband, Jason Wyatt," she said. "I'm Rynna."

"Bob Kemper," he said. "This is a great little place, isn't it?"

"Oh, yes, it's wonderful," Rynna agreed. She was a little blurred with fatigue and passion, and although it was an effort to be polite, she was able to smile into this stranger's face as if her love for Jason was something she could share with the whole world.

Not more than a dozen more words were exchanged, and Bob Kemper went in the opposite direction when they left the café. Afterward, Rynna couldn't remember his face or the color of his hair. Jason was silent on the way back to their bungalow. Rynna, bemused by love, didn't even notice. As soon as the door was closed behind them, he said, "What was that all about?"

"What?"

"You know what. That Kemper character."

"He was the man on the beach."

"I know that. The same man twice in one day. Accidentally runs into you, twice in one day?"

She shrugged. "What difference does it make? He was only being polite. Why are you upset?"

"I'm not upset," he said grimly. "I don't have any reason to be upset. Do I?"

"Of course not," she said. She didn't understand what he was saying, but it wasn't important. She tried to change the subject, to tease him into smiling, but to no avail. "What is wrong?" she demanded.

"Nothing is wrong," he said with an edge of sarcasm in his voice. "I'm on my honeymoon, and my wife is already flirting with every beach bum who happens by."

"Jason!" She laughed. The accusation was too ridiculous to take seriously. "I was not flirting with him."

"What happened on the beach?"

"Nothing. I barely spoke to him."

"Whatever you said, he obviously found it encouraging."

"I didn't say anything to him. He recognized me, that's all. I was a familiar face, so he came over to say hello. You're making something out of nothing, less than nothing."

"I'm not stupid, Rynna. I saw the way you looked at him."

She was so bewildered she didn't even think of defending herself. She wasn't conscious of having regarded Bob Kemper at all. His face was a dim blur. She loved Jason, saw only Jason, and she didn't understand why he was speaking to her this way, why he was getting angrier by the second.

"I'm not going to stand for this," he said, his face flushed, his eyes dark with rage.

Shocked and just beginning to be frightened, she stammered, "Don't talk to me like that."

Jason, her beloved Jason, her gentle, loving husband, came toward her with murderous fury in his eyes. He struck her.

Rynna was so surprised she didn't react, didn't back up or lift her hands to protect herself. Her defenselessness infuriated him further, and he hit her again.

And then it was over. Like a summer storm that blows up quickly and passes over, his anger vanished. He was immediately contrite, humble, wretched. He helped her to the bed, sat beside her, held her hands and kissed them, offering abject apologies. "God, Rynna, I'm so sorry. I'm so sorry. It's just jealousy, stupid jealousy. I love you so much. I don't ever want to lose you. It's only because I love you so much. If I didn't care for you the way I do, you couldn't make me so angry."

Rynna, with her head still reeling from the blows—they were not slaps—thought, Why is this so familiar? Where have I heard this before?

For the next few days, Jason's every word and

action was aimed at making up to her for that single moment of violence. He was so gentle, so solicitous, so lovingly considerate. She was reassured, lulled into forgiveness. She put the ugly incident out of her mind. She was deeply in love.

The second time she didn't even know who it was she was supposed to have flirted with. She couldn't remember smiling at a man, looking at a man. Why didn't Jason believe she could see only him?

Again he was desperately sorry afterward. Again he was so good to her, so wretched about having hurt her. Again, even as she covered the bruise on her cheekbone with makeup before they went out to dinner, Rynna forgave him.

The third time he didn't accuse her of anything specific. The conversation was so innocent she didn't realize what was coming. She was changing her clothes after coming back from the beach, and Jason was watching her. She liked the feeling, not precisely seductive, but somehow sensual, of having him watch her dress.

They were talking, as they often did, about memories they didn't share, about their lives before they met. She was telling him something amusing and inconsequential when she sensed he was not listening. She glanced at him, and he was watching her with an intent but unfocused expression, as if he was thinking about something else. "A penny for your thoughts," she said lightly.

In a matter-of-fact tone, not at all accusing or judgmental, he said, "You weren't a virgin when we were married. Tell me about the men you had before me."

By then she might have had the sense to be frightened, but instead she was amused. "What are you talking about? There weren't any men before you." She smiled, reassuring him as if he were a child who needed soothing, "You are the only man in my life, Jason, my only lover. I'm the one who should be jealous. Tell me about the women you've had." She didn't really want to hear anything. She was only teasing. She finished buttoning her blouse and picked up her hairbrush.

"Oh," he said, "now you'll tell me about the double standard."

"I wouldn't dream of it," she said. "It's all so unimportant. Nothing else matters, only you and me." She brushed her hair with quick strokes and smoothed it over her ears.

Jason smiled as he got to his feet, and she had no inkling, no premonition. "You are such a liar," he said, and his tone was so commonplace she couldn't grasp the meaning of the words. He grabbed her roughly and kissed her without a hint of tenderness.

"Don't," she said. "You're hurting me."

If he heard her, he gave no sign. "I'll show you who you belong to," he said and shoved her toward the bed. She lost her balance, fell backward, and hit her head against the headboard. Jason grabbed her, his fingers biting into her arms, and deliberately banged her head against it again. When he released her she fell back on the pillows, too stunned to move.

He raped her. There was no other word for it.

****

This time the bruises wouldn't show. Rynna had a painful lump on the back of her head, but the real pain was not physical. She locked herself in the bathroom for three hours, deaf to Jason's pleas. Her face was unmarked, but it didn't matter. She was not going out to dinner anyway. She would never go to the beach again, so it didn't matter if her swimsuit wouldn't hide all the bruises. She took a long, hot bath and cried herself out, and then she sat staring at the green-tiled walls and contemplated the wreck of her life.

Jason was sick. Jealousy was a sickness. She was sick too. She had been attracted to him, and surely the signs had been evident. How could she not have known what he was capable of? He was so charming, so easygoing, but that façade was a cover for other things, things she had seen and not acknowledged. She had seen examples of his selfishness, his impatience. God, what a fool she must have been, to mistake impatience for grand passion.

Which was worse, to leave him or to stay? She was not unique. She was like any other battered wife. If she stayed with him and let him treat her this way, she was as sick as he was. Had she done something to provoke him this last time? Had she said something? Was the way she spoke to men unintentionally provocative? Could Jason, the outraged husband, be justified?

No. No. No. Rynna covered her face with her hands. How had it all become such torment? She was not at fault. She had behaved properly.

Jason had a problem, but as his wife it was her problem too. Could she get him to accept professional help? To admit he needed it? He would repeat the same old refrain: *It's only because I love you. I don't mean to hurt you. It's only that I care so much.* God, what a line that was. How many millions of women were told those lies again and again and wanted to believe them and let the abuse keep happening?

He had never hurt her while they were courting. Perhaps he had been a little rough, a little impatient once or twice, but she had been in love. His devotion was exciting. *Damn. Had* she encouraged it?

No. No. Again and again she rehashed the same thoughts, and again and again she acquitted herself. She was a fool, but she did not deserve this.

She didn't want to stay here any longer. No matter how happy they had been here, it was ruined now. She could never stay in this bungalow without reliving the sickening crunch of her head against the headboard. She had given herself to Jason so willingly, so lovingly, but now she could remember only the brutality of rape. Everything was ruined. The honeymoon was over.

She wanted to go home to Stonebridge. The house that had once been a prison to her now beckoned as a refuge, a haven. Jason would be all right there. He couldn't want to wreck his life, to be condemned for a few minutes of violence out of weeks of sanity. No Bob Kempers were at Stonebridge to trigger his anger. He would have her all to himself.

God, what was she thinking? Was Stonebridge to be her prison? Was she to be one of those pathetic women who were afraid to speak to the mailman for fear of provoking their husbands' rage? No. Not a chance. If she and Jason were to live together, he would have to promise to seek professional help. Otherwise she could not live with him at Stonebridge.

The isolation that beckoned her now would destroy her. Even Ted and Ellery would have to leave if he couldn't control his jealousy. Was it the isolation of Stonebridge that drew him to it? Was that why he wanted to live there after they were married? So he could have her all to himself? With a chill of fear, she remembered him telling her about his father: "He wanted her all to himself, and finally even that wasn't enough. He didn't want her to have a thought in her head that didn't belong to him."

So he killed her.

If she let him, Jason would kill her.

But no, no. She was not Rosalind. Jason was not Alex.

He wept and begged her to forgive him. He swore it would not happen again. He seduced her with words, as he had in the beginning. She gave him one more chance.

Chapter Fourteen

Returning to Stonebridge was like coming home. Rynna had forgotten how impressive a house it was, and now it was hers. She marveled again at the clean lines of its architecture, the magnificent old stone, and the rich colors of the interior walls. She breathed in the familiar smells of polished wood and old fabrics. Stonebridge. Home.

She headed directly to the music room. It was as she remembered it, warm and inviting, filled with the subtle scent of roses. Rosalind welcomed her home. Rosalind's presence comforted and sustained her.

Jason came in behind her, and as if a light had been switched off, the warmth vanished. Rosalind was gone. She was never present when he was. This was the first time it been demonstrated so clearly, but now Rynna remembered missing something the night they met, when they played piano together.

She was disturbed by the implications, but she understood that it was only natural. Jason was a child when his mother died. She had no reason to identify this tall, handsome man with her small son. To her, he was more likely identified with his father. It was sad, but it was logical. She must not be unnerved by accidental associations.

Next she went upstairs to see Ted. He was just the same, sitting at his desk with his books and typewriter.

Her first instinct was to give him a big hug, but she was restrained by a confusion of feelings. Instead she leaned against the desk, gazing into those familiar blue-gray eyes, and said, "Hi, Cousin, did you miss me?"

His only reply was a faint smile, and then he said, "Are you all right?" He was appraising her with his eyes.

She thought, How does he know? What does he know? but she said lightly, "Of course I'm all right. Don't you like my tan?"

Again the same faint smile was all the answer he gave.

She tried again: "Did you get my postcards?"

"I lived for your postcards," he said with his so-familiar note of irony.

"Did you finish the book?"

"No," he said. No excuses, no explanation, just, "No."

"What have you been doing all this time?" she asked, exasperated.

"Minding my own business," he said.

"Damn it, Ted. I said it was all right for you to stay until the book was finished. But I expected to see some progress. Now you're dragging your feet, and you think you can make me feel guilty about trying to throw you out of the house."

"*Are* you trying to throw me out of the house?"

"It's my house."

"Technically. Tell me to leave. Tell me to get the hell out of *your* house—if that's what you want."

"Don't do this, Ted. I just got home. I'm glad to be home. I'm glad to see you. But I don't understand. What's going on? Tell me the truth."

"The truth? You won't like it. I know what you'll

say."

"Tell me."

"Jason."

She almost laughed. "You want to stay because of Jason? My God, you hate him. What's the matter? You won't have anybody to fight with?"

"I don't trust him, Rynna. I don't know what he wants, but I won't leave you alone here with him."

"Don't be absurd. He's my husband. You're afraid to leave. You're looking for excuses." She had slipped a little into Jason's point of view. Ted isn't living in the real world, he had said. Ted wouldn't have the nerve to kill Grandmother. He trades on his disability.

"I told you you wouldn't like it."

"Damn it, Ted, you cannot go through life blaming Jason for everything."

"Not everything," he agreed. "Credit where credit is due." She was desperately tired of this same old refrain, but at the last minute she caught the edge in his tone, the expression in his eyes. Something else was behind this, something more.

She looked away, trying to sort out her confused feelings. She needed to take hold of her life. She could not let things slip beyond her control. She would begin here. "I think it would be better if you left," she said, "but I'm not throwing you out. Take whatever time you need. Stay out of Jason's way. I don't want to listen to your bickering. All right?" She turned back toward him and gave him a level look.

"All right," he said, and then something in the way he gazed back at her stirred her memory. She flushed with embarrassment when she recalled what had passed so briefly, so intangibly, between them on her wedding day. Did he remember too? Was he remembering now? She'd had a brief conviction that he was in love with her. Was that possible? His hatred of Jason, his reluctance to leave Stonebridge?

"Ted," she said tentatively. "If I…" She didn't know what to say. She wanted to apologize, but she had done nothing to apologize for. He had done nothing either. He had been the soul of discretion and probably wasn't even aware he had given himself away. Was it fair to let him know she knew? What did she know? "I don't want to lose you as a friend," she said finally. "I know how you feel, but…"

She stopped, as if she had come up against a stone wall. He clearly didn't know what she was talking about. Didn't he know? He had made his opinion of consanguinity pretty clear. If he objected to her marrying Jason, who was only a second cousin, he could hardly admit to anything but familial affection for her. Or was she imagining things? He was staring at her, puzzled, and she no longer knew what had put this idea in her head.

"What is it?" he asked warily.

She shook her head. "Nothing," she said. "Forget it."

And then she remembered her own tears and Ted holding her hand, comforting her, saying, "Sometimes pain is the only way to know you're alive."

"I'm sorry," she said impulsively and left the room as quickly as she could.

****

During the first few months of their life at Stonebridge, Jason was the model husband. Things were so much better that Rynna could only puzzle over her own sense that something was missing. She missed him when he was in town during the day, and a little rush of excitement still gripped her when he came through the door in the evening. He told her in generous detail of the events of his day, keeping no secrets, holding nothing back. He showed a patient, intent interest in everything she was doing in the house, helped her with remodeling decisions, and offered his own impeccable taste. He was loving companion, careful provider, considerate lover, the perfect husband. Nothing was lacking, nothing was wrong.

She had made a terrible mistake.

He loved her. A woman couldn't ask for more love. He surrounded her with love. He smothered her with love. She could not escape.

She no longer loved him.

No matter how tenderly he treated her now, she couldn't forget the Bahamas. She thought he must have forgotten. He never alluded to it. Neither did she. That awful moment was distant now, forgiven, set aside. But she did not forget. He had made heartfelt pleas and promises, and she had given him another chance. It would never happen again. And yet she was terrified.

To make matters worse, they had been careless about birth control. By the time she knew the marriage was a mistake, she was already pregnant. She was afraid to tell Jason.

Ted stayed on—he still wasn't finished with the book—and Jason tolerated the situation. Ted heeded her advice and stayed out of his way, so few opportunities rose to aggravate the feelings between them. He stayed out of Rynna's way too, most of the time. She couldn't tell whether he was working toward his eventual departure or not. She had breakfast with him occasionally after Jason left for an early court appearance, but she refrained from asking him any pointed questions. They talked about books they had both read, and sometimes they argued the way they always had, but too much had changed. She wanted Ted to leave, and she wanted him to stay. She didn't know what he wanted. Sometimes she didn't care. They didn't talk about Jason. It was too difficult.

For the time being, peace reigned at Stonebridge. She knew it would not last.

It didn't.

One night, not long after she knew for sure she was pregnant, Rynna lay awake beside Jason in the master bedroom, the room that was once Grandmother's. They had redecorated it, erasing every trace of her strong personality. Only the handsome paneling and the antique four-poster Edmund Randolph had slept in remained. The walls were now a warm cream with chocolate trim. It was beautiful…and empty.

Jason lay on his side, facing her, breathing evenly, peacefully asleep. He always slept especially well after making love to her. The house was silent. Everyone was asleep. Only she was restless, wakeful, tormented, filled with bitter regret. Her marriage was over, and she had to carry on with it anyway. That was the worst part. It was like walking around after she was dead. If only she could lie down and decently die. She had always thought suicide was cowardly, and she was too strong-willed to just quit. But sometimes she wished she could die, so she wouldn't have to go on with this.

With great bitterness she revisited her vision of marriage with Jason before the wedding and in the early weeks of their honeymoon. It had all looked just like this, exactly the way she was living now, in every detail. But it had been viewed through a blissful haze that had left her. She had fallen out of love with her husband, but didn't that happen to most people sooner or later? The honeymoon ended sometime, but they could still be friends, lovers, companions. They could still be happy.

She was desperately unhappy. She couldn't fault Jason's recent behavior, but she no longer wanted to go through the motions. She was lonely. Stonebridge was so damned empty now. She was lonely even while he was making love to her. She bitterly considered the phrase. What they had shared in the beginning, under that blissful haze, was very special, something people usually called love. Love, a most elusive, much misused word. She had no idea what it meant, but it was nothing to do with Jason, not for her, not anymore. Jason had killed love.

She was clearheaded enough to see that he had not changed. Only she had changed. The bitter truth was that he was a lousy lover and always had been. Blind, stupid Rynna—devoted, worshipping Rynna, the perfect little bride—had found him masterful, skillful, passionate. He was impatient, arrogant, and selfish. She didn't think he was ever intentionally brutal, except that one time in the Bahamas, but neither did he have any conception of what real love was. And she, like the little idiot she was, had been pleased by his possessiveness. She had wanted to belong to him. What a fool she had been. What a price she was paying.

Had Rosalind experienced this? Rosalind too had married for love, had seen Alexander Wyatt through a rose-colored haze, and had chosen to give herself to him. She defied her family to move away with him, into exile, and to a lonely death. Did she suffer like this, even when Alex was a model husband? Did she lie awake and weep bitter tears when she was carrying Jason? Did Alex say all the right words, as Jason did? Did she at last recognize her marriage for the hollow shell it was? Or did she continue to love him desperately, never understanding what was happening? Did she understand that he was going to kill her, that sooner or later he had to kill her to finally make sure of her, to put her where his authority was beyond question, his possession absolute?

I won't go blindly, she thought. I will not let Jason kill me. But he was killing her already, a slow day-by-day death that could last twenty, thirty, forty years. If she didn't go insane first, he would kill her in the end.

Rosalind. Help me.

She glanced at the clock. It was 2:10. She caught her breath. Could Rosalind help her? Did she want to help her? If she could, if she had the power…

Rynna eased out of bed carefully, quietly, without disturbing Jason, and put on a robe. She slipped down the hall to the room that was hers before she married him. Pamela's room. She sat on the bed in the dark and waited, breathing deeply, calming herself. She would be still, open, receptive, and Rosalind would come. The minutes passed slowly, silently.

Bright, shimmering notes rose from the music room below. Rosalind played the opening phrase of *Für Elise*. When the last note died, Rynna detected the faint scent of roses in the silent room. She was warmed, comforted, soothed. Rosalind was so close she could have touched her, but her eyes were open in the semi-darkness, and there was nothing there. Nothing she could see. Rosalind was present, but she had no power. Jason held all the power.

The door opened so suddenly she jumped. "What are you doing in here?" Jason demanded.

Rynna stood up, her heart pounding. She tried to recapture the calm that had sustained her moments before, but she was unaccountably terrified. "I couldn't sleep," she said.

He switched on the light, and she flinched and put a hand up to shield her eyes from the glow. "What?" Had he not heard her, or did he want her to repeat it anyway? More likely he wanted a different answer.

"I couldn't sleep," she said again. 'I didn't want to wake you, so I came in here. I was just sitting here."

He glanced around. "Pamela's room."

"My room," she said. "I mean, it was my room when I first came."

"Your place is with me," he said.

"Yes, Jason," she agreed. Did he hear the note of mockery in her voice? Did she want him to?

"What are you doing in here?" he asked again.

"Nothing. Let's go back to our room. I'm sorry I disturbed you."

"I woke up, and you weren't beside me," he said. "I expected you to be there, Rynna."

"Let's go back to bed," she said. She was both resigned and strangely excited.

"I would like an answer first," he said. He was perfectly composed, very civilized. A man was entitled to a straight answer from his wife.

If she told him the truth, he would be angry anyway, so what was the point? "I couldn't sleep. I came in here because I'm used to it, and I didn't want to bother anybody."

"You're lying," he said.

She was lying. He would think so anyway, but in fact she was, and she couldn't stop the guilty flush in her cheeks. "Don't badger me, Jason. You don't want to hear this. You wouldn't believe it anyway."

"I am not badgering you," he said. Of course he wasn't. He was much too civilized. "Tell me the truth." He grabbed her arm, his fingers biting into her flesh. She resigned herself to the necessity of wearing long sleeves tomorrow to cover the bruises.

"Don't, Jason. You're hurting me."

"I'm not hurting you. You are such a goddamned little liar, Rynna."

"I'll tell you the truth," she said, "but you won't believe it."

"I'm in no mood for games."

"No games, then. I came in here because you can hear the piano in here. If someone is in the music room playing the piano, you can hear it in here. I don't know why, but it's true. You can ask Ted. He noticed it too."

He stared at her as if she had lost her mind.

Maybe she had. She stumbled ahead anyway. "During the night, this time of night, sometimes I hear the piano. Nobody is there, but I hear it. Oh, yes, you think I'm crazy. Of course you do. Ted does too and probably Cecile. But it's true. Ask Lucy why she won't dust in the music room. She believes in ghosts." She was babbling hysterically, but at least now she was telling the truth.

"No, I don't think you're crazy," he said. "I think you're a lying little—"

"It's Rosalind," she blurted before she thought.

"What?"

"The presence I feel, the ghost Lucy is afraid of, it's Rosalind."

"Rosalind," he said dangerously. He was still holding her arm too tight, and he pulled her closer.

"Your mother…your mother is in this house." He couldn't possibly believe it, but it was so wild it might have distracted him. "I know it's hard to believe," she went on. "It was for me too, at first, but it's the truth, Jason. Try to have an open mind."

"An open mind," he mocked. "I guess we both know what you would like me to be open-minded about, don't we? Naturally, I don't believe a word of this fairy tale, but it is appropriate, isn't it? You are two of a kind, you and my dear mother. Isn't that so, Rynna? Isn't that the real truth you can't manage to tell? You and Rosalind. Faithless women are all alike."

She was trembling in spite of all her grim resignation. "I am telling you the truth," she said desperately. "I have never been unfaithful, and you know I haven't. You know it's true when you're thinking straight. You are always sorry afterward, don't you remember? Can't you see it's a sickness? You need help."

"God, that's rich," he said, enjoying the joke. "You are the sick one, my darling little wife. Leaving my bed in the middle of the night and inventing tales about the house being haunted, for God's sake. You're not even a good liar. What are you good at, Rynna?"

"Jason…"

"Ghosts. A truly pathetic lie, my sweet, no style at all. Ghost stories to cover up your grubby little trysts."

The word was so old-fashioned he might have learned it from his father. "For God's sake, Jason," she burst out in a tone she hoped would reestablish reason, "who am I supposed to be having a tryst with in Pamela's room at two o'clock in the morning?"

"I told you I was in no mood for games."

"Be serious, Jason."

"Very well, let me try to guess. You've been awfully solicitous of Cousin Ted."

"That is really sick."

"Does he do you any good, or does that matter? You can't handle a real man, can you?"

"Stop it."

"You're not telling? I should ask him, then." He let go of her and strode toward the door.

Rynna came after him and grabbed his arm. She was fighting back for the first time, reckless and lightheaded. "Don't you dare," she said through her teeth, now as furious as he was.

He was stronger, of course. He evaded her easily and again roughly grabbed her arm. "Come on." he said with a grim smile. "Let's get Ted in on this, see what he has to say for himself."

She tried to wrench herself loose, but he half-dragged her out into the hall. "No," she cried, her voice coming out in a harsh whisper. She was terrified the noise would awaken Ted and he would be drawn into this one way or the other. "No!" She sobbed and kicked out at Jason, trying to loosen his grip. She managed to land a kick on his shin, and he cursed and let go of her arm.

His hands immediately went for her throat. He was still pulling her toward Ted's room, and they were near the top of the stairs, struggling, swaying together on the landing. In a blinding flash of memory, Rynna recognized the vision she'd had in the music room.

It was not Rosalind's memory. It was her own premonition. She struggled to pry Jason's fingers from her throat and succeeded enough to take a gasping breath and choke out a few desperate words. "You're just like your father," she said.

He let go of her abruptly, and she almost fell, and then he hit her so hard her vision blurred, and she did fall to her knees, groggy and sick but somehow relieved. Now the worst would happen. Now it would end. She didn't much care if he killed her.

He hit her again and again and again. She didn't care.

This time he offered no abject apology, no tears, no pleading. When he was finished with her, he left her lying in the hall and strode back to their room. The key clicked in the lock. He had locked her out.

She spent the night in Pamela's room, grateful for its dim silence. She thought Rosalind came to comfort her, but it was more likely she dreamed it. Did she dream that Rosalind was not entirely powerless, that she was gathering and conserving strength for some future confrontation?

Chapter Fifteen

In the morning Rynna waited until Jason left the house to return to their room to dress. She did the best she could with the bruises on her face and wore a long-sleeved, high-necked blouse to hide the marks on her neck and arms. Studying her throat in the mirror, she noted with clinical detachment that he could have killed her. They were strong, the Wyatt men. Alex had broken Rosalind's neck. The bruises weren't too noticeable, but she was a little worried about the swelling of her lower lip. She could ring for Cecile and put some ice on it, but then Cecile would know. Cecile would know anyway. She was keenly observant. Rynna hoped to God Ted wasn't.

She ate breakfast alone in the dining room, cereal and orange juice and warm cinnamon coffee cake. Marie had a strange expression when she poured the coffee, but of course she said nothing. Marie was a good girl, discreet and obedient. Nevertheless, servants would talk. Rynna couldn't do anything about it. They would gossip about her and Jason as they had about Rosalind and Alex. Some say he's just like his father, Cecile had told her. Just like his father.

Ted came in before she was finished, and her careful makeup and breezy breakfast table conversation were wasted on him. He helped himself to toast and tea, and then he took a good look at her. He seemed a bit hungover, and she was relieved—he must have taken one of his pills last night and slept through all the commotion. She was glad but didn't like to think he had been in pain. "Are you all right?" she asked

"Yes, fine," he said absently. "Are you?" He was staring at her, and she tried not to give herself away, but...

"He hit you?" His voice rose in an incredulous rage she had never heard before. In all his bitter campaign against their marriage, he had never shown this depth of anger.

They're all alike, after all, Rynna thought. Rage is always underneath.

"I'll kill him," he said, and he sounded as if he would. She believed he would.

"I want you to leave," she said. "This time I am telling you to get out."

"No, you aren't," he said.

"Please, Ted. This is between me and Jason."

"Between you and—my God."

"Seriously, Ted, I want you to leave."

"Not unless you do."

"I'm not leaving Stonebridge. Grandmother left it to me. She wanted me to live here."

"Grandmother didn't know Jason."

"I'm not leaving."

"Then throw the son of a bitch out."

"He's my husband. He needs help."

"Oh, God, yes, he needs help. He's not going to get it from you, is he?"

"Please calm down and listen to me. I will not leave Stonebridge, and I can't leave Jason, not yet. I want you to leave. It will be better that way, for all of us. You can't help me, and you will make things worse if you—"

"You are an idiot, Rynna. You really are." He picked up a piece of toast and then dropped it again. She almost expected him to throw it.

"I am asking you, as a friend, to do as I ask."

"As a friend," he repeated. "I have been a better friend to you than you know, for all the good it's done either of us."

"Now you're going to say, 'I told you so.' I know you warned me, but you didn't know this would happen, did you? In any case I have to live my own life. I have to make my own mistakes."

He shook his head. "Costly mistakes."

"Yes, all right, but my mistakes. Stay out of this, Ted."

"I will leave if you will, or if he does. I swear I will mind my own business, Rynna. I will stay the hell out of your life. I don't give a damn what kind of trouble you get yourself into next, but for God's sake, get rid of Jason before it's too late."

"He is my husband," she said. "Do you understand? I married him, for better or worse."

"And he promised to love and to cherish."

"He does."

"My God, Rynna."

"He does. In his own mind he is the best husband in the world. Most of the time he is. Even you would agree." She couldn't quite keep the bitterness out of her voice. "Regardless of whether I knew everything I was getting into, I married him of my own free will. Till death us do part."

"I'll kill him for you," he said, and although his voice was heavy with sarcasm, he was almost serious.

Rynna had been living with Jason too long. She couldn't resist such an opening. "Like you killed Grandmother?" she asked and was immediately as contrite as Jason usually was. "No, oh, no, Ted, I'm sorry. I know you didn't."

He rolled back from the table, his face pale.

"Don't leave. Eat your breakfast."

"I've lost my appetite," he said and left her alone.

Rynna sat for a long time with her head in her hands. Why did everything always go so wrong? Finally, she followed Ted upstairs. His door was open, and she strode in without knocking. "Ted," she said, taking her courage in both hands, "there's something else I have to tell you. Another reason I can't leave Jason. I haven't told him yet." She waited for some response, but he just sat where he was, his back to her, waiting. "I'm pregnant," she said at last.

"Christ," was all he said, and she thought she should leave now and not mention it to him again.

Instead she stood uncertainly in the doorway. "Ted?" She stepped further into the room. "Are you crying?"

"No, of course not," he said, but she couldn't see his face. After a moment, he said, "You never do things by halves, do you, Rynna? One disaster after another."

"I don't think having a baby is a disaster."

"His baby," he said with bitter distaste.

"It's my baby," she said. She couldn't blame him for his reaction. She did not want Jason's child, not Jason's.

"Get rid of it," he said, and then, before she could protest, "No, of course you wouldn't. I know you wouldn't." He put his hands to his face. "Jesus," he said, sounding much the way she had felt after Jason hit her.

Finally, he faced her. "You haven't told him?" he asked.

"Not yet. I'd better tell him tonight. It wouldn't do for him to hear it first from somebody else."

"I wouldn't tell him,"

"I know, but I should have told him first."

"You're afraid of him, aren't you?"

"No."

"Yes, you are. You should be."

"I'm no more afraid of Jason than I am of you, of the anger I see in you, the way you go at each other. It will only get worse. I think it would be better if you left."

"I'm not going to leave," he said. "If I did, there would be nobody on your side."

"That's not true. Cecile is here, and Lucy."

"What do you think they can do?" he scoffed.

"What do you think *you* can do?" And quickly, hoping to deflect his angry response, she added, "Rosalind is on my side."

"What?" He stared at her. "God, not that again."

"I know she's here, and she knows Jason better than we do. She tried to warn me."

Ted shook his head. He didn't know what to make of her stubborn delusion about Rosalind. "She's dead," he said. "Her husband killed her. I don't want the same thing to happen to you."

Rynna gazed out the window, across the lawn toward the trees. How could she convince him she was safe when she didn't *feel* safe? Yet she was certain the danger would be greater if he stayed at Stonebridge. Danger to him, danger to her.

"It's funny," she said, thinking aloud. "Jason told me about his father's jealousy. He said Alex tried to kill him once. He said he wanted her all to himself. He didn't want her to have a thought in her head that didn't belong to him. He knows Alex was insane, but he doesn't recognize the same thing in himself."

"Jesus," said Ted feelingly and then, trying for a matter-of-fact tone, "They say abused children become child abusers. Knowing it's wrong isn't the same thing as being able to control it."

She was appalled. Child abusers? "You don't think he would hurt the baby?"

"Rynna," he said. "Get a divorce."

She could only shake her head numbly. If she could convince Jason to get professional help, their marriage might survive, and her baby would have a devoted father. If not, she would never be safe from him. A divorce would not free her. It was only a piece of paper.

****

Against all her advice, Ted joined them for dinner.

"To what do we owe this unaccustomed pleasure?" Jason asked. "May we expect a pronouncement?"

"Not from me," Ted said sullenly.

"Oh, please," Rynna said, putting her hands to her head. Would they both behave like this all evening? She couldn't bear it.

"Nothing to announce?" Jason insisted. "Nothing to celebrate? You haven't finished the legendary masterpiece? You're not thinking of leaving us? Not tired of living in my house?"

"It's not your house," Ted snapped. "It's Rynna's house. If it was your house, I wouldn't live here for five minutes."

"That's good to know."

They all sat in silence while Marie spooned steaming broccoli soup into bowls, laid warm rolls on the bread plates, and retreated without a word.

"Jason," Rynna soothed, reaching across the table to touch his hand. She could feel Ted's eyes on them. These were not the circumstances she would have wished for, but she was afraid to wait any longer. She couldn't trust Ted to keep his temper. "I do have something to announce," she said. "I wanted to tell you later, when we were alone." She risked a glance at Ted. "But there's no reason Ted shouldn't know too." She smiled at Jason, playing her familiar role as loving wife. "Darling, we're going to have a baby."

His face lit with pleasure, and Rynna grew lightheaded with relief. She sat smiling while he rose and came to her chair to embrace her and kiss her intimately, oblivious to their hostile audience. "That's wonderful," he said. "It's wonderful, Rynna. I can't believe it." He kissed her and then leaned back to see her face. "Are you all right? Do you feel all right?"

"I feel fine," she said, laughing, filled with relief. "I'm glad you're happy about it. I wasn't sure…"

"Of course I'm happy. I've never been so happy. We did it, didn't we? This calls for a celebration." He glanced at Ted and for once showed no anger, no derision. "Let's celebrate," he said. "Let's have champagne. Ring for Marie, will you?"

"Rynna shouldn't drink," Ted said.

"What?" Jason was still smiling, but he was annoyed by the unexpected opposition.

"If you're pregnant, you shouldn't drink champagne," Ted said.

"Nonsense," Jason said. "A little champagne never hurt anybody. Don't be a killjoy, Cousin Ted." He rose and rang the bell himself, and when Marie came in he said expansively, "Bring us a bottle of champagne. We're celebrating."

They drank champagne and toasted "the next heir to Stonebridge" while the soup got cold, and Jason was elated and charming, his most endearing self. She was certain he didn't remember anything about the night before. She was puzzled by the ease with which he could forget ugly scenes that scarred her memory.

She could understand men who beat their wives only when they had been drinking and didn't remember after they sobered up. But Jason almost never drank, and if he did have a glass of wine with dinner it made him more relaxed, more easygoing. Where did the anger, paranoia, and jealousy come from, if not out of a bottle? And where did it go? How did it vanish so quickly after it drove him to violence? If she mentioned it now, would he know what she was talking about? If he did, what would he remember? The way he spoke to Ted made it clear he didn't recall his accusation in Pamela's room, or had never taken it seriously.

Marie served the main course of duck à l'orange, and Rynna relaxed a little and tried to enjoy the party atmosphere of the meal, but she was not surprised when the civility between Ted and Jason was finally stretched to the breaking point. Jason refilled her champagne glass, and Ted said, "I don't think Rynna should drink so much."

"Mind your own business."

"He's probably right," she said lightly. "Too much alcohol isn't good for the baby. Anyway, I'm not used to it."

"Drink it. Mr. Demeray is not in charge here."

"She said she didn't want it." Ted's voice held a

dangerous edge.

"That's not what she said, and I told you to mind your own business."

"Gladly. But it you mistreat Rynna, you'll answer to me."

"Oh, yes," Jason sneered. "What will you do?"

"Jason, don't." She put her hand on his arm and struggled to keep her voice steady, reasonable. She didn't want to provoke him, not tonight. "It's not important," she said, as if urging him to ignore a slight to her. "Don't let him spoil the celebration." She leaned toward him confidingly, presenting a united front.

Jason kissed her and acceded to her wishes, but he couldn't resist a parting shot as Ted backed away from the table. "Rynna is my business," he said. "Don't ever forget that."

Ted didn't reply, but she understood the look he gave her. He was not likely to forget anything.

Chapter Sixteen

In bed that night, Rynna lay in Jason's arms, and he talked dreamily of their future. The moment was one of the best of their marriage, but already she realized this child did not mean the same thing to him as it did to her. He was not interested in her plans for the baby. He was indifferent to the idea of converting Pamela's room into a nursery, and he didn't want to discuss names. The child was not real to him. Her pregnancy was a fact, and it was important to him as an achievement. He had proved his manhood. He, Jason Alexander Wyatt, would be a father. The child was incidental.

Rynna was wise enough to play it his way. She busied herself with her own plans, poring over decorating magazines and articles on childcare, but she didn't discuss them with him. As long as he was happy, proud, pleased with himself, her life was more pleasant.

Ted was at least interested enough to listen to her sometimes. He couldn't forget the baby was Jason's, and on the whole he wished it hadn't happened, but there it was. When asked, he would give his opinion on wallpaper for the nursery or the choice of names. He thought Rosalind was a bad idea, Pamela a little better, and no, he absolutely would not assent to Theodore, even if Jason would have.

"Kids ought to have their own names anyway," he said one morning as they lingered at the table after breakfast.. "He'll be burdened enough with this family's history as it is." He let her expound on the relative merits of anesthesia and natural childbirth—Jason had fallen asleep in the middle of the discussion the night before— and then confessed, "The whole thing scares me silly, Rynna."

"Why?"

"It just does. I don't know where people find the courage to go through all this."

"It doesn't take courage, Ted. Being careless is enough. After that you don't have any choice."

"Yes, you do," he insisted. "I admit the alternative takes courage too, but that's not the point."

"You're not scaring me, Ted."

"Of course not. You're as brave as they come."

"I don't know about that, but I'm not afraid to have a baby. Childbirth isn't that risky, not anymore."

"It almost killed my mother," he said.

"That's your problem, then. You listened to her story too often. Dr Moran says I'm in perfect health, and I feel great. You have nothing to worry about, believe me. I'll loan you my copy of *Childbirth Without Fear*."

"And after the baby is born, what then? Aren't you afraid of that, of the responsibility?"

"I know what you mean, but no, not really. I'm looking forward to it too much."

He shook his head. "That's what amazes me. You're walking right into the line of fire with your eyes wide open."

"And don't have the sense to be scared? Your poor mother traumatized you at an early age."

"Maybe she did. I wouldn't wish my childhood on any parent."

"But they loved you." Without ever knowing them, on the strength of Ted's testimony and a few snapshots in the family albums, she considered William and Clara the standard of parental love she and Jason should strive for.

"Yes, they did, and they went through hell. I'll never forget what Clara suffered when she thought I might go blind."

"Blind?" Rynna echoed. He was almost infecting her with his belief in the nameless terrors ahead of her. If something was wrong with the baby? The baby's eyes?

"Blindness is sometimes a complication of arthritis in children," he explained. "I'm just nearsighted like everybody else, but Clara suffered with the possibility for weeks."

Clara slipped a bit in Rynna's estimation. "She shouldn't have let you see that," she said. "No wonder you feel the way you do."

"I'm glad Pamela didn't hand *you* any complexes," he said.

"I never gave her any trouble."

"But I notice she didn't repeat her mistake."

"I don't think my parents wanted more than one child. They spoiled me rotten, though."

"That's obvious," he said dryly, and Rynna rose, dropped a light kiss on his forehead, and headed upstairs to consider the nursery walls.

A few days later, Jason brought home an old college friend who was in town for a few days. Kenneth Grant was enough like Jason to be his brother—they had been fraternity brothers. He possessed the same outrageous charm, flattering and funny. He and Jason talked about people she didn't know, but always in a way that included her and invited her to laugh with them. They enjoyed a pleasant evening, lingering over dinner and then adjourning to the music room. Rynna played requests, and Kenneth Grant marveled at her talent, and Jason stood next to her, proud and pleased.

She played *Für Elise*, feeling daring, glancing at Jason to see if he recognized it. He didn't, not as far as she could tell. While she was playing it, Grant studied the portrait over the mantelpiece. "It looks like you," he said. "Sort of. Is it supposed to be you?"

"No," she said, laughing. "It's Jason's mother."

"At a very young age, obviously. Sure looks like you. But you're related, aren't you?"

"We're second cousins," she explained. "His mother and mine were first cousins. We have the same great-grandparents."

"Sounds confusing. She sure looks like you, anyway."

"I don't think so," Jason said. His manner stiffened, but Grant didn't appear to notice.

"You know what they say—a girl just like the girl that married dear old Dad."

Either this man was more stupid and insensitive than he appeared, or he didn't know his old friend as well as he claimed. She would have liked to know more about Jason's past, about what he was like when Grant knew him, but she wasn't going to learn anything from him.

When he left, he said, "Don't get up, Rynna," and she stayed where she was, playing softly, while Jason saw him out.

As soon as Jason came back into the room, even before he opened his mouth to accuse her, she knew she was in trouble. "I should at least be able to bring a friend or a client home for dinner once in a while," he said, "without you throwing yourself at him like that."

"You're insane."

"I am insane," he agreed, "to keep loving you when you are such a lying slut."

Rynna refused to answer his accusations. They were not to be taken seriously. "I'm not going through this anymore. If you don't get help, professional counseling, and learn to control your jealousy, I'll divorce you."

"Like hell you will." He grabbed her wrist and yanked her up from the piano bench to face him. "Try it and see how far you get. I know every lawyer and every judge in this county, and who do you think they'll listen to? Whose side do you think they'll take? You just try it. Get Kenny Grant to represent you, if he's infatuated enough to take me on. I'll get Stonebridge for a start, and I'll get custody of my child. I'll win a custody suit before the child is even born. It ought to be an interesting case, don't you think?"

"I don't believe anything you're saying," she said, keeping her voice level. "I don't think you do either. I don't want a divorce, and I certainly don't want Kenneth Grant. I think he's a bore."

"You played up to him all evening."

"No, I did not. I made an effort to be agreeable to your guest, and that's all. You're the only man I want."

He pulled her against him, and one hand gripped the back of her neck in a way that really frightened her. He could have broken her neck so easily. He kissed her, and she relaxed in his hold, faking a willing response. "God, you are a tramp," he said. "I'm warning you, Rynna, if you try to divorce me…"

"I don't want a divorce. I just want you to—"

"Shut up," he said. "You remember what I said. I warned you. If I can't have you, you can be damned sure nobody else will."

"Jason, please. You know I love you." He kissed her again, still holding her head in his rigid grasp, and with his other hand he unbuttoned her dress. "Not here," she said faintly. "The servants."

"To hell with the servants," he snarled. "This is our house."

She couldn't bear to have him take her here, in Rosalind's music room. "Let's go upstairs," she urged.

He gathered her in his arms and carried her up the stairs. Like Scarlett O'Hara, Rynna thought, on the edge of hysteria. He didn't hit her, and this time was not so bad. She couldn't call it love, but it wasn't rape either.

Afterward, Jason slept as peacefully as he always did. Even though her wrist still throbbed from his earlier violence, a thrill of amazed pride overtook her. *I can control him.* She could, sometimes at least, deflect his anger. It was like the feeling she'd had, early in their honeymoon, of having the power to arouse and please him. If she could do this much, maybe she could convince him he needed help. She thought it was a turning point.

It wasn't. One morning he accused her of having an affair with Dr. Moran. The idea was so ridiculous she laughed, but icy fear was already growing in the pit of her stomach. She couldn't laugh him out of this. She couldn't reason him out of it. They were in the bedroom, and she had just finished dressing. It might be safest to go downstairs before this could escalate.

"Don't try to deny it," he said, his eyes dark with a familiar anger and hatred. Where did it spring from?

"I'm sick of your lying, your sneaking around and trying to lie your way out of it."

"That's fantastic. Can't you see that it's crazy, a fantasy? It's all in your mind. It's not possible."

"Stop lying, goddamn it. It's not enough that you are a conniving little tramp who betrays me again and again."

"Jason, please."

"Shut up. I told you to shut up. Shut your lying mouth, or I'll shut it for you." He lunged, his fist raised to smash into her face, and she raised her hands to protect herself. If he scarred her face, if he left bruises…

Thwarted, he tugged at her hands and then, outraged, rammed his fist into her chest and, as her arms came down instinctively, into her abdomen. Rynna screamed, dropped to her knees, and bent forward to shield the baby, and at the same time she covered her mouth to stifle her own cries. Nobody must hear. Nobody must know.

"Oh, God, Rynna!" He was beside her, kneeling on the floor, drawing her into his arms, cradling her. "I'm sorry. I'm so sorry. I didn't mean it. I didn't mean to do that, I swear. I didn't mean to hurt you. Please, Rynna, please, speak to me, darling, please forgive me. I didn't mean to. It's only because I love you so much. I swear to you it will never happen again."

The words were all so familiar.

She lay in the darkened bedroom, keeping her breathing shallow to avoid arousing the pain that was finally ebbing, fading. Jason, chastened and pliant, had followed her instructions, yielded to her wishes, and left her in peace. She had forbidden him to call Dr. Moran, and his anxiety to do so made it clear he had already forgotten how this had begun.

The baby was all right. She thought the baby was all right.

Her mind went over and over the same thoughts again and again. She couldn't stop the cycle of memory, speculation, and imagination.

He didn't know what he was doing. He never did when he was like that, but more specifically in this case, he didn't remember she was pregnant when he hit her in the abdomen.

Jason's own words: *He tried to kill me once. He wanted her all to himself.*

Over and over, she relived it, how his fist came at her with such force, such rage. Her muscles tensed with the memory of pain and terror, and she would have to breathe carefully again.

She wanted to sleep, but her eyes remained open in the cool dark. Cecile had brought her an aspirin and laid a cool cloth on her forehead because Jason had said she had a headache. Nothing disturbed her. Everyone stayed away and kept quiet. Where were they? What were they doing? What were they saying? Did Cecile know? Were the servants talking about her, about Jason? Where was he? Was he still upset, weeping, consumed with guilt? Or had he gone to town, to work with his briefs, his dry legal ideas? Was he indifferent to her pain, or had he forgotten her already?

What's to become of us? How long can this go on?

Where was Ted? Had he heard her scream? Did someone tell him she was ill, lying down with a headache? Or did someone tell him the truth? Not Jason. If Cecile knew, would she tell Ted? Would she have to tell him? Would he guess? She reflected bitterly on his warnings, He was always warning her, and always about the wrong things. He'd told her not to marry Jason, but he didn't know Jason was capable of this. He'd told her having a baby was risky, frightening, but he didn't know Jason might...

No. Jason didn't know what he was doing.

Around and around, over and over, again and again.

She thought about killing him, and that was a surprise. She had never entertained the idea. She didn't think, Maybe I'll kill him. She didn't wonder, Could I kill him? She simply considered the ways she might do it, if she were going to—and of course she was not. These thoughts were merely a mental exercise, an idle game. She could never do it even if she wanted to. She would never get away with it. She might someday be desperate enough, frightened enough, but not yet. More importantly, she wasn't angry enough. She was only trapped and hopeless.

Her head was filled with nightmare images, and some of them were terrifyingly real and vivid. They were as clear as the vision in the music room, and she prayed they were not premonitions too. She didn't know which ones frightened her the most. She must not think about them. She must not believe they could materialize.

Sgt. Chandler, thin, edgy, unsmiling, rising from an awkward, half-crouched position beside her husband's inert body. "He's dead." *Who killed him?* Rynna followed Sgt. Chandler's gaze, but she couldn't see the murderer.

If I were going to kill Jason, I would...

"I'll kill him," Ted had said. "I'll kill him for you."
Who killed Grandmother? What did Jenny know?

Ted's wheelchair, empty, lying on its side, one

wheel spinning crazily.

"Rynna is my business," Jason said. "Don't ever forget that."

Wire-rim eyeglasses like Ted's, stark against a polished floor, one lens shattered, bright spatters of blood across the floor, across the glass.

She would try to surface, to wake up screaming, but she was not asleep, not dreaming.

The baby was all right.

Jason didn't know what he was doing.

Over and over, until her head really did ache.

That evening, when they were both calmer, when Jason was still contrite and careful of her feelings, they talked about their future. "I want to stay with you," she said, not sure herself how much of a lie it was, "but I'm afraid to. If you don't get professional help, I don't know what I'll do."

"I will," he promised. "I'll see somebody. I'll ask Dr Moran to recommend somebody."

The last thing he would do was ask Dr. Moran. He would have to do better than that. "Please, Jason," she said. "This is important. If you want to save our marriage, if you want me to continue as your wife—"

"I'll do whatever you want," he said with fervent sincerity. Oh, yes, he could be very sincere. "I promise. I don't want to lose you, Rynna. You are the most important thing in the world to me."

Maybe she was. Maybe he meant what he said. But as the memory of the incident faded, his intentions would dim. Other factors would come into play—his career, his reputation. He couldn't afford a scandal, a whisper of doubt. Rynna did not lose hope, but she knew the chances of his carrying through on this were slim. She considered making an appointment for him herself, but if she did, would he keep it? If he went, without the will to accomplish anything, would it be a waste of time?

So long as peace reigned between them, she let it slide. She had his promise. If necessary, she could remind him of that. In the meantime, she didn't need to rock the boat. He had sworn it would never happen again.

Chapter Seventeen

One bright August morning, Rynna came into the library and found Ted busy with Grandmother's books. They were his now. According to the provisions of the will, the house and all its contents belonged to Rynna, with the exception of the furniture in Ted's room, which he had bought with his own money, and all the books, which were his to dispose of. He had mentioned the possibility of giving some of them to the public library, since Grandmother's taste in literature had run to the type of novel neither he nor Rynna cared for. He had put off the task of sorting through them for months now, but here he was, putting dusty volumes in cardboard boxes. She hoped it meant he was ready to leave Stonebridge. She would miss him, but she had not forgotten those nightmare images.

"Good morning," he said cheerfully enough, glancing at her and back to the book in his hand. "Some of this stuff is downright awful."

"I remember," she said, thinking of the hours she had spent reading to Grandmother. "Is it all right if I sit in here? I wouldn't get in the way."

"Sure," he said.

Rynna sat in Grandmother's favorite armchair and pulled out the baby afghan she was crocheting. She wasn't very good at it, but it was a suitable thing to learn. Jason didn't like her to do it in the evening—he preferred to have her complete attention. She worked intently and then glanced up. Ted was watching her speculatively.

"What?"

"Nothing. You look so comfortable sitting there, hopelessly domestic."

"That's how it's supposed to look. Don't you want one of the servants to help you?"

"No, I don't." He had started with the lower shelves, which was awkward enough, but it was the top shelves she was concerned about.

"Can I help?"

He glanced up, amused. She would have had to stand on the ladder and hand the books to him, and of course he wouldn't let her do that. He was worse than Jason about treating her like a helpless pregnant woman.

"I'll manage," he assured her. "You just sit there and work on that—whatever it is."

So she did. She sat and crocheted and mulled over names again in comfortable silence. Occasionally Ted would read her a particularly dreadful title. When he was quiet for a long time, she would look up and find him browsing through one of the books. Most of those ended up in the boxes destined for his own collection. He didn't have space left in his room for any more books. He *would* have to move out.

Robert Edmund Wyatt, after the grandfathers? William?

"What was your father's middle name?" she asked.

"Charles." William Charles Wyatt. Charles Jason Wyatt. She somehow assumed the baby was a boy and hadn't spent a great deal of time on girls' names. Ted was right. The child should have his own name. To call it William or Pamela might be unfair, but who remembered Robert or Edmund? *Bobby Wyatt.*

The baby stirred. "Ted, come here," she said, holding her hand out. He didn't appear to understand, and she said impatiently, "Come on."

"What's wrong?"

"Nothing. Just come here." The wheelchair was a nuisance. They couldn't get close enough except with it set sideways to her chair. She took his hand in both of hers and held it against her abdomen. "Can you feel that?"

He shook his head.

"Wait…there. Did you feel it? It's a miracle, a real one, a scientific miracle. You should appreciate that." She spoke lightly, feeling an uncomplicated kind of affection for him that was somehow involved with her feelings for the baby. He had told her abused children became child abusers. Wouldn't beloved children grow up to be loving parents? Wouldn't Ted make a good father? Then she saw his face, the expression in his eyes. "Ted? What is it?" He shook his head, unable to speak. She was still holding his hand. He didn't pull away, but he tensed. "You really are afraid, aren't you?"

"No," he said. "It's just…you don't understand."

No, she didn't. Or maybe she did. Everyone he had ever loved—Pamela, William and Clara, Sylvia, Edwina. "They all left you, didn't they?" she said, considering what he must be thinking. "Poor Ted."

He jerked away, abruptly, angrily. "Don't say that."

"No, I didn't mean…I'm sorry. I just meant…"

He rolled away, back to the bookshelves, and picked up a slim volume, trying to shut her out, withdrawing to the safety of books.

"I do understand. It's no wonder you don't want to

give any more hostages to fortune."

After a moment, he relented enough to answer her. "Don't make too many assumptions," he warned her. "Anyway, nobody gets to choose, do they?"

"No." She considered this. You couldn't choose, but you could try. Some people just kept trying. "Is that why you told Grandmother you wouldn't marry and have children?"

He shook his head, and the old familiar irony crept into his voice. "You never give up, do you, Rynna? You're never satisfied until you think you know everything."

"That isn't true."

"True enough. Anyway, I'm afraid I made that decision for more practical reasons. I wouldn't do this"—he touched the wheels with an emphatic gesture—"to any child."

"But arthritis isn't hereditary, is it?"

"There is a genetic factor, a predisposition. My children would be susceptible, at least."

"You could adopt children."

"It's not easy, and it's harder if you're in a wheelchair." He wasn't complaining. He was being practical, and his tone was matter-of-fact, as if he were giving a lecture on the subject. He was putting distance, as real as the physical distance between the armchair and the bookshelves, between himself and her, between himself and her baby. Jason's baby. "Anyway," he continued, "it's always a risk."

"That's what you keep telling me."

He didn't hear the teasing note in her voice. He was too intent on one of his favorite subjects.

These were just excuses. Nobody would choose not

to have children for such reasons. If Ted's arthritis was heredity, it must be a recessive gene. Or had William and Clara not lived long enough to be obviously affected?

"Hereditary diseases aren't the worst," he said. "At least you know what the risk is. It's the unexpected, the things nobody knows enough about to predict or prevent."

Rynna only half listened. She was counting stitches, and she had heard it all before.

He wasn't attending to what he was saying himself. His mind was on Grandmother's books.

"Miscarriages and stillbirths for no apparent reason," he went on, an all-too-familiar litany. "Mysterious things they still can't explain. Birth defects, crib death—"

"Ted…"

"—like what happened to William and Clara's child."

"What?"

"I must be crazy to say all this to you now, in your condition. It doesn't scare you though, does it?"

"Ted, what did you mean—William and Clara's child?"

"William, Jr.," he said, still sorting through the books.

"What are you talking about?"

"Didn't Pamela tell you about that?" he asked.

"If she did, I don't remember."

"Well, all right, it's not a very long story. The baby just died. Nobody knows why. Now they call it crib death, which just means they don't know what caused it."

"Poor Clara."

"She had a difficult pregnancy anyway, and she damn near died in childbirth. But it had nothing to do with that. The baby was perfectly healthy. One morning he just didn't wake up."

"How awful," Rynna said. He was right. It didn't scare her. Nothing like that would happen to her. She had lost a stitch and frowned as she worked to fix it.

"They didn't think she could have another child, and he wouldn't let her go through it again anyway, but they wanted a child. Clara wanted a baby desperately. William wanted a son. That's why they adopted me."

"What?" She looked up, disoriented.

"We were the same age. They picked up where they left off."

"They adopted you," Rynna repeated. She couldn't understand what he meant. "Adopted you?"

"Didn't your mother tell you this?"

"No, Ted. Nobody ever told me you were adopted. Nobody. I thought…"

He was completely unconcerned. He leaned down and put two more books in one of the cardboard boxes.

Rynna took a deep breath. "Do you know who your real parents were?"

He was a little annoyed, as if she was missing the point. "William and Clara were my real parents," he said.

"I know, but…" She was waiting to feel something, waiting to understand. Slowly, slowly, it came into focus. She was seething, and it wasn't about a lost stitch.

"What's the matter with you?" he asked. "Rynna?"

"Why didn't you tell me?" she asked.

"I assumed you knew. It wasn't a secret."

"You should have told me. It should have occurred to you I might not know. You should have told me, just in case."

"Why? It doesn't matter, Rynna. It never mattered to me. I never thought it made any difference to Grandmother."

No? "When she said she was leaving the house to me, you said, 'That's not the reason.' Is that what you meant?"

She didn't even hear his answer. In the car on the way to Grandmother's funeral, hadn't he said…?

At least my name is Demeray. That may be a technicality…

It was only a technicality that she and Jason weren't named Demeray. Wasn't that what he meant? That his own name might be a mere formality, a lie, never occurred to her.

As for the Demeray bloodline…

"God damn you," she said, an inexplicable anger taking hold of her. "God damn you, Ted."

"What's wrong? Why are you angry?" He stared at her, amazed by this unexpected reaction.

"You should have told me."

"Why does it matter to you? Nothing's changed. Adoption is perfectly legal, Rynna. We're still cousins."

Cousins. Cousinage—dangereux voisinage.

"I'll never forgive you for this," she said.

"For what?" He couldn't understand why she was upset, and she didn't really know herself. Her marriage to Jason was a lie, and being pregnant didn't help. She had reason enough to be edgy, but why was she upset that Ted was adopted? No, not that he was, but that she hadn't known he was, that he hadn't told her? "Rynna?" He abandoned the books and approached her, hesitating, not understanding. "What is it?" He was completely bewildered.

Why was she so furious, so suddenly tearful? Why did she want to hit out at him, to get back at him? What had he done?

Then she had the answer. Her head came up. She blinked back tears and met Ted's eyes. "I married the wrong cousin," she said.

He smiled faintly and waited, trying to understand what she'd said, willing to see the joke. Was it a joke? "What—what do you mean?"

What did she mean? "I don't know. I don't mean anything." She evaded the stunned, questioning expression on his face, gathered her needlework, rose swiftly, and strode out of the library before he could say anything to stop her.

He called after her. "Rynna..."

She kept walking, as if she hadn't heard, but his voice echoed in her head.

Rynna...

****

Rynna walked along the river, just rambled for a long time, and tried not to think at all. The weather was fine, and it was good for her to stretch her legs. Dr. Moran had said it was the best exercise. The baby wasn't heavy enough yet to slow her down. She could walk quickly, strongly, without tiring. She thought about how easy it was, how pleasant, how much she took such things for granted. What she did was not important. The important thing was she could do it if she wanted to. She could do whatever she wanted, whenever she felt like it, without even thinking about it. Nobody ever fully appreciated things like this until they were gone.

But he didn't mind. He said he didn't.

What—what do you mean?

Of course he did.

Rynna...

She didn't cry. She was through crying. She lifted her face to the sun, savored the warmth on her face. She was still alive. She could still feel the sun. Nothing had happened to her. Nothing had ended.

What do you mean?

What did she mean? What had she said? *I married the wrong cousin.* What did that mean? Nothing, it didn't mean anything. The whole idea was nonsense.

What was Ted thinking? What had she done?

I married the wrong cousin.

But she didn't love Ted either. Yes, of course she did. She loved him as a friend, as a cousin, nothing more. But he loved her, or he might have if he wasn't afraid to. No, he couldn't love her. She belonged to Jason, and she had taken Stonebridge from him. They were friends. Under the circumstances, he had been very decent to her. But he didn't love her. He didn't want to give any more hostages to fortune. And she couldn't suddenly fall in love with him just because it no longer qualified as incest. Could she be so desperate for love? Of course not. If she were in any way capable of loving him, she would have fallen in love with him a long time ago, in spite of their being cousins. She could not love him. Nobody could love him. He was too difficult, too stubborn, too well-armed with defenses and evasions. He was impossible.

What was in that face that she could love?

She remembered little things she had absorbed unconsciously. His intent blue-gray eyes behind those wire rims, his rare smile, his expressive voice, the way he moved his head, his lank blond hair. The way he had kissed her on her wedding day.

No, she had no reason to love him.

He would take her away, though, if she asked him to. He had said he would, more than once. He would help her escape, and he wouldn't expect anything in return. He never did. He would never try to hold her, hold onto her, the way Jason did. But it wouldn't be fair to him. She couldn't expect anything from him. She had behaved irresponsibly, selfishly. She had never stopped to think.

Why hadn't he told her?

It doesn't matter. We're still cousins.

Nobody had told Jason either. Jason didn't know. If he did, he would have used it a long time ago.

She would not think about Ted. She would not think about anything. She would just wander along the river in the sunshine, for the exercise. The day was so pretty. She would continue until she was tired, until she was calm.

Nothing's changed.

They had not been raised together as cousins. He was a stranger. He had always been a stranger. Being cousins, second cousins, hadn't stood between her and Jason. She and Ted were no less cousins now. He was right—it didn't matter. She had nothing to blame him for.

What had she said to him? *God damn you, Ted. I'll never forgive you for this.* And: *I married the wrong cousin.* After that, what could she say? He might be angry, hurt, confused. She would have to talk to him again, to apologize. But not yet. She couldn't face him yet.

When she finally returned to the house, she was tired enough to sleep for an hour before she had lunch delivered to her room. She couldn't eat, though, not even the hot, creamy potato soup. She wasn't hungry. She had to keep her strength up. She had to take care of the baby, but she couldn't eat anything.

Ted didn't come to see her. She could not go to him.

He must have finished with the books, because a man arrived to pick up the boxes for the public library. She didn't go downstairs to check, but Cecile told her he had come and gone. He had taken the boxes away, and Lucy had been upset about the cigarette ashes he had dropped carelessly on the library rug.

Dinner was routine, ordinary, a simple meal of spinach soufflé and a green salad. The familiarity was a kind of boredom, so it was a strain to get through it. Jason was annoyed by her inattention. "Who are you thinking about?" he asked.

She awoke with a jolt. Was she in danger? Had she forgotten how to feel danger? "Don't start. I'm just tired."

"Who was here today?" he asked dangerously, insistently.

"Nobody was here."

"You're lying. I could smell cigarette smoke in the library."

"Oh," she said, relieved. Was that all? "The man who came to get the books. Cecile said he was smoking."

"How old is he?"

"I don't know. Ask Cecile. I didn't see him. Stop this, Jason. You promised you wouldn't…"

"You promised to forsake all others."

"Leave me alone. I have a headache." She wasn't hungry anyway. This battlefield was easy to abandon. She rose coolly, without hurrying, and climbed the stairs.

She didn't know how he would react. She didn't care. The entire day had been too much strain, too much confusion. She only wanted to sleep.

Jason came into the room and closed the door behind him.

"No," she said, before he could begin. "Don't." She was awake now, alert, conscious of danger. He came immediately to where she stood, and she backed up instinctively but didn't raise her hands to protect her face. She expected him to hit her at once. She preferred it that way, a sudden blow, before she had time to dread it.

Instead he shoved her against the wall and his hands circled her neck, his thumbs digging into her throat. "You are such a liar, Rynna, such a lying little slut."

"Jason," she whispered. "Please."

"I'm not going to hurt you," he said smoothly. "But you know you have it coming, don't you? Don't you?" His tone was silky, his eyes dark, dangerous. She was terrified.

"Yes, Jason," she whispered.

His hands slid from her throat to her shoulders, but she was still trapped against the wall. She knew what would happen. She knew what came next. He wouldn't hit her. This time sex would be enough, and she would rather he hit her. The ordeal would be over sooner. No, it was more than that.

She would rather he killed her. Why didn't he kill her and get it over with?

"I'm not going to hurt you, "he promised again.

Ted thinks I'm brave, she thought. But she must not think of Ted. She must not think of anything.

Jason did hurt her, but it was not intentional. She

didn't care anyway. It was only pain. *Sometimes pain is the only way to know you're alive.* She wept in bitter hopelessness after he was asleep, but no, the tears were not for mere physical pain.

I would rather he killed me.

Chapter Eighteen

In the morning, after Jason left, Rynna stood for a long time under a hot shower, as if she could obliterate him from her mind by erasing every trace of him from her body. How much soap and water would it take to rid her of the feeling of his hands around her neck?

Her mind skipped from one thing to another. She couldn't control her thoughts. Too much effort was required, too much will.

Who knew Ted was adopted, now that Grandmother was gone? The servants? Dr. Moran would need to know for his medical history. Baxter? Would Dr. Moran or Mr. Baxter know who his biological parents were? Adoption records were sealed, but it could have been a private arrangement.

Was Jason bluffing when he said he would get Stonebridge if she divorced him? Did she own Stonebridge free and clear, or did he, as her husband, have rights to it?

Ted was afraid of life. No, he wasn't. He had the steady courage of a survivor.

If Jason had just killed her, she wouldn't have to think about anything.

Ted had lived at Stonebridge like a recluse as long as Grandmother needed him, but he had his own life, his own work. Before he started spending so much time on the book, he must have lived a different kind of life. He had friends at the university. He had once been engaged to be married. He had studied in France. Why had he stayed after Grandmother died? To finish the book? For her? If she knew what had happened with Sylvia...

Jason knew, but even if she could ask him, she couldn't trust the answer. He was such a liar. Even his handsome face was a lie, a trap. What a fool she had been to fall in love with him. What did it mean—love? Just a word? No. Love had nothing to do with words. She and Jason had exchanged all the right words. He was a wonderful man if you wanted somebody to romance you, sweet-talk you, to stand up with you in church, to carry you over a threshold. What was that worth, after all?

I married the wrong cousin. Ridiculous, as if she had arrived here planning to marry one of them, to marry anyone. If she had, it would be true. Jason was better-looking, but Ted had more money. She had Stonebridge, and if she had married him, if such a thing had even been possible, her children, as he had pointed out, would be called Demeray. Except he didn't want to have children. He hadn't been serious about her hypothetical children. He wasn't serious about much of anything, except Jason.

After a while, feeling calmer, stronger, she dressed and brushed her long hair. "You should let your hair grow," Ted had said that first day, rudely, in his cool, offhand way. Cecile would gladly brush it if she rang for her, but she wanted to be alone. When she did ring, it was to have a breakfast tray brought to her room—tea and toast, which was all she could stomach. The servants would think nothing of this. Her pregnancy was a handy excuse for so many things. In fact she was avoiding Ted. Was he avoiding her?

Finally, too bored and restless to stay in her room

any longer, she headed downstairs. The weather had warmed up, and the thought of hiking down to the river in such bright, relentless sunlight made her head ache. She retreated instead to the music room, her favorite place.

She stood for a moment studying Rosalind's portrait. Perhaps a resemblance did exist, at least when she wore her hair up. Or was it something else people saw when they looked at her and were reminded of Rosalind? In some strange way, she and Rosalind were related by more than blood.

She sat at the piano but didn't touch the keys. She wanted to play for her own comfort, but caution constrained her. She must not disturb Ted. He had assured her, long ago, that her playing wouldn't disturb him. But she had been a stranger then, a guest, restless and resentful, hunting for something to do. She had not said to him, "I'll never forgive you for this."

The night she met Jason, Ted had gone to her bedroom to listen to her play, to check out the acoustics—a sensible, scientific test of her theory. He had told her he could barely hear the piano in his own room. If she played now, would he hear her? She hadn't heard the typewriter yet this morning. If he was not working, not concentrating, would he recognize what she was playing? If she played *Vilia* for him, would he appreciate it as a peace offering?

She couldn't decide what to do. Rosalind, she thought, help me. Give me strength. Was that blasphemy? Rosalind was in the room, though. She could feel her presence, smell the faint scent of roses. Rosalind could always comfort her. Comforting, encouraging.

"Really?" Rynna whispered. She closed her eyes,

trying to draw her closer, as close as she had sometimes been in the darkness of Pamela's room. "Ted?"

Light footsteps approached in the hall, and she leafed through the sheet music as if she were searching for something to play. Lucy came to the door with a trivial question about the household accounts. She was polite, a little apologetic, sorry to have disturbed Mrs. Wyatt, hoped she was feeling all right.

"I'm fine, Lucy." Where had she acquired that tone of polite dismissal? From Grandmother? She wasn't sure she wanted to be good at this job—mistress of Stonebridge.

She couldn't put it off any longer. She must talk to Ted. She must behave like a mature, civilized adult and apologize. With a sense of weary inevitability, she climbed the stairs and knocked on his closed door.

There was no reply. He probably knew it was her, recognized her knock. But the silence frightened her a little. She had not seen him in twenty-four hours. He might be ill.

"Ted?" she called. Still no answer, but somehow she knew he was there. He heard her. He was deliberately ignoring her. She tried the doorknob. It wasn't locked. Cardboard boxes lay around the room, as others had the day before in the library. He was marking the top of a box with a black felt pen and didn't even glance up. "What are you doing?" she asked, coming into the room as if she had a right to do so. Her house, his room.

"Getting ready to leave," he said tonelessly. "That's what you want, isn't it?" He glanced up to see her reaction, but without much interest.

She ignored the question. "I have to talk to you."

Ted picked up a book, glanced at the title, and let it

fall into a half-filled carton. The careless, emphatic thump it made was like a slap. "You talk too much," he said.

"I know," she said. "I'm going to do it again." She reached for the door.

"Don't close it," he said and when she did anyway, he shook his head and picked up another book.

She stepped toward him, and he looked up, annoyed and resentful. He was not bad-looking. His face was aristocratic, if not a Demeray heritage. Not an easy, approachable face like Jason's. He would be hard to reach, harder to love. Instead of what she was thinking, she said, "It's funny. I never would have guessed you were adopted. I always thought you looked like your father. Your hair is the same color."

Exasperated, he put down another book and faced her squarely. "Look, Rynna, don't... What do you want?"

"I don't want anything from you. I just want you to know that what I said yesterday... I was confused. I didn't mean anything. I...things have been pretty bad with Jason lately, and..."

"Did he...?" He flared up again—his fury was so close to the surface—and she cut him off with a dismissive gesture.

"It doesn't matter anymore what he does," she said wearily. "I know what Rosalind went through. In the end, she may have been better off dead."

"Don't talk like that," he snapped. "If he..."

"I don't want to discuss Jason. I just wanted you to understand that I wasn't thinking straight. I'm sorry about what I said." He was silent, and she couldn't tell what he was thinking. She wasn't sure whether she could continue this conversation, but something in her life must be made clear, finally. Everything was confused. Couldn't she make one thing simple? "It wasn't just that—Jason, I mean—or what you told me. I've never been sure of your feelings for me, especially since my wedding day. Do you remember?"

He remembered. He watched her, waiting to see where she was headed, his fair skin slightly flushed.

"You don't trust me, do you?" she asked. "No, of course you don't. Oh, Ted, I'm sorry."

He looked away. "Stop crying," he said, although she wasn't, not really. He sounded annoyed.

Tears bathed her face, but she didn't feel anything. She didn't know where they came from. She brushed impatiently at them, trying to appease him. She had gone too far after all. She had lost Jason, the Jason she had fallen in love with, and now she would lose Ted as well.

"What is it?" he said in a softer tone. "Come here."

She started to sit in the awful cane chair but thought better of it. She sat on his bed, which wasn't much more comfortable but brought her closer to him. "I've done everything wrong," she confessed.

He shook his head.

"I should never have married him."

"I'm not going to say—"

"You told me so. I know. I don't know what to do. I've ruined my life. I feel as if I've ruined yours too."

"No, of course you haven't," he said. He was surprised, a little shocked, but something else was in his voice, something she couldn't put a name to.

"Yes" she said. "I don't deserve your friendship."

"Rynna," he said with uncharacteristic gentleness. "We'll always be friends." He gathered both her hands in his, a warm gesture of friendship, and she was greatly comforted. This was the right thing to do after all, to apologize, to admit her confusion, to clear the air. Now they were close again, sitting together, talking quietly. He was silent, holding her hands, gazing at her gravely.

"What are you thinking?" she asked.

He didn't answer at once. He was considering whether or not to tell her. He wouldn't just blurt it out the way she did. He had to think it through first. Finally he said wistfully, "I would really like to kiss you."

Her first reaction was a swift stab of panic. *No, please.* She had made one mistake already. She could not go through this again. Then she calmed herself and considered that one kiss was not a lifelong commitment. He was scared too. Of course he was. He hadn't missed her hesitation, and he would not have pressed her. She tried to joke the way he did. "Why don't you try it," she suggested, "and see what happens?"

He ignored her flippancy. It was enough that she was willing. He leaned toward her, still holding her hands, and kissed her shyly, tentatively—a boy's kiss. She had been kissed with greater boldness by a fourteen-year-old boy with braces on his teeth. She was both touched and disappointed. Whatever had happened on her wedding day was a fluke or her imagination. She thought, almost gratefully, that this would come to nothing after all.

Ted let go of her hands, removed his glasses, and laid them on the edge of the desk.

"Why, Miss Jones," she said, still trying to joke. If it's a joke, it can't hurt.

"Shut up," he said, not in the dangerous, bullying tone Jason would have used, not unkindly, but grimly, as if to make her understand this was no joke. He could see her perfectly well at this distance without his glasses, but he looked blind and defenseless without them.

He kissed her again, more expertly, rather sweetly. She was on the edge of a precipice. This was going to be serious. But she did love him—as a friend at least. She had to protect herself with words. His silence was too dangerous. "Not bad for a man who's out of practice," she said.

"Shut up," he said again. The wheelchair made it awkward, and he moved to the bed to sit beside her.

Rynna glanced involuntarily at the closed door. He had told her not to close it. It wasn't locked, but the servants would not intrude.

"Don't be afraid," he said.

"I'm not."

He caught her hands again and placed a kiss in each palm. She closed her eyes, feeling giddy, and he kissed her eyelids, her cheekbones, and returned to her lips to kiss her like a lover, sweetly, tenderly, with carefully controlled passion. Jason's demanding, sometimes bruising kisses had been exciting at first, but now they were only a prelude to rape. No, she must not think of Jason now, not now. Ted was holding her face between his hands, and something terribly serious was happening, something dangerous. Why was it dangerous?

When they stopped, breathless and shaky, Rynna leaned her forehead against his, her long hair swinging forward. She had the strangest sensation of falling into him. She had lost her balance, but she was safe. He put his arms around her, and she couldn't fall.

"I shouldn't say this," she began when she had caught her breath a little.

"Then don't," he said. He stroked her hair, brushed it back from her face, and pulled away from her so he could see her expression and make sure she was all right.

She was not all right. She was in terrible danger. But this dangerous stranger was only Cousin Ted, her best friend in all the world now. It was all right. She could say anything now, even the truth. He kissed her again. "You're a better kisser than Jason," she said.

He was surprised, pleased, annoyed, not sure she was serious. Then he realized she was serious and didn't know how to take it.

She didn't even care if he was going to be angry. Anger, passion, it was all the same. With Ted, she had nothing to fear. They were in grave danger, but she was safe with him. She could say whatever she liked. She didn't have to worry about how he would react.

He took it like Ted, with a quip. "But he's a better dancer." he said. "He also happens to be your lawfully wedded husband. I think we'd better cool it."

She breathed deeply, steadying herself. He was right, of course. "Now it's all true," she said. "Everything Jason accused me of."

"Damn Jason," he said.

"Damn Jason," she agreed. "I wish I had never let him touch me. I wish…"

"Don't," he advised. "It isn't worth it. It doesn't matter."

Didn't it? "But I'm married to a man you despise," she said. "I'm having his child. I'm fat and ugly."

He laughed, sounding boyishly amused.

"But don't you mind?" she asked, trying to see his face. "Don't you mind about the baby?"

"No, Rynna, I don't mind." He was still amused. She

couldn't understand why it was funny, but it was better than anger.

"Ted, really?" she insisted.

He groaned and hid his face in her hair. "You are a pain in the neck," he said. "You always were."

She couldn't imagine why those words should make her smile, but they did. "Kiss me again," she said.

He kissed her again. "Thou shalt not covet thy cousin's wife," he said.

"Did you?" she asked. "All this time?"

He shook his head. "Demeray's Rule: Don't think about what you can't have."

She was amazed by this, by his self-restraint and his constancy. She was still confused about her feelings, but he wasn't. She couldn't remember how she had come to this point in her life, but here she was. This blond stranger sitting so close to her, holding her, kissing her—this was really difficult Cousin Ted, who had made her life such hell with his stubborn opposition to her marriage. She had always cared for him in one way or another, hadn't she?

"I love you," she said.

"Yeah, sure, that's what they all say." She didn't understand. Didn't he think she was serious? Or was it still too dangerous, too scary to be serious about? He glanced at the half-empty bookshelves and reached for his glasses, still holding her with one arm around her shoulders. "Now I *should* leave," he said.

"No, I don't want you to."

"It's what you wanted all along."

"But now..."

"You are the greediest woman I've ever known," he complained. "You had to have Jason, in spite of all my warnings, and now you want me too."

"I don't want him," she said.

He sobered. "Come with me, then. You don't have to stay with me. I don't expect that. All I want is for you to be safe."

Rynna sighed and rose, putting distance between them. Time to be practical now. "I'll tell Jason you're packing," she said, "but don't leave yet. Give it a few days. I need time to think."

"Rynna, I'm sorry if I—"

"Don't be sorry," she said quickly, fiercely. "I do love you, Ted."

He nodded without conviction. Why didn't he believe her? He hadn't said he loved her either. Did he? "What do you know about love?" he asked bluntly.

Rynna was devastated. What did she know about love? Not much.

Later, after she had time to think it over in peaceful solitude, she did understand that he was wiser about this than she was. They were moving too fast on a course that could be disastrous for both of them. She had made the mistake of using Jason to try to escape from Stonebridge. She must not make the same mistake again. She couldn't use Ted to escape from Jason. He offered her sanctuary without strings to keep her from committing herself to another mistake.

She had allowed Jason to sweep her off her feet because it was easier than making it on her own. Could he, then, be blamed for considering her his possession? Ted didn't want to possess her. He didn't want to shelter her from life. *Sometimes pain is the only way to know you're alive.*

She had been hurt. He had been hurt. They could

make it together only by each being strong enough to make it alone.

She didn't want to go through it all again, especially not with someone as difficult as Ted. She was still married to Jason, still a bride, and she had promised to keep only unto to him as long as they both lived. The idea was unbearable now, but she had meant it when she made the vow. Wouldn't her feeling for Ted be equally changeable, equally risky? She certainly didn't want to marry him. If she could get free of Jason, she never wanted to be married again. Ted wouldn't want to marry her anyway. He hadn't even said he loved her. She was only a temptation he was finally unable to resist.

If you think marriage is such a bed of roses, I'll marry you. And she had said, "Don't be ridiculous." She had thought he was joking. He *was* joking. But she had dismissed the idea so decisively based on the assumption that they were first cousins, too closely related by blood to consider marriage even a possibility. But he knew otherwise and assumed she did too. He must have thought she had other reasons. She did: She was in love with Jason. She was not in love with Ted. But she needn't have been so scornful. He might have thought she had another reason. He might have thought...

I'm a goddamned cripple. So what? Yes, he was right. It didn't matter. Ted was Ted, after all. He was not an invalid. He would never be dependent on her. He was pretty damned determined not to be dependent on anybody. If she were willing to marry him, the wheelchair would make no difference.

She let herself briefly consider what it would be like to be married to him. He was not Jason. Jason—his physical beauty, his charm, his successful career—was a sham. He had no substance. There was steel in Ted, what her mother would have called "character."

As for sex—well, she couldn't ask him. There might be difficulties, but surely... *Does he do you any good?* That was so like Jason.

She wasn't going to marry Ted anyway. She was daydreaming. She couldn't give herself to him, to any man.

She avoided him the rest of the day, restraining the impulse to just go and find out if she had imagined this. A world of difference stood between what she felt now and the real dread she had experienced the day before, knowing she must finally face him. *What do you know about love?*

When Jason came home, she was attentive, the dutiful wife. She found it easier today. She had more energy somehow. She had played this part so many times. It was not so difficult, was it? The difficult part was to restrain the instinct to flinch from every casual touch.

He didn't try to make love to her. If he had, she could have put him off for a few days. She could have a headache. She could feel ill because of the baby. But she would have to give in eventually, if she didn't want him to suspect, to find out. She would have to make a decision soon.

That night, in a confusion of dreams and wakeful anxiety, she received a clear image of Jason against a dark backdrop, raising his hand. He held something, a dark shape. Danger. A gun? A knife? But Jason didn't own such a weapon. Did he?

Chapter Nineteen

In the morning, rested in spite of her disturbed sleep, and hungrier than she had been in several days, Rynna headed downstairs to the dining room for breakfast. Ted was at the table, as on so many other mornings, with a book beside his plate, eating a poached egg and fruit. He needed a haircut, she observed critically. He was dressed casually in slacks and an open-necked shirt with the sleeves rolled up, a shirt she had given him for his birthday, light blue and expensive. She had the impression he didn't like it much, but he wore it sometimes. He was indifferent to such things and never cared what she wore either.

"Good morning," he said gravely.

She smiled. She couldn't help it. He sat before her, like a hundred times before, and just seeing him made her smile. She stepped over to him, brushed his hair away from his face with an intimate gesture she would never have dared before—he would never have sat still for it before—and kissed him warmly.

He caught her hand and looked up, cool and questioning.

She thought, This is some silly, schoolgirl crush. It was idiotic to become infatuated with this man now after living under the same roof with him for more than a year. *Never mind.* She kissed him again.

"Hey," he said.

"I don't care. I love you."

"Six months ago you were in love with Jason."

"I don't care," she said, smiling.

"Six months from now…"

"I don't care. I love you."

"Are you sure?" He was still looking up at her, which put him at a disadvantage, so she sat down and pulled her chair closer.

"Yes," she said.

He considered her for a few more seconds, watching her face, and then caught his breath. "Thank God," he said, and Rynna leaned over to kiss him again. He smiled then, his rare genuine smile. "What would you like for breakfast?"

"Anything. I'm starving." She was, but she was hungrier to talk to him. She had so much to say to him, as if she hadn't seen him in weeks.

Ted rang the bell, and Marie came in, her face respectfully blank. If she noticed they were sitting closer than usual, she gave no sign. "Yes, suh?"

"Mrs. Wyatt is starving," he said. He was careful not to glance at Rynna. "Eggs, oatmeal, biscuits. She's eating for two."

Marie smiled at Rynna, said, "Yes, suh," with perfect politeness, and left.

"She doesn't give anything away," Ted said.

"What do you mean?"

"I mean you can't tell what's on her mind. Be careful."

"With Marie? I trust her. I think she would be on our side anyway."

"She's afraid of Jason," he said.

"So am I. But Marie won't say anything."

218

"Not if she doesn't know anything," he agreed. "Be careful, that's all."

"What are you going to do, Ted? Are you really going to leave?" He rubbed his eyes tiredly, and she thought, He didn't sleep any better than I did.

"I'm looking at apartments on Friday," he said. "Fred Sullivan arranged it."

"Can I go with you?"

"That would look pretty, wouldn't it?"

"We're cousins," she reminded him. "It's the least I can do."

"We'll see," he said. Pamela used to say that. It usually meant no. He handed her a cup of tea and asked, "Did you know Ellery is leaving?"

"No, he didn't say anything to me."

"He wouldn't. He's been considering it for a while anyway, and he and Jason had a few words."

"About me, I suppose."

"You aren't surprised."

"No surprise, Ted. He accused every man I ever looked at or didn't look at. Even on our honeymoon."

"Jesus. I always knew he was a bastard."

"He suspected you too, before he had any reason to, but I guess he decided cousins don't count."

"This one does," he said dangerously.

Marie came in with Rynna's breakfast. Neither of them could think of anything noncommittal to say, and the awkward silence was somehow incriminating. When she was gone again, Rynna said, "I'm sorry about Ellery. He's been with you a long time."

"With Grandmother," he corrected.

"What will you do?" She buttered a warm, flaky biscuit.

"Sell the Bentley," he said. "Unless you want it."

"No, thanks." What would she do with such a car?

"Buy something more practical," he continued. "Smaller."

"Can you drive?" she asked, surprised.

"Of course I can," he said, as if she should have known. "Can't you?"

"Yes, of course."

"Good, I wouldn't want to try to teach you. You don't take direction very well."

"Cheeky," she said.

They lingered over breakfast, talking, and then Rynna asked him to come to the music room. It was important to her, but she couldn't have made him understand why. He looked at Rosalind's portrait as they came in, and she faced him, standing beside it.

"Yes," he said, answering the question she hadn't asked. "More than ever."

"You said once that Jason wasn't marrying me—he was marrying Rosalind.

"For which you slapped my face," he reminded her.

"I know. I'm sorry." She bent swiftly and kissed the corner of his mouth, right where she had hit him.

"Well, you always had guts," he said.

"That's one way of putting it. You said I looked like her."

"I'm way ahead of you," he said. "I didn't even know her. She was just a name, a family story, and the portrait in the music room. I never saw her in the flesh, but I don't think she was half as beautiful as you are."

"Flatterer," she said, but she was pleased. She sat at the piano and ran her fingers over the keys. She played *Für Elise,* and the first few notes sent a shiver through her. She performed well, better than she thought she was capable of. Rosalind was close, her spirit strong. She closed her eyes and let her take over. Yes, it was all right. She was calmed and comforted. Rosalind approved. Rynna had held back, afraid to complicate her life, but there was no need. She had instead simplified it.

When she stopped playing, Ted met her eyes, unsmiling. He appeared uneasy. Did he sense something too? "That was terrific," he said, a shade too late to be convincing.

"Ted," she said. "If I ask you a question, a serious question, will you tell me the truth?"

"Maybe," he said cautiously.

Rynna leaned forward confidingly and asked in a half-serious stage whisper, "Are you gaslighting me?"

"No," he said, laughing. "I wouldn't dare."

While he was off guard, laughing, she asked, "Will you tell me about Sylvia?"

"No." He would brook no nonsense.

"Never?" she asked seriously.

He changed the subject. "Play something else," he said. "Anything."

She played "Chopsticks" to make him laugh.

"God, I hated to practice," he said.

"Grandmother told me. She said you were like your father."

"That's true. He didn't have the patience either."

"Ted, didn't you mind being adopted? It seems so strange. You always cared more about the family history than Jason or I did. Don't you wonder about the people who gave you up?"

He shrugged. "I never thought it was important."

"You are so sensible sometimes. I can't think why I

love you."

"Nor can I," he said.

She swung around on the piano bench and held out her hands. "Kiss me anyway," she said.

Serious, unsmiling, he set the wheelchair at an angle to the bench so he could lean across the armrest and kiss her properly. Rynna again had the sense of falling toward him, into him, so his blood would run in her veins, bright bubbles like champagne in her blood. A most extraordinary feeling, like nothing she had ever known with Jason, even in the beginning. She clung to him desperately, afraid to let go.

"Jesus," Ted said, when he could breathe again. "We damn well better stop this."

"No, Ted. No. I love you."

"But we can't do this. We can't. If we have to wait, we'd better start now. It won't get any easier."

"I don't care." She didn't care about anything else either. She only wanted him to hold her. For another long, desperate moment they kissed with a terrible urgency, as if the entire universe centered here, as if nothing else mattered, as if they were not in grave danger.

"Damn." Ted held her a little longer, his face in her hair, and then said again, "Damn. No more, Rynna. It's too hard. It's too risky."

"You're afraid," she said. It was not an accusation.

"Damn right I am." He sat still, catching his breath, and then touched her face, brushing the back of his hand lightly against her cheek, a gentle, intimate gesture. "I could make such love to you," he said.

Rynna closed her eyes, still feeling his hand after he withdrew it. *I could make such love to you.* Not a boast, but a wistful promise.

After being married to Jason, she wouldn't care if he couldn't. But that wasn't entirely true either. She would have much preferred a celibate life to continuing to live with Jason, that much was true. But he had awakened in her a desire he couldn't satisfy, and her love for Ted was becoming intensely physical. She could tell from the way he kissed her that it was the same for him, but he had been schooled in patience and self-control for so long. He had himself on a leash, but now she could hope he would be able to give her what Jason only knew how to take.

She was sitting still with her eyes closed, and Ted couldn't resist kissing her one more time. He held her face between his hands and touched his lips to her closed eyelids. Her emotion was almost painful, and she clutched his shoulders, leaning on his strength. His lips held hers for a long, heedless moment and then...

"Jesus," he whispered and rolled the wheelchair back so abruptly she almost fell, almost didn't recover in time.

Lucy was standing in the doorway. Surprised, flushed with guilt and happiness, Rynna didn't know if Lucy had seen anything, if Ted had heard her coming and moved away in time, or if she even needed more evidence than was plain on their faces.

She gave no sign. "I'm sorry to disturb you," she said smoothly, "but there's a telephone call for you. It's Mr. Wyatt."

"Thank you, Lucy," she said, trying to sound calmer than she was. They hadn't even heard the phone. They would have to be much more careful. She risked a glance at Ted as she rose from the piano bench, and he was watching her, both irony and a kind of warning in his eyes. They would have to remember that Mr. Wyatt still had every right to expect her to answer when he called. They had no rights at all, legally or morally. Rynna was a married woman, and Ted was not her lover, not her blood cousin, maybe not even her friend.

Jason was too excited to notice if she was a little distracted. He was calling to tell her he was bringing two guests home for dinner. They were in town to do business, down from Washington, something Rynna didn't understand—mining rights, corporate law. "There's a lot of money in this," Jason said. "We need to make a good impression."

"But, Jason, it's such short notice. Mrs. Lester has the night off."

"This is important," he insisted. "Tell her she can have the next two nights off instead. Ask her to make a chocolate pie, would you?"

"Yes, all right. I'll ask her."

"And listen, one of these guys is a geologist, and he knows Ted. I mean he's heard of him. Some scientific mumbo jumbo in the journals. Ask him to join us for dinner. It might help."

"Yes, darling."

"Thanks, Rynna. I love you. I'll see you tonight."

"Yes," she said, but he had already hung up. She stood in the hall holding the receiver and feeling numb. She didn't know if she could bear the strain of this. After what had happened the last time, with Kenneth Grant, how could she help Jason entertain two strangers? She would be afraid to be too friendly, too interested in them, but if they could help Jason's career, how would she dare to be cool to them? And Ted—she had not been in the same room with both Ted and Jason since the night she told Jason she was pregnant. So much had happened since then. So much had happened in the past few days, the last twenty-four hours. Was it possible to play the loving wife, the gracious hostess, with Ted sitting a few feet away?

"What is it?" He had come up behind her. "Bad news?"

She shook her head and replaced the receiver. "No, just people for dinner. He wants you there too. One of them knows you or something." She gazed at his familiar face, her friend, her lover, Cousin Ted. "Are you famous?" she asked.

"Not even a little. Jason's the one who wants to be famous. He has all the ambition in the family."

Rynna put her hand to her head. "Let's not talk about him," she said. "I don't know if I can do this anymore."

He was immediately serious, concerned. "What can I do? Would it help if I…?"

She shook her head. "No, it's all right. I can handle it. I'd better talk to Mrs. Lester. I'll see you later." She glanced around quickly. Lucy was not lurking in the hall. "Is it safe?" she asked.

"It's never safe," he said, and she knew it was true. She left without kissing him and headed to the kitchen to consult with Mrs. Lester. She had plans for the evening, of course, but Rynna soothed and flattered and promised—she was becoming an expert at this sort of thing—and left her planning the chocolate pecan pie, always Jason's favorite.

She consulted with Cecile about what to wear. What would impress her husband's colleagues without provoking his jealousy? A new distance had opened between her and the young maid. They had been such good friends once. Did Cecile know or suspect something? Or had her own restraint driven a wedge between them? Once she could have told her what she was feeling, but no more. Cecile still admired Jason, and Rynna could not have admitted she no longer loved him.

Later she went to Ted's room. He was working at his desk, but the door was open. She rapped lightly for form's sake, and he didn't even glance up. "I would advise you to stay out of here," he said.

"I was never very good at taking advice, though." She came into the room but didn't close the door. "I'm here on business, I promise."

He lifted his head. "Whose business?"

She ignored the question. "About dinner," she began.

"I'll behave myself," he promised. "I'll be civil to Jason and his friends."

"And wear a tie."

"A *tie*?"

"Yes, a tie. You can wear the one you wore to my wedding if it's the only one you have, which would not surprise me. It will look all right with that shirt. The cuff links, too."

He raised an eyebrow. "You're going to start running my life now, is that it?"

"I wouldn't dream of it. It's important to make a good impression. It's important to Jason. At this point, what is important to him is the law of the land."

"I know. I'll be careful. You be careful too."

"I will. Don't worry."

He shook his head. "I don't think you know how to protect yourself."

"What, from Jason? I've had a lot of practice."

"From Jason," he agreed soberly, "and from me."

She was surprised and touched. He still didn't believe she loved him. She wouldn't set him straight now, in his bedroom with the door open. Discretion must begin somewhere. "Don't worry," she said again and left the room.

Chapter Twenty

Ted and Rynna ate lunch together, and in a way it was a dress rehearsal for dinner. They knew they had aroused Lucy's curiosity, and they both behaved as if they knew someone was listening at the door. Mrs. Lester had outdone herself with savory bean soup and tuna noodle casserole, and it was easy to devote their attention to the food. The conversation remained low-key and neutral, nothing Jason could have objected to, nothing inappropriate to cousins.

Rynna tried not to stare at Ted and restrained herself from so much as touching his hand. They were friends, after all. They had been friends for a long time. She shouldn't find it so hard to resume that simpler relationship.

He still had not said he loved her, and she tried not to mind. Jason said it all the time, and what was it worth? Words that were used, overused, abused—what value did they have? The same was true of endearments, which she and Ted never used with one another. She still accorded Jason, as her husband, the perfunctory *darling* and what did it mean? Nothing. Ted didn't like to be called anything else. Grandmother was the only one who had called him Theodore, and Grandmother was dead. She had told Rynna once that he had resisted being called Teddy even as a baby. He clung to that absurd monosyllable as he did to his favorite technicalities—his financial independence, his ability to walk, the Demeray family name.

Words of love had not become natural to them, and that would be an advantage when she talked to him in front of Jason tonight. She would make no accidental slips. Jason wouldn't be able to tell that "Ted" was now an endearment to her.

But she would not be able to help looking at him. Jason would find it suspicious if she avoided his eyes altogether. What would be the greatest risk?

Damn Jason's career anyway.

****

The evening was fairly successful in spite of Rynna's concern.

The geologist, Henry Norris, was a homely and graceless young man, inclined to abrupt interruptions and boring monologues, but she discovered she actually liked him. She had no illusions about the reason. He was not the least bit charming and paid no attention whatever to her, but she was dazzled by the attention he paid Ted. He hadn't expected the wheelchair, but he didn't let it faze him. He stuck out his hand and said, "Dr. Demeray?" with real enthusiasm.

"Ted," he said at once. Rynna was startled. She didn't think he had a Ph.D., but she wasn't sure. He wouldn't have bothered to tell her.

The other man, Osborn—she never did get his first name—was a corporate lawyer with a polished manner that should have put her at ease. Somehow it didn't, but at least she could answer intelligently when he paid her compliments and explained what he wanted Jason to do.

She couldn't understand what Ted and Henry Norris were talking about over dinner, and Jason would have found it suspicious if she tried. She could barely risk the temptation to just look at Ted for no good reason. She didn't want Jason to notice her paying more attention to either of the guests, and still less did she want him to see anything between her and Ted. It was a challenge to listen to what Osborn said to her, to smile and answer skillfully, to be a credit to her husband, and at the same time try to ignore Ted's voice patiently fielding Norris's questions.

The meal was calculated to impress—French onion soup, and squash and pomegranate salad, followed by stuffed pork chops, twice-baked potatoes, and ending with chocolate pecan pie. Pretending concern that their guests had enough to eat or the coffee was hot enough, Rynna could glance casually at Ted, who was not impressed by Norris's enthusiasm. He was not famous, he said, not even a little. Who was this strange man who knew his name from something he had read? And what did this have to do with Jason?

She found it easy to feign exhaustion when the evening was over.

"I think it went well," she said to Jason when they were alone. She sat at the dressing table and watched him in the mirror as he undressed.

"Yes," he said. He appeared to be satisfied. He was a little preoccupied, but it was business on his mind this time. She scanned his face for danger signals, but she thought she was safe.

When he was ready for bed, he came up behind her, brushed her hair back from her face, and studied her in the mirror. "Will this mean moving to Washington?" she asked, holding very still. A coiled spring inside her was wound so tight that if he touched her, she would break into pieces.

"No," he said, not at all distracted. "It might mean spending some time there, but the real work will be in Brenford." He bent to kiss the angle of her jaw and rubbed his cheek against hers.

"Jason," she said faintly.

"You're all tensed up," he said. "What's wrong?" He frowned, watching her face in the mirror. His eyes were so dark, so dangerous. She thought wildly, If you hit me again, if you ever hit me… What? What would she do? Go to the police? No. Tell Ted? God, no. She was trapped. Nobody could help her except herself.

"I'm really tired," she said. She kept her voice steady and casual with some effort, but she didn't need to fake exhaustion.

Jason studied her a little longer, a shade suspicious, but in the end he kissed her on the cheek, said, "I'll take a rain check," and climbed into bed.

Rynna lay awake beside him for a long time, oppressed by his unwelcome presence. She avoided thinking of Ted. It was too painful. Her feelings about the evening were so confused, even without that. Was this development in Jason's career a good thing? The strain was too much. She could not bear it. But sleep eluded her. She wished she could get up and go into Pamela's room or downstairs to the music room, but it wasn't safe. Jason might wake up. She had to stay here.

She found no comfort in the room she shared with him, the room Grandmother had died in. Rosalind would not come to her while she was with him. She was alone.

She did sleep, finally, but she was still tired and strained in the morning. Jason, before he was even fully awake, drew her into his arms, and she instinctively shoved him away and sat up.

"What the hell." He scowled and grabbed for her arm, but she eluded him and ran into the bathroom and was thoroughly sick.

She didn't usually have morning sickness, but surely she was entitled. She splashed cold water on her face and glanced at herself in the mirror. She looked pale and exhausted, but not really ill.

"Are you all right?" Jason was standing in the doorway, watching her. "Shall I call Dr. Moran?"

"No." She steadied herself. "I'm all right, darling. I feel better now."

He came in, moving slowly, watching her in the mirror.

She wasn't afraid, but she didn't want him to touch her. "Having a baby is a lot of trouble," she said. He probably knew she was trying to deflect his attention.

He bent to kiss her forehead with casual possessiveness. "I'll see you tonight." Rynna stayed where she was. She didn't answer or even raise her head. He had only brushed her forehead lightly with his lips, but she was trembling. She thought he had left, but he spoke again from the doorway. "That goddamned baby better take after me."

Rynna didn't answer. Yes, it was likely their child would resemble him, and he or she would be beautiful. Still exhausted, she brushed her teeth, showered, went back to the bedroom, and dressed. She didn't feel safe until she knew Jason was gone, when she saw for herself that the Ferrari was not in front of the house.

She sat on the bed, trying not to think, dreaming a little, and her mind drifted inevitably to thoughts Jason must not know about. Was Ted having breakfast downstairs, or was he in his room, still asleep or already working? She could almost see him at his desk, his blond head bent over his work. She could see the line between his eyes when he frowned, the shape of his ears, his rare grin, his fine, well-shaped hands.

"Ted," she said half-aloud, alone in the room. Where was he? What was he thinking? He was so far away when he wasn't with her. She closed her eyes and imagined again the touch of his hand, the light brush of his fingers against her cheek. *I could make such love to you.*

She opened her eyes, and the new extension telephone was right in front of her. Her hand was already on the receiver. She considered calling Baxter, but his loyalties had been to Grandmother. He would of course advise her, as he would advise Jason or Ted, but he could never take sides.

Ted, her hands in his, so serious. "I love you," she had told him confidently, but he couldn't accept it, not yet. *Yeah, sure, that's what they all say.*

Rynna lifted the receiver and called Cy Harris. She made an appointment for the following day, Friday, the day she intended to help Ted hunt for an apartment. She would not have to explain a trip to town, a few hours absence, to her husband or to the servants. "I don't want Jason to know about this," she told Cy.

"No, of course not." He was a lawyer. Lawyers were used to privileged communications. He knew Jason, and he didn't much like him. He would not betray her.

Cy hung up first, and just before she replaced the receiver Rynna heard a faint click. Was she imagining things, or had somebody else been on the line? No, surely not. Who could it be?

She had breakfast with Ted, and except for one

quick kiss of greeting, they behaved discreetly, like cousins. Rynna didn't care. She just wanted to sit in the same room with him, to talk to him about unimportant things. She helped herself to toast and oatmeal from the sideboard and sat as close as she dared. She asked him to explain what Norris and Osborn wanted and understood that it involved the buying up of mineral rights without making it clear the corporation was involved.

"Is it legal?" she asked.

"Of course it's legal. That's why they need Jason and Osborn, to make sure it's done legally."

"But it isn't right, is it?"

"We'll see," he said.

What did he mean? She studied his bland expression. He was keeping secrets too. "Ted," she said, "you wouldn't…" She didn't know what she wanted to ask. Would he fight Jason? *Could* he? Did she want him to?

"We'll see," he said again. She didn't know what he planned to do, but she did know one thing—Jason underestimated his adversary.

****

At dinner that night, Jason was full of plans and ideas, and Rynna managed to ask intelligent questions, based more on what Ted had explained than on what she understood from her husband. Jason was at his best, charming, witty, lovingly deferential. A woman who couldn't make a happy marriage with such a man must have only herself to blame, Rynna reflected. This was the man she had fallen in love with. Why was it no longer possible to feel anything for him?

They climbed the stairs together, arm in arm, and she told herself it was possible to go on with him, to give up this illogical, hopeless, foolish passion for a man who didn't love her, who wouldn't even tell her flattering lies.

"What are you thinking about?" Jason asked. "*Who* are you thinking about?" he added with the faintest stress.

"What?" she asked vaguely, as if she didn't understand, as if she didn't know what was happening. She sat at her dressing table and picked up the hairbrush. Jason liked to watch her brush her hair. He liked her hair long, a long dark cascade of hair like Rosalind's.

He was not to be distracted. He came up behind her, plucked the brush out of her hand, and grabbed her wrist, holding it cruelly tight. "Tell the truth, or I'll break your arm."

"Stop this," she said through her teeth. She had played—had been—the outraged innocent so many times. The situation was so familiar.

"I'm not joking," he said, and his fingers tightened painfully on her wrist. "I could break your arm so easily, my love. You have very small bones, very fragile."

"Let go of my arm. You promised you wouldn't do this again. You promised me you would get professional help if you can't control your jealousy. I have never been unfaithful to you, and you know it. When you are thinking straight, you know it."

She met his gaze in the mirror, and after a moment he faltered. "I—I'm sorry," he said, and the pressure on her wrist eased. "You know I love you. It's only because I love you."

"I'm tired of hearing that." She rubbed her bruised wrist.

"That I love you?" He stared at her, a dangerous flush in his cheeks.

"That you can't help being jealous, threatening me, hitting me because you love me. If you loved me, you wouldn't want to hurt me."

"I don't," he said, and he sounded so penitent, so sincere, as he so often did. "I don't want to hurt you, Rynna. I swear to God I never want to hurt you. I don't know what comes over me."

"See a doctor, Jason. Find out."

"Yes, I will. I don't want to lose you."

Rynna took a deep breath. "All right," she said. "We'll talk about this tomorrow." Tomorrow she would know where she stood legally. Tomorrow she would have real guarantees, or she would leave him. Tomorrow she would be in the position of strength, and she would make the threats and the ultimatums.

"I love you," he said, putting his arms around her, pulling her back against him, his face in her hair. It made her skin crawl. "You know I love you, don't you?" Yes, he loved her, in his way, as a trophy, a possession. "Come to bed," he said and when she sat still, reluctant but unresisting, he gathered her in his arms and carried her to the bed.

She didn't protest, allowed him to lay her on the bed and kiss her with rough urgency. It would be wisest, easiest, to simply give in, to let her mind go blank and go through with it, as she had so many times, and she almost managed it. "Stop," she said, holding him off with the strength of desperation. "Not tonight. Please, don't." He withdrew, angry and surprised. "Please, Jason. I don't want to tonight. I just feel… I'm so tired."

"You're always tired lately," he said. "You don't really think I buy that, do you?"

"Please be patient with me. Tomorrow we'll talk.

Tomorrow—"

"You are lying," he said in a tone of absolute conviction, and Rynna could not defend herself. She was lying.

"Jason…"

"You little slut," he said. "You lie to me every goddamned day. You lie all the time. There is somebody else. That's why you don't want me. I'm your husband, and if I want to make love to you, I will. You're not going to put me off so you can—"

"Stop it, Jason. You know what you're saying isn't true."

"Goddamn it, I will not be betrayed. Tell me the truth. Who is it?"

"There's no one. There's never been anyone."

He hit her twice, very hard, in the face.

Half an hour later, when her nose had stopped bleeding and the ice had eased her swollen lip, all she felt was relief. Tomorrow one way or another, her life would change.

****

In the morning, Rynna pretended to be asleep until Jason left. She didn't think she had fooled him. She studied her face in the mirror and carefully covered the traces of violence with makeup so neither Ted nor Cy Harris would have to know. She wasn't sure she could deceive Ted anyway, but she had to try.

He was at the breakfast table when she came in. She studied him thoughtfully. Who was he? Cousin, friend, lover? Intelligent, stubborn, cynical—he was all that. Why did she love him?

"Are you all right?" he asked, holding out a hand to her, and she squeezed it and leaned over to kiss him briefly before she sat.

"Yes," she said and directed her attention to tea and toast and oatmeal. When she glanced up, he was watching her, grave, unsmiling, his bacon and eggs forgotten. "What are you looking at?" she asked, keeping her voice light.

"You. Are you sure you're all right?"

"I'm fine. What do you mean?"

He scowled. "Rynna, please don't playact with me. When you pretend nothing is wrong, I really start to worry."

"Nothing is wrong, Ted. I'm all right." She sipped her tea, keeping the cup steady by sheer force of will.

Exasperated, he was silent for a moment and then said bitterly, "Is this what you want, then? Do you want me to move out and pretend I don't know what's going on here?"

Rynna closed her eyes, feeling hopeless, exhausted. They must not begin like this. She must be strong. She must be in control, and she must use every ally she had. "All right," she said. "Jason and I aren't getting along, but I can't talk to you about it. You'll get angry. You always do, and then you're no different than he is. You're just as unreasonable. You'll want to go after Jason or something, some stupid macho act of revenge. You want to fight over me."

"No, that's not true."

"Oh, isn't it? Jason isn't even satisfied to be married to me. He has to lay claim to me over and over again. God help me if I speak to another man, think about another man. It doesn't make any difference to him whether he makes love to me or beats me senseless. It's all the same to him. It's proof of his domination, his possession."

Ted said nothing, dared say nothing.

"Do you want to possess me?" she asked more evenly.

He helped himself to tea, buying time. "No," he said firmly.

Half convinced, half exasperated, Rynna said, "You're only saying that because you think it's what I want to hear."

"I'm not going to deny that."

She sighed. "Maybe it's true. Half true. Maybe not." She spread jam on her toast but couldn't manage even a bite. "For some idiotic reason, I love you anyway."

"Idiotic," he agreed. "But on the whole I think…better me than Jason."

"Pretty sure of yourself."

"No," he said. "Pretty sure of Jason."

Rynna took a deep breath. "If I tell you something, will you promise not to lose your temper?"

"It's very likely," he said, "that you can't tell me anything I haven't imagined."

Yes, she'd been afraid of that. "He hit me last night," she said. "I wanted him to hit me."

And that he hadn't imagined, hadn't expected, didn't yet understand.

"If he hits me, if I provoke him and he hits me…"

Ted put his hand on hers. "Go on," he said, his voice a little strained.

"Then he's satisfied. It's over. He's proved his point. It's enough. He doesn't have to make love to me. There's no difference to him between violence and passion. He's just laying claim to me. Last night, especially last night, I asked for it."

Ted's hand tightened on hers, but he said nothing.

"I didn't want him to make love to me. The last time he did was the night after you told me you were adopted. I was knocked out, really confused. I didn't know how I felt about you yet, but I knew I would rather he killed me."

"Jesus, Rynna," he protested, not angry, but dazed. "Did you think that would matter to me? Did you think I would rather he beat you?"

"No," she said. "No." Had she? She didn't like to think what it must be like for him, lying in bed down the hall, night after night. But no, Demeray's Law: Don't think about what you can't have. *Thou shall not covet thy cousin's wife*. But that was before she had allowed him to…what? To hope? What had she offered him in exchange for further entangling him in her situation?

It made no difference. He was exactly the same. He was still Ted. He argued and evaded and hid behind cynical humor, but he was always Ted.

She loved him. It didn't matter why or how or where it would lead. She simply loved him. She no longer remembered when he had not been important to her. When did she begin to love him? When he held her hands and asked wistfully if he could kiss her? When she married Jason and he went through the wedding rituals against his will, for her sake? When he kissed her goodbye in that surprisingly intense way?

No. She knew exactly when it was, although she hadn't suspected it at the time. In the moment, on the day of her arrival at Stonebridge, more than a year ago, when he studied her in his grudging, critical way and said rudely, bluntly, "You should let your hair grow."

So she did. Not for Jason. Not to look more like the

music room portrait of Rosalind. For Ted. And then blindly, stupidly stumbled into something she called love for Jason, something she accorded the name of love. Because first cousins must not fall in love.

Revisionist history, she thought, shaking her head.

"What are you thinking?" Ted asked.

"Nothing. I love you. Eat your breakfast." Didn't they have years ahead of them in which to explain and understand? If she could free herself from Jason, didn't they have a future? Perhaps. One step at a time.

Chapter Twenty-One

Shortly after breakfast, Ted and Rynna set out for town to look at apartments near the university. Not, as far as the servants or Jason were ever to know, to keep an appointment with an attorney. They held hands in the car, not caring whether Ellery could see or not, but didn't talk much. They were setting out on an adventure. Ted was quiet, serious, but yes, a little excited, as she was. Like children, like lovers.

He sighed, and she asked, "What are you thinking?"

He glanced toward Ellery. "I hope we don't have any more cousins," he said.

"Not yet."

He looked at her face and then out the window. She didn't know yet what he thought about the baby, aside from his fears for her. "Still working on names?" he asked.

"Yes and no. I've almost decided."

"On what?"

"Robert Edmund."

He was surprised, but he smiled, pleased and boyish. "Grandmother would have liked that," he said.

Ted and Ellery waited in the car while she kept her appointment with Cy Harris. The building was some distance from Jason's office and near enough to other places she could reasonably have visited—Dr. Moran's office, Grandmother's dressmaker—that she didn't worry about the Bentley being seen on the street.

Cy had a professional, detached demeanor. If taking sides against an old rival gave him any pleasure, he did not let on. He had no illusions about the fight Jason would put up if he was challenged, but he was reassuring about her right to Stonebridge and any future question of custody.

"If he suspects you of infidelity, he will use it to try to prove you an unfit mother," he explained, "but the courts still favor the mother, even if her past conduct is in question. Unless he has a lot of solid evidence, he doesn't have a prayer. He hasn't established a relationship with the child."

A lot of solid evidence. Which Jason might imagine he had, but in fact he had none, not a scrap. Unless he called Ellery and Lucy and Ted? Ellery wouldn't betray them. Lucy? What had she seen? The whole truth of what had passed between her and Ted was proof of nothing. They were kissing cousins. But she could not bear to think they might question him under oath about his feelings for her.

When she got back in the car, he took her hand and said, "Okay?"

"Okay. If I file for divorce, Cy will represent me. On grounds of cruelty. It's my word against his, of course."

"I can testify—"

"I'd rather you didn't," she said, and they exchanged a look of too transparent understanding. Some things were better left alone.

Fred Sullivan had lined up several apartments with the aid of the university housing director. The first one was unsuitable, only nominally wheelchair accessible, very dreary, and musty smelling. "I hope they're not all like this," Rynna said. "This is depressing."

"It's not so bad," Ted said, glancing around.

"I knew it," she said. "If I left it up to you and Mr. Sullivan, you'd live in a dingy hovel."

The next one was a lot better. The apartment was on the second floor of a new building, only a few years old and clean and well-maintained. She almost protested that the first floor would have been more suitable, but the elevator was swift and modern, and the second floor offered a pleasant view of the tree-lined edge of the campus.

The biggest drawback was the manager, a stout, voluble woman, who stared rudely at the wheelchair and asked a lot of unnecessary questions. "Y'all fixin' to live here together?" she asked.

"No," said Ted coolly. "This is my cousin, Mrs. Wyatt."

Mrs. Katz clearly didn't believe that. The previous tenants, she gave them to understand, had been quite irresponsible. After they moved out, the carpet had to be replaced and the bedroom repainted. "At their expense," she said with a stern expression. She wouldn't be taken advantage of. In the midst of her monologue, a young boy appeared in the doorway and told her she was wanted on the phone. "Oh, all right," she said grudgingly. "Take y'all's time," she said to Ted and Rynna. "Have a good look and talk it over. When y'all've decided, come on downstairs and let me know."

"Thank you," Ted said soberly, but as soon as she was out of sight he grinned at Rynna.

"She's awful," she said.

"She's great," Ted countered. "The previous tenants…quite irresponsible."

"You might think it's funny now, but she's the sort to make a nuisance of herself if you move in."

"She thinks we're planning to shack up."

"We wouldn't want to disappoint her, would we?" Rynna said. The manager and in particular her assumption about their relationship had put her on edge.

"Rynna, you know I didn't mean anything."

"No, I know you didn't, but she did." She strolled around, examining the furniture. "It is a nice place," she said. "Certainly better than the first one."

"Do you think I should take it, then?"

"Do you like it?"

He glanced around and shrugged. "It's okay."

She sighed. "You're hopeless. Ted, you do know you can afford much better than this?"

"But I don't need anything more than this," he said, as sensible as ever. "What would be the point?"

Exasperated, she asked, "What will you do with Grandmother's money?"

"Put it to work."

"What do you mean?"

"What I just said. Put it to work. That's what money is for, isn't it? Not to spend on a lot of things you don't need."

Amazed that this had never occurred to her, Rynna persisted. "Create jobs you mean? Invest in industry, things like that?"

"Things like that," he agreed, and something, some slight evasion in his tone, tipped her off.

"You're going to fight Jason," she said with conviction. "You'll use Grandmother's money to stop him from tearing up the valley."

He pretended surprise. "Good idea," he said.

Rynna, overcome by a mixture of feelings, bent swiftly and kissed him. "I love you," she said.

Ted caught her hand and squeezed it, holding her there, but didn't answer. "Let's check this place out."

The apartment was clean, well-lighted, and nicely furnished. The doorways were wide, the shelves low enough. The kitchen was small but had a gas stove and a cozy breakfast nook. The bedroom, newly painted a muted shade of green, was comfortable and attractive, with a sturdy double bed and enough space for a good-sized desk.

Rynna sat on the edge of the bed. "Not bad," she said. "It's certainly more comfortable than your bed at home."

"I like it that way," he said.

"I'm sure you do. Come here and try this one. See if it's firm enough."

Her suggestion was a reasonable, logical one, but he stayed where he was. Rynna was conscious of an undercurrent of strain, but not sure what was wrong. He glanced at her and then away, pretending an interest in the curtains.

"Don't you like it?" she asked.

"Yes, it's fine."

And then she understood, or thought she did. They were alone in this apartment, in this strange, welcoming room with its comfortable double bed. The manager had left them alone here, and considering her verbal style, she was likely to be on the phone for an hour.

When was the last time Ted had made love to a woman, any woman? Sylvia? How long ago now? And why assume he and Sylvia had slept together, when she and Jason had waited until they were married? How long had he wanted to make love to *her*? When he said he hadn't coveted his cousin's wife, did he mean he hadn't allowed himself to think about it? After Jason, who made so much of nothing at all, it was hard for her to believe Ted could be immune to sexual jealousy. But when she said she wished she had never let Jason touch her, he said, "It doesn't matter." He had done everything he could to stop her marriage, and he had certainly looked on her wedding day as if it was more than he could bear. Because she had done it against his advice, or because he was in love with her?

Did he love her? He had never said so. But he wanted her, and she wanted him. At this moment, it was too much for her. "Ted," she said and waited for him to meet her eyes.

"Don't think about it," he advised.

"Why not?"

"Just don't."

It wasn't good enough. Rynna rose and went to him, took his face between her hands, and kissed him in a way that left no doubt of her intentions.

"Jesus," he said, shocked. "Not *here*."

"We could go somewhere else," she said. She was thinking of a hotel but didn't say so. It would sound cheap, furtive. She didn't want that, not with him. But she did want him, and it was clear from the way he gazed at her, taking her hands, that he shared her desire. They were nearly at the point of no return, but Rynna made the same mistake she always made. She talked too much. "As far as Jason and the servants are concerned," she said, "we spent the day looking at apartments. Ellery wouldn't…"

"Are you saying," Ted asked slowly, "that you want

to go to a hotel with me and then go back to Stonebridge, back to Jason?" So he was not immune after all. And just like that, it was over. The moment passed.

"Ted, don't be angry," she said.

"I'm not."

"But I don't see…"

"I'm not real keen on adultery," he said.

Adultery. She didn't think of it that way. It was only a legal concept, meaningless. "Another technicality," she said, half amused.

"Not to Jason it isn't."

She was incredulous. He cared little enough for Jason's feelings. If that was the best reason he could come up with… She was hurt by the rejection. But Ted wouldn't lie to her, would he?

"Are you sure that's the reason?" she asked. "Not because…"

He leaned in and kissed her. "Now shut up," he said. "This is hard enough."

"Do you really mean you wouldn't make love to me as long as I'm married to Jason?"

"As long as you intend to remain married to him."

"If I filed for divorce…?"

"I don't want to push you into it," he said. "I don't want this to sound like blackmail. You have to make your own decision about Jason. Until you do… Do you understand?"

"No," she said, "but it's all right. You're probably right. You usually are."

"Am I?" He smiled and said, almost shyly, "I'm sorry. Do you still love me?"

"Yes, damn it." She went to the window and stood gazing at the view, the apartment's best feature. She had no claim on him. If she didn't want him to possess her, she couldn't try to possess him.

What if Sylvia hadn't left him? What if he had been already spoken for when she came to Stonebridge? She had no right to him. He was not hers.

Other women would be in his life now. His students, colleagues—aggressive young women who weren't related to him by blood or adoption. And she, who had been so sure only a few days ago that he was impossible to love...

Ted, watching her, but surely unaware of the trend of her thoughts, said, "I want to ask you a question."

She said, "Go ahead," but kept her gaze on the trees.

"It's sort of hypothetical, and you don't have to answer it if you don't want to. But if you do, I want you to give me an honest answer."

"Yes, of course." She gave him her full attention, curious now.

"I don't want you to say what you think I want to hear or try to spare my feelings."

Rynna gave a surprised half laugh. When did she ever spare his feelings? When, in all the months they had known each other, had they been careful with each other?

"If you leave him... I mean if you were divorced from him now, if you were free of him, if Jason was no longer in the picture..." He waited, and she gestured for him to go on. "Would you marry me? I mean would you even consider it? Not the Demeray fortune, but just me, Ted Demeray, teacher and textbook editor?"

As if, for God's sake, *that* made any difference. Rynna's eyes blurred with tears. He was so damned serious, so composed, and it almost sounded as if he were trying to talk her out of it. He wanted an honest answer.

After rejecting her advances, he had the nerve to ask her, half-seriously, if she still loved him, and now he was proposing—if it could be called a proposal. Surely she had the right to ask. "Ted, do you love me?"

He didn't answer at once, and she didn't know what he would say. *What do you know about love?* He wouldn't say what Jason would say, what most men would say: "Of course I do." She would get an honest answer too. "Yes," he said finally and then, quickly, "Would you?"

If Jason didn't exist, would she give up her hard-won, newly appreciated freedom for such a man as this? "Yes," she said. "In a minute."

"Yeah?" He met her eyes, still serious, bur curiously excited, like a young boy.

"Yeah," she said softly, smiling at him. "But…"

"I knew it wouldn't be that simple," he said.

"You know I want children. It's important to me. Regardless of what happens with Jason, I'm still going to have his child. Jason's child. I can't change that."

"It doesn't matter."

"Don't say that. Of course it does. If we were married, you would have to be a father to Jason's child."

She remembered Ted saying, "If you married me, at least your children would be called Demeray." Grandmother would like that.

"He would be your child," Ted said. "If we were married, he would be our child."

"He might look like Jason."

"Or you or Rosalind or William or Pamela," he said, crossing his arms. "What difference does it make what he looks like?"

"That goddamned baby," Jason had said, only

250

yesterday morning, "better take after me."

Ted was right, of course. He ought to know. If children learn by example, he knew how to love a child who was not, in a merely biological sense, his. He was afraid of the risks, but he had asked her anyway.

"If we were married," she said, "I would want your children, but I understand how you feel about it. I would be willing to take the risk, but if you're not, we could adopt a child, a little girl?"

"We could try," he said, and it was not an evasion. It would be difficult, but he was willing to try.

"I love you," she said and went back to kiss him, leaning over, holding her hair back from her face. She sighed. "There's something else we'd have to deal with."

"What?" He clearly had no idea.

"This," she said, touching the arms of the wheelchair.

"Oh." He was surprised, not that she had brought it up, but that he had forgotten to do so himself. "Do you mind?"

"Do *I* mind?" she asked, with a little gasp of incredulous surprise. As if she were the one who had something to put up with. Knowing it was dangerous, she asked, "Did Sylvia?"

He didn't much like the question, but he answered her. "I don't know. I suppose she did."

"No, of course I don't mind. It is a nuisance sometimes, though."

"Yes," he agreed with a breathless laugh.

"Ted, do you remember when I first came to Stonebridge? I was down by the river, and you came—"

"And asked if you were going to jump in."

"You leaned against a tree and talked about my

mother. Was it a good day?" she asked, searching his face. "Or were you showing off?"

"Both," he said, and seeing that it wasn't really what she wanted to ask, he continued soberly, "You can ask me anything, Rynna. If I don't want to answer, I won't, but I'm not going to smack you for asking. My name is Demeray, not Wyatt."

Rynna knelt on the floor in front of him, gazed into his face, and put a hand gently on his left knee. "Does that hurt?"

"No."

"I'm afraid I'll hurt you," she confessed.

"Don't be. I'll let you know if there's a problem."

"Will you? Promise?"

"I promise if you'll do the same. Tell me what the problem is, Rynna."

She considered. What was the problem? She wasn't sure. She was feeling her way through unexplored territory. "Will it get worse?" she asked.

"I don't think so."

"You hope not," she said. "And nothing can be done? Dr. Moran said—"

"You talked to Moran about this?" He wasn't pleased.

"I knew you wouldn't like it. I told him not to tell you. When you were arrested—"

"I was not arrested," he said. It was a technicality, but he could be so stubborn about such things.

"I mean when Grandmother died."

He interrupted her brusquely, suddenly tired of the subject. "I'll never be able to dance, Rynna. Is that what you wanted to know?"

She shook her head. "Dancing," she said, casually

dismissing those pleasant romantic evenings with Jason, "is overrated." Thank God she wasn't as much a fool as Sylvia. Sighing, she got to her feet and returned to the window. "We've been up here a long time," she said, glancing out at the lovely, sunlit day. "She'll expect you to take it, you know."

"If I do," he said, watching her, "I will always see you standing at the window." That didn't sound, did it, as if he believed she would leave Jason? For a few minutes they had dismissed Jason, talked bravely of a world in which he didn't exist. But he did. She was still married to him.

"Oh, Ted, I do love you," she said fiercely. "Why is everything so hard?"

When he didn't answer, she strode out of the bedroom, out of the apartment, and he followed her in silence. They went downstairs and found the manager.

She was still on the phone, but she covered the mouthpiece and asked if they had made up their minds. She stared frankly at Rynna, as if she assumed the decision rested with her, and Ted surprised Rynna by giving her an inquiring glance, as if he thought so too. "It's not my decision," she protested.

"We have a couple of other places to see," Ted explained. "I'll let you know."

"Yeah, well, I can't hold it, mind, if somebody else wants to take it."

"I understand," he said. "Thank you."

When they returned to the car, Ellery was leaning against it reading a newspaper. He gave no indication of noticing they had been inside an unusually long time.

They were not to have another such opportunity to talk alone at the other apartments. The owner or manager was always with them, asking and answering questions, showing off the good points, glossing over the problems.

At the third place, the manager was a wiry man in his fifties who greeted them cheerily and then said to Ted, "You were in Korea, huh?"

"No," he said politely, "I wasn't," and he gave Rynna a look that said, See, I told you.

In the end, he decided to take the second-floor apartment with the pleasant view and the talkative manager, and they went back and settled the details.

Coming back through town, they pàssed the courthouse, and Rynna said reluctantly, "I should…" Ted glanced at her and then leaned forward to tell Ellery to stop at the Brenford Professional building, where Jason had his office.

She rode the elevator up alone to say hello, to remind herself of Jason's existence. As usual, he had no memory of last night's ugly scene. He kissed her, and she could feel the soreness of her bruised lip, where he had hit her. With Ted she hadn't even noticed. She colored guiltily just for thinking of him. How could Jason always put her in the wrong?

Fortunately, he was busy and self-absorbed, as always. She told him they'd found a suitable apartment, and he said, "Good." He told her about the deal with Norris and Osborn, and she only half attended, but gradually it dawned on her what he was saying. A possibility existed, nothing definite yet, but a real possibility that he would fly to Washington to talk to some other people *this weekend.*

Rynna's head fairly reeled with the possibilities. "Tonight?" she asked.

"I don't know yet. I'll call you. I'm sorry,

sweetheart. I'm really distracted by all this, I know. I hope you didn't have any plans?"

"No," she said with wifely generosity. "No, of course not. Mrs. Lester is off anyway. If you can make it, we'll put something together." She was as distracted as he sounded. *If Jason doesn't come home tonight...* She managed to put it out of her mind and kiss him goodbye.

"If I don't see you later, I'll call," he said. "I love you."

Oh, do you? What do you know about love?

She didn't tell Ted about the possibility of Jason going to Washington. What if it didn't happen? What if it was a trick? What if it was true, and she and Ted were alone in the house tonight? Not really alone, of course— the servants.

Whether Ted noticed her preoccupation or had other things on his mind, they didn't talk in the car on the way back to Stonebridge. He held her hand lightly in his, but scarcely glanced at her, watching the scenery. It was a beautiful day.

Chapter Twenty-Two

Jason called shortly before he would have been expected home and said he was flying to Washington. He wasn't even coming home to pack a bag. He wouldn't need much. He would stay with Osborn. "When will you be back?" Rynna asked, sounding even to herself like an anxious wife. She *was* anxious.

"I don't know. Probably Sunday night. I'll miss you."

Yes, I just bet you will. She couldn't respond in kind, but did manage to say, "Goodbye, darling," convincingly enough. She should have been an actress. This new development meant she couldn't talk to him tonight about their problem. Did he remember they had a problem? She didn't like to postpone the confrontation again, but a surprising lightness filled her now that she didn't have to face it yet.

When she told Ted, he followed at once the direction of her thoughts. "Don't borrow trouble," he advised.

They ate dinner together, and it was pleasantly relaxed. Mrs. Lester was off, and they opted for the simplest fare—cold ham and cheese, with tomato basil soup. The conversation was nothing Jason could have objected to—as if the afternoon had never existed—but they shared an ease, a freedom, in the knowledge that Jason was not and would not be at Stonebridge tonight.

****

In town, Jason finished with his paperwork, grabbed a sandwich between phone calls, and prepared to leave for Washington. He kept a shaving kit in his desk, and that was all he needed besides his briefcase.

In the hall outside his office, he met Vic Preston, one of the friendly circle of young attorneys who had been the center of his world before he met Rynna Dalton. They hadn't seen each other for a few weeks and chatted briefly about their respective cases, and then Vic said, "I saw your wife today."

"Yes, Demeray is moving out of Stonebridge. Rynna is helping him find an apartment."

Innocently, casually, Vic went on, "In the Langton building. She didn't see me, though. She was getting off the elevator."

"The Langton building?" Jason repeated.

"Yeah, you know, the new building, where Cy Harris has his office."

"Oh, yes." He recovered quickly. "Her doctor is over there." Which was true enough but did not explain why Rynna was in the Langton building.

"Oh, yeah, I heard y'all were expecting," Vic said as they stepped onto the elevator. "I guess you want a boy?"

"Of course," said Jason, although his mind was elsewhere.

Vic got off on the second floor with a casual goodbye. Jason waited until the doors closed behind him and then pressed the button to return to the fifth floor.

****

Ted and Rynna adjourned to the music room after dinner, and she sat at the piano and rested her hands on the keys but didn't begin to play. Something was not right. She didn't feel like playing tonight, and she didn't know why. Rosalind?

"What's wrong?" Ted asked.

"I don't know. Not in the mood, I guess." She stroked the keys lightly, tried the opening phrase of *Für Elise*. The hair on the back of her neck prickled. What was she doing, trying to frighten herself? She looked back at Ted. "Why don't you come here and help me. We could play 'Chopsticks' together."

He came closer but didn't join her on the bench. "I don't think so," he said. "You will never make a musician out of me."

"We have the whole evening," she said. "Tell me what you would like to do."

He said nothing, but took her hand and held it, his gaze on their interlocked fingers.

"What? Don't tell me you want to go to your room and work on your book."

"No."

"What, then?" She was touched by his silence and something like shyness in his tone.

With his other hand he caressed her face softly and then leaned closer to kiss her. "This," he said and kissed her again.

"Ted…"

"No, I know. It's dangerous." He sighed. "Somehow, in this room, it's harder to remember that."

Rosalind's favorite room. Did Rosalind want them to be together, or did she only want Jason out of their lives? "Do you want to go upstairs?" she asked. He could make what he liked of that.

He shook his head, and then he kissed her again, and she found herself falling, tipping over the edge—into danger. He had let go of her fingers, and his hands were in her hair. He could not get enough of her. He stopped abruptly, still holding onto her, his breathing uneven. "I'm sorry," he said and then desperately, sweetly, "I love you."

Rynna snuggled closer, her face hidden against his shoulder, his arms holding her safe. He had said it, and without prompting. She was filled with a confusion of emotions: gratitude, compassion, a shared sense of danger. She kissed him and tasted tears on his lips. Were they his or hers? His. She touched his face, comforting him.

Ted had finally had enough.

"It's not easy being in love, is it?" she asked. "It hurts."

He didn't answer. He just held her. After a few minutes, he said quietly, more in control, "I'm sorry. I didn't mean to do this. I don't want to make it any harder for you."

"No, you're not. It's not your fault. I wish we could be together tonight."

He was very still, and she could feel his heart beating against hers. Then he withdrew slowly, rested his hands on her shoulders, and gazed into her eyes. "So do I," he said.

She knew he meant it, and she knew nothing was going to happen. Yielding to the temptation would only make everything harder. So long as Jason was part of her life, so long as she still had to face him, they must not put him in the right.

Again she had a sharp sense of danger, like a warning. Rosalind.

"Let's go upstairs," she said. "Would you mind if I

came to your room, just to talk? Or don't you trust me?"

"It's myself I don't trust," he said. "But, yes, let's go upstairs."

He went first, and Rynna stood in the doorway for a moment before she switched off the light. Danger. There was danger.

Rosalind was disturbed.

****

Jason let himself back into his office. His secretary had already left for the day, and nobody else was around. Everyone knew he was on his way to Washington. He put the shaving kit back in the desk. He was not going to need it. He sat for a long time without stirring and then unlocked the small right-hand drawer of the desk. Nobody else knew what he kept in it. Nobody else had a key. Not even his faithful secretary. Not even his loving wife.

From the drawer he retrieved a small, deadly handgun.

****

Rynna ambled around Ted's room, scanning the shelves, half empty now, most of the books packed into cartons. "Talk to me, Ted," she said, running her fingers over the bindings, some of them a little dusty, some of them well-used.

"About what?"

"Anything. I just like to listen to your voice. Tell me about your book. When will it be finished?"

"It's finished," he said.

She looked at him sharply. "Really finished? You lied to me?"

"No, I didn't. I told you why I didn't want to leave Stonebridge."

"Tell me about it, then. Tell me about rocks and things."

"It's not everybody's idea of fascinating subject matter."

"Sort of an acquired taste? Then maybe I should acquire it. Just start talking."

So he talked, and sometimes she attended, and sometimes she understood, and sometimes she simply listened to his familiar, calm voice. She left the shelves and sat on the floor at his feet and rested her head against his knee. "Is this all right?" she asked, and he laid his hand on her head without stopping the flow of words.

After a while he shifted a little, found a position that was more comfortable for both of them, and stroked her hair lightly while he continued his explanation.

When he stopped talking, Rynna didn't move.

"Are you asleep?" he asked.

"No. Keep talking. Tell me something else. Tell me about your childhood."

"You've heard about my childhood. You've had family history up to your ears."

"I'm not talking about the Demerays," she said. "I want to hear about you. Tell me what it was like to grow up here. Tell me what kind of a kid you were."

He had to think, and then he started talking again, not in the detached, professorial tone he had used when he was telling her about his work, but softly, intimately, leaning a little forward, his hand protectively smoothing her hair.

****

Jason parked on the road and strode up the driveway, his footsteps muffled by the soft ground at the edge. A light was on in Ellery's room above the garage, out of earshot of the house.

He had waited long enough for most of the servants to be safely in bed. When he finally let himself in the front door, only Lucy heard him. She was surprised, but said only, "Mr. Wyatt, we weren't expecting you."

"I still have to fly to Washington," he said, "but I need to pick up some things first. Where's Mrs. Wyatt?"

"Upstairs, I think, sir. Shall I…?"

"Don't bother, Lucy. I'll get what I need and let myself out. You go on to bed." He tucked a bill into her hand to insure her discretion.

Lucy, surprised, even a little offended, hesitated, and then accepted it. "Yes, sir," she said and withdrew.

The house was quiet, except for a faint murmur of voices from upstairs. As he crossed to the bottom of the stairs, Jason didn't notice the light was on in the music room.

****

"Did you hear something?" Rynna asked, lifting her head a little.

"No, did you?"

"Maybe not." She looked up at him. "Are you all right? You look tired. What time is it?"

Ted glanced at his watch.

The half-open door slammed back against the wall with a nerve-shattering crash.

Jason stood in the doorway, the dimly lit hall behind him, his familiar figure as hazily unreal as an image in a nightmare.

Chapter Twenty-Three

"Jason," Rynna stammered, stunned, terrified. He could not be here. He was in Washington. They had been discovered, caught. No, they had done nothing.

He came into the room with the slow, unhurried movements of a man who knew exactly what he was doing. "So," he said, his eyes dark, his voice dangerously deep and icy. "Now we have the truth." He closed the door behind him, and the latch clicked with dull finality in the still room.

Rynna would have scrambled to her feet, but Ted's fingers clenched in her hair, and his other hand closed on her arm, keeping her still. "Don't," he said calmly.

"Mister Demeray," Jason said with an exaggerated, sarcastic politeness, "kindly take your hands off my wife."

For a few seconds, while she sat in stunned silence, caught between them, Ted didn't react. Then, as if he had just become aware of his grip on her, he let go of her hair. His fingers eased on her upper arm, not holding her, yet not releasing her. He leaned a little toward her as if they were alone and murmured an apology. He smoothed her hair where he had rumpled it.

"You bastard," Jason said, trembling with rage, holding his voice steady with effort. "In my own house."

"Rynna's house," Ted said quickly.

Jason grabbed her arm fiercely and yanked her to her

feet. Sickened by the threat of too familiar violence, terrified of the danger to Ted, she managed to face him with her chin up.

"I suppose the child is his," he said.

She shook her head and, taking courage, said, "I wish it were. I wish it were anybody's but yours."

"You did your best," he said coldly. "Didn't you?"

"No," Ted said. "She has been faithful to you." He was not afraid of Jason. His face showed mostly defiance, and something else, the old enmity that had always existed between them. He glanced at her, not unaware of her danger, and added, with his faint, ironic smile, "Technically anyway."

His nonchalance was too much for Jason. He let go of Rynna and struck Ted with a fierce, backhanded blow that nearly knocked off his glasses.

Ted didn't even flinch, but she did. All the times Jason had hit her, she had been too stunned to feel much pain, but a shock went through her when he hit Ted.

Before Ted could react, Jason grabbed him by the throat.

Immediately, Ted's hands went around Jason's neck, choking him with unexpected strength, the two of them locked in a fierce, violent struggle.

"Stop it," Rynna cried. "Ted! Jason! Stop it!"

They more than hated each other now. They thirsted for blood. They would have gladly killed each other, now that their murderous rage, so long civilized into submission, had been unleashed. The fight wasn't even necessarily about her.

However serious he may have been at the time, what Ted had told her about Jason was what he believed now—he had killed Grandmother and somehow cost him

Sylvia.

And Jason knew Ted, so long discounted as the idle dreamer, the bookish, crippled cousin, was after all capable of taking from him the one thing he would never be willing to give up.

They weren't even aware that the fight was unequal, and maybe it wasn't. The wheelchair bucked and lurched dangerously, but it was Jason who faltered, his face taking on an unnatural purplish shade. His hands slackened on Ted's throat, and he was gasping for breath. He let go and shoved Ted back with one hand while the other tugged frantically at the fingers digging into his windpipe.

Rynna's vision darkened, as it had when Jason choked her, but she managed to reach for the cord next to the bed to ring a bell in the servants' hall. She was afraid they would kill each other if they were not stopped. Lucy could ring for Ellery or call the police. She was afraid to leave the room to run down the hall to call from the extension in the master bedroom.

Jason, at first too surprised by Ted's strength to recall his own advantage, finally stopped struggling and kicked Ted in the shin with vicious force.

Rynna cringed, but whatever Ted suffered, his face showed only grim determination.

Desperate, Jason kicked him again and thrust his knee into Ted's with all his strength.

Ted swore and let go.

Jason backed away, and they faced each other warily, both out of breath. Jason bore distinct, reddish bruise marks on his neck, and Ted was clearly hurting, pale and sweating from the pain in his knee.

The fight was not over. Nothing would ever be

finished between them. Rynna couldn't stop this without help. She tugged the cord again and then ran to the door and wrenched it open.

Even in her anxiety she was conscious of the terrible chill on the landing. The air was so cold, not as in a draft, but as if all the warmth were being drawn from her. "Lucy!" she screamed, and hugging herself against the unnatural chill, she hurried back into the room.

Jason was approaching Ted with the respectful caution he would have accorded a rattlesnake, and with the same confidence that he could defeat him. He might have underestimated his enemy, but he was not dissuaded.

"Jason, don't." Rynna grabbed his arm and tried to hold him back.

He threw her off easily, but she had at least distracted him. "I'll take care of you too, you little bitch."

He raised his hand to strike her, and Ted swung the wheelchair around and slammed it viciously against Jason's legs. Jason staggered back, breathless with pain and surprise.

"This is between you and me," Ted told him. "Leave her out of it."

Jason wisely kept his distance, but he said, "She doesn't want to be left out of it." Recovering a little, a new and menacing tone creeping into his voice as he circled slowly closer to Ted, he continued, "You want to watch this, don't you, Rynna?"

"Please stop, Jason."

"You'll like this," he assured her without taking his eyes off Ted. "You like old movies, don't you? Do you remember the one where Richard Widmark—"

"No!" she cried, knowing exactly what he meant,

and in the same second he made a grab for the wheelchair. Ted swung the wheel into him, but Jason dodged and got behind him. Even then, he didn't find it as easy as he expected. Rynna grabbed at his arm, and he flung her aside, but Ted's resistance was harder to overcome. Still trying to stop him, she yelled as loud as she could, "Lucy, where are you? Call the police!"

Jason shoved her aside and struggled with Ted for control of the wheelchair. He maneuvered it, little by little, with a nightmarish inevitability, toward the landing and the top of the long, curving staircase.

In a chilling flash, she recalled her earlier vision, those distinct nightmare images: Ted's glasses shattered on the floor, drops of blood, the wheelchair overturned.

But Ted, whether he had seen the Richard Widmark film or not, was not about to be shoved down the stairs. When they neared the top step, he grabbed the railing and hung on.

The wheelchair did overturn, and Jason, tripped by his own momentum, nearly fell over it.

Rynna ran to Ted where he was holding onto the railing, on his feet now, out of breath but unhurt. "You are insane," she said to Jason.

"And you, my darling wife, are a liar and a whore."

Ted pushed away from the railing, and she grabbed his arm. Whatever he had in mind, she was sure it would have been suicidal.

Jason, unnerved, was not so sure. He stepped back, watching them both, and then he put his hand inside his coat.

"Oh, Christ," said Ted, even before Jason brought his hand out again, holding the unmistakable dark shape of a compact revolver.

267

Rynna gasped but stood her ground. For several seconds, nobody moved. The only sound was the slowing whir of the wheel, still spinning between them.

"Let go of his arm," Jason said. "Move away from him. I'm not going to hurt you."

She had heard that before. The scene was all too familiar—except for the gun. She stayed where she was, clutching Ted's arm.

"I'm not going to hurt you," Jason repeated, his voice smooth but unconvincing. "Just do what I say. I only want what belongs to me. Step away from him." When she didn't immediately obey, he raised the gun a little.

Ted said, "Go ahead, Rynna. Do as he says."

She glanced at him—he looked stubborn, determined, not afraid even now—and back at Jason.

Jason let the gun drop a few inches and asked irritably, "Why is it so damned cold in here?"

Ted took advantage of his distraction to pull out of Rynna's grasp and reach for the wheelchair, intending to right it.

"Leave it," Jason said sharply and leveled the gun directly at him.

"Okay," Ted said. "Take it easy." He kept his voice level, reasonable, but Jason understood he was being humored.

"Shut up," he commanded and with a dull snap he cocked the gun.

"Jason, please," Rynna entreated.

"Get over here," he told her. "Right now." Without taking his eyes from Ted, he moved toward her, grabbed her wrist, and dragged her to the top of the stairs. "Are you going to tell me the truth now?" he asked. "Or shall

I break your arm?"

His fingers tightened until she feared the bone would snap, and she could ease the pressure only by yielding, letting him draw her closer.

"Don't. You're hurting me."

"Jason, what are you doing?" Ted asked. "Think what you're doing."

"I told you to shut up," Jason snarled, and the gun discharged.

Half-deafened by the awful bang, week-kneed with horror, Rynna looked at Ted. Jason had missed—on purpose, surely?

Ted was backed against the railing, holding on with both hands. When he shifted his weight, the railing creaked ominously. He gave her a look that said clearly, Don't do anything foolish.

"Another word out of you and I'll blow your head off," Jason threatened. "How many times?" he asked her, fury in his voice, his fingers biting into her wrist. "How many times behind my back in my own house, you and high-and-mighty Cousin Ted?"

"Never. I swear to you. There has never been anything between us." A lie. Could he tell it was a lie? "I have never been unfaithful to you. Never."

"You know I don't believe that. You have always been a goddamned whore, haven't you? I should have known it wasn't safe to let him stay here."

"Jason, for God's sake, I have not been sleeping with Ted."

"No? What were you doing in his room?"

"We were talking. Just talking."

"Like hell you were. What were you doing in Cy Harris's office?"

For a second, Rynna was too surprised to answer. How did he know? "You threatened me," she reminded him. "You said if I divorced you—"

"You are not going to divorce me," he said menacingly. "I'll kill you first. Do you understand me? If the baby is mine, nobody else is going to raise it, and if I can't have you, nobody else will. You belong to me. Do you understand?"

When she didn't answer, he tightened his grip until she cried out with the pain.

"Do you?"

"Yes," she said faintly.

"Remember that," he said. "You are mine, and I'll kill you before I'll let anybody else have you, least of all Demeray."

Rynna stared at him, trembling. This terrible stranger had once been her handsome, devoted husband. This was still Jason. Some remaining hint of the man she had loved was still in his eyes. She inhaled deeply and risked everything on the simple truth. "I love him," she said quietly.

He was stunned. He had expected submission or another lie. He dropped the gun, and his hands went around her throat, choking her.

For a moment Rynna could only think of the gun. Ted was safe as long as the odds against him were hopeless. But if he could somehow get the gun…if he tried to reach the gun…

"Goddamned whore," Jason said through his teeth.

He was so strong, so desperately angry. He could break her neck. He could kill her, just as he—just as *Alex* had killed Rosalind. At the top of the stairs, just like this, struggling…

No. She would not give in to horror, to the dizzying sense of *déjà vu*. In this precarious position, so near the top of the stairs, the only weapon she possessed was her own courage.

She would rather die with Ted than continue living with Jason.

No. She would live. She would not allow this to happen.

Not again.

In that moment, someone came out on the landing beyond Jason, the dim figure of a woman, emerging from the dark hall. For a second, Rynna thought Lucy was finally responding to her summons.

It was not Lucy.

A tall, slender woman in a rose-colored dress stood before them, a woman in her late twenties, with thick, dark hair swept up in an elaborate coiffure. Her skin was pale, her eyes dark and blazing. There was nothing insubstantial about her, nothing ethereal. She was very beautiful.

Whatever it was—ghost, trick, or illusion—it was not her imagination. Behind her, Ted said with sharp conviction, "Rosalind."

Rosalind.

Jason hadn't seen her. She was behind him. He glanced from Ted to Rynna, confused by what he saw in their faces, and slowly, reluctantly, still holding Rynna by the throat, he turned to look.

The apparition stepped swiftly toward him, and he released Rynna so suddenly she staggered back and almost fell. He put a hand to his face, as if to shield his eyes from a blinding light. "What the hell?" he said and immediately grabbed for the gun he'd dropped. Rynna hadn't acted fast enough to get it first. He fired at Rosalind, but the bullet slammed into the wall beyond.

Rosalind did not falter. She stood a few feet from Jason, not speaking, and gazed directly into his eyes. Face to face with him after so many years, it was clear she was not seeing her once beloved son. She was seeing his father, Alexander Wyatt, the man who had destroyed her love with jealousy long before he took her life.

Jason, everything else forgotten, even the weapon in his hand, stepped backward, staring, unable to take his eyes from her face. He was aware enough to keep a few safe inches from the edge of the stairs, but he had forgotten something else. He took another step backward and another.

In the last split second, Rynna shouted a warning— "Jason!"—but it was too late.

He took one step too many, and he stumbled over the wheelchair where it lay half blocking the top of the stairs, one wheel still spinning slowly. He lost his balance and fell heavily against the banister above the top step. The old wood snapped beneath his weight with a splintering crash. He fell backward off the staircase to the unyielding hardwood floor of the hall below.

The sickening thud that followed would haunt Rynna's dreams for years to come.

Rosalind swept forward, rested her hand lightly on the railing, and stared down at Jason before she turned back to the other two. A hard glitter of triumph shone in her eyes.

Too dazzled to feel anything and more or less holding each other up, Ted and Rynna stood face to face with the ghost of Rosalind Demeray Wyatt.

She gave them a smile of benediction, and then she

was gone.

The warmth of the house returned, a benevolent warmth like the welcome Rynna had first sensed in the music room. No trace of the apparition remained. Only a faint scent of roses.

Rynna could tell nothing from Ted's grim expression. "Now do you believe me?" she asked shakily.

He didn't answer. "It's over," was all he said.

She hid her face against his shoulder. His hand was on her hair, and finally she heard footsteps below, followed by Lucy's startled cry.

Ted said calmly, "Call the police."

Was it over? She was safe. Jason was dead. Whatever the future held, she and Ted would face it together. A whole world lay beyond Stonebridge.

But...

The child, Jason's child, shifted restlessly in her womb.

It was not over.

Author's Note

Some readers might consider the term "gaslighting" an anachronism, as it didn't become widespread usage until the 21st century. My friends and I were using it more than a decade before it first appeared in *The New York Times* in 1995, though, so I don't think it's unreasonable to suppose that Rynna could have come up with it independently any time after the film *Gaslight* was released in 1944.

A word about the author...

Linda Griffin retired as Fiction Librarian for the San Diego Public Library to spend more time on her writing, and her work has been published in numerous journals. In addition to the three R's—reading, writing, and research—she enjoys Scrabble, movies, and travel. This is her eighth Wild Rose Press publication.

http://www.lindagriffinauthor.com/

www.ingramcontent.com/pod-product-compliance
Lightning Source LLC
Chambersburg PA
CBHW070101030726
47506CB00002B/545